DARK ALLEGIANCE

THE LAST WARD: BOOK THREE

SHELLEY RUSSELL NOLAN

ODYSSEY
BOOKS

Published by Odyssey Books in 2021

www.odysseybooks.com.au

A Cataloguing-in-Publication entry is available from the National Library of Australia

ISBN: 978-1-922311-85-6 (pbk)

ISBN: 978-1-922311-86-3 (ebook)

Cover design by Andreea-Elena Vraciu

For Mum, always and forever.

ONE

J ACKSON SLOWED THE ALL-TERRAIN VEHICLE AS HE SURVEYED the gates to Harlington.

The closed gates.

It was just past midday, so the gates should have been open and a team comprising the town's security guards and wardens waiting to assess those incoming and outgoing. Instead, several guards in the Harlington blue and gold uniforms stood on top of the guard post that ran along the front wall to the left of the gate, staring down at Jackson's ATV with grim expressions on their faces.

Stopping the ATV completely, Jackson turned to Lieutenant Max Carstairs, who sat in the passenger seat, his brow furrowed as he stared at the closed gates. The young warden had never been a freak, so his eyesight wouldn't be as good as Jackson's, but he'd still be able to tell the Harlington guards were not happy to see them.

'I take it this is not normal operating procedure?'

Strong wind buffeted the ATV, though it did little to affect the sturdy vehicle, but outside the dirt swirled across the road, dried grasses and stubbly trees bending in the eddies. Jackson had radioed ahead to let Captain Murphy know they were coming, putting down the non-response to interference from the storm brewing overhead. Now he was thinking the radio silence might be due to another reason.

Carstairs' frown deepened. 'The town gates are only closed from dusk to dawn, or when there is a potential threat alert. But that's never happened in the entire time I was stationed here.'

Bandits preyed on some of the smaller communities, but none of them were stupid enough to take on a town of Harlington's size, one with not only a force of security guards, but a full contingent of wardens as well.

Not sure if it would do any good, Jackson grabbed the radio and attempted to get through to the Harlington Ward one more time.

The crackle of static was the only response—from the radio at least.

A grating noise carried to them over the wind as a crack appeared in the centre of the gates.

The gap was not wide enough for a vehicle to drive through, but more than sufficient for three men to slip outside. Jackson studied them as they strode toward the ATV, heads bent against the wind. The one in the middle, in Ward armour, was Captain Murphy. Instead of being flanked by two of his wardens, his escort were members of the Harlington security force.

Jackson leaned back to look into the rear of the ATV. 'Lieutenant Jensen, you and Michaelson remain in the vehicle. Keep your eyes open and be ready.'

Ready for what, he didn't say as he indicated for Carstairs to exit the ATV. They moved to the front of the vehicle, waiting for the welcoming committee to make their way to them. Jackson kept his eyes slitted against the dust stirred up by the wind. The dark clouds overhead pressed down on him and he felt a few drops of rain. They would need to get the situation sorted before the dark clouds emptied their load right on top of them.

When he was one hundred metres away, Captain Murphy waved the men escorting him to a stop and continued forward on his own, mouth down-turned.

'You shouldn't have come here, Kyle,' Murphy said, his voice pitched low. 'Didn't you get my message?'

'Clearly not.' Jackson spoke softly as well, aware Murphy would have no trouble hearing him, even over the wind, unlike the Harlington guards.

Murphy grimaced. 'It's all gone to shit. Once word of Butcher's death hit High Command, they went into damage control. Acting-General Stratton has put a freeze on all Ward activities while he and the colonels sort out what went wrong and vote for the next general.' He pulled his shoulders back. 'It seems General Butcher's aide destroyed a lot of his files before anyone thought to stop him. I've been recalled to explain my actions and face possible court martial, as has Captain Landry. We leave in the morning.'

Muscles tensing, Jackson narrowed his eyes. 'I take it your message wasn't asking for a rescue.'

Murphy snorted. 'The only way to clear my name, to clear all our names, is to tell the truth.' He looked over at Carstairs and winced.

'I'm sorry, Lieutenant. I was unable to keep your name out of the firing line. I have orders to take you in for immediate trial as a deserter. If I see you, that is.'

Carstairs stiffened. 'Sir?'

'You were never here. Either of you.' Murphy turned his attention back to Jackson. 'My orders are to take you in as well, hence my message telling you to stay away.'

'Even if we had received your message, we still would have come. We have a box of Hannah's vaccine with us, to cure your freaks. Then we need to take some of their blood, if they're willing to share.' With Councillor Dillon out for his head and those of his wardens, Jackson had felt it was more prudent to get what they needed to create more of the vaccine from Harlington rather than Brimfield.

They would need to return to Brimfield eventually, to enable them to spread the cure more effectively, but that would come once they had a stockpile of the vaccine.

Murphy shook his head. 'I'm afraid that will be impossible. Even if I were to go against High Command on this, the Harlington Council would never let you step foot in town, let alone get near the freaks. The Over-Council has put out a broadcast with your name on it, demanding your immediate surrender. Failing that, it gives the councils permission to use whatever force is necessary to take you into custody.'

Jackson rubbed the back of his neck. 'Let me guess, Councillor Dillon is behind this.'

'Doesn't matter who's behind it. Orders are orders. If the two dolts behind me had a clue who you were, all three of us would be facing a firing squad right now. I told them you were wardens from Alston, here with a private message from High Command, one they couldn't rely on getting through with the recent spate of storms playing havoc with our communications network.'

It was Jackson's turn to grimace. 'You're risking an awful lot here, Murphy.'

'Not as much as I could.' Face bleak, Murphy heaved out a sigh. 'What Butcher and Templeton did was wrong, but cleaning this mess up is not going to be an easy task. I know you want to get started on curing the world, but if I were you, I'd lie low for a time. Wait until Landry and I have had a chance to tell the real story to the colonels. When you and your wardens have been cleared of any wrongdoing, then you can see about spreading your cure to the rest of the towns. I only hope I'll be back here at Harlington by then to see this brand new future of yours firsthand.'

From the bitter twist of his mouth, Murphy didn't believe

he would ever get to see that bright future, and Jackson didn't blame him. He'd seen how one general could destroy everything he had worked toward. As much as he hoped whomever got voted in as the next general had more foresight, he couldn't count on it.

'Good luck,' Jackson said, holding out his hand.

Murphy gripped his hand and gave it a firm shake before turning to Carstairs. This time, he leaned in and clasped the young lieutenant on the shoulder.

'You have a good head on you. Make sure you keep it there.' Then he turned around and walked back to his escort. Not stopping to wait for them, he strode toward the gate at a quick pace, making them scramble to keep up.

Carstairs turned to Jackson. 'Now what?'

'Guess we get to go to Brimfield sooner than planned.' His smile was grim as he contemplated the difficulties that lay ahead. With Hannah demanding he find others to share the load of supplying the blood needed to make her vaccine, he didn't have much of a choice.

If all the Wards and towns were locked against them, curing the freaks was not going to be an easy prospect.

TWO

Justice pulled the heavy box toward her, coughing at the dust she stirred up as she peeled back the cardboard lid. The smell of damp and musty books rose in the air and she held her breath as she reached inside to pull out the first one, skimming her eyes over the faded cover.

There was no telling how long the Legion had stored these books. Barrett had discovered them on a foray deep into the mine while looking for supplies with Leon and some of the other former construction workers. He'd thought Hannah would find them useful, but it had been Justice whose heart had raced at the sight of the long disused library.

The Legion had spent countless resources, in both money and lives, in their effort to stop her from fulfilling the destiny Gaea set out for her before she was born. She was hoping this library would contain information she could use to decipher the Earth Goddess' last message to her. For try as she might, she had not been able to understand how she was to wash clean the sins of the fathers to give mankind the second chance she had already died for once.

Daniel Zarb's book had been more focused on the lore that surrounded her creation and the act of judgement. A judgement she thought she had delivered in this very compound, only to discover after her death that it had not been enough. Sure, her sacrifice had cured the man she loved and enabled Hannah to use Jackson's blood to create her vaccine. But mankind was still on the same path to destruction as they had been.

Somewhere, she had failed to complete a final step, the step that would truly give mankind hope of a better future. All her sacrifice had done was buy them a little more time. But as each day passed with her no closer to understanding what her task was, Justice knew the days of everyone she cared about were numbered.

She had to find out the truth of her purpose.

This was the last box of books. Those she had opened earlier had revealed a mismatch of fiction and nonfiction texts, none of them related to her or her purpose.

This was her last hope, and she continued to hold her breath as she pulled out book after book and scanned the covers.

The box was half empty before she took her first breath, a wave of dizziness swamping her as she stared at the set of gold scales embossed in dark brown leather. Just like Daniel's book, the scales matched the birthmark covering her right palm.

Hands shaking, not daring to hope in case what she'd found was a copy of the book she already had, Justice carefully opened the cover. The writing within was faded, the pages crinkling as she leafed through them. Some of them were stuck together, and she gingerly prised them apart as she scanned the words printed on them.

It was a different book.

Her gasp spilled out before she could help it.

'Did you find something?'

Hope brimming inside her, Justice looked over to where Hannah was standing in front of one of the stainless-steel tables in the centre of the lab, her hands on the elaborate microscope taking up most of the available space.

'I think so. At least, it isn't a copy of Daniel's book. But I don't know if it will help us yet.'

Her friend took a thin slice of glass smeared with a whitish substance out of the view spot on the microscope and carefully placed it on the table. Then she wiped her hands on her lab coat and came over to peer at the book in Justice's hands.

'What does it say?'

Justice frowned as she peered at the faded writing, angling the book to take advantage of the brighter lighting in the lab. Unlike the rest of the compound that made do with solar lights and lamps, this room had fluorescent lighting. Considering the Legion scientists had been behind the creation of the freak virus five hundred years earlier, and had been working on a way to control the infected ever since, it made sense that this room would be better lit than everywhere else.

That was why Justice had asked Barrett to bring the boxes of books there rather than try to examine them in the mine or the room she shared with Jackson.

Hannah hadn't been too impressed at the idea of cluttering up her immaculate workspace with musty old books, but she'd let Justice have a table in the corner. She knew how important it was to find a clue to what Justice was supposed to do next. Though Justice knew Hannah still thought her vaccine had already answered one part of the puzzle.

Justice hoped that when she found out what the bit about facing the past meant, she would also gain insight into the rest, to see if Hannah was right, or if blood still had a part to play in ensuring the future of humankind.

All her hopes rested on the book in her hand, and as she leafed through the pages, her excitement grew.

'It's talking about me, about what I would need to know to fulfil my purpose.'

'Really? It has all the answers?'

'We're not that lucky. It is more of a guide meant for my teacher, for the one who would train me to dispense justice.'

'And who would that be?'

Justice's excitement dimmed. 'Brother Owen.' Tears filled her eyes. 'He was the head of the monastery where I was raised until I was ten. I had lessons with him every day, even before I could talk, where he would tell me stories about what life was like before the virus was unleashed, and the state of the world since. It was because of his teachings that I knew I was supposed to visit each town and observe the people so that Gaea could assess humankind through me and determine what her justice would entail.'

'But how does a teaching manual help you figure out what Gaea meant?'

'It doesn't. But it does give me a clue.' Justice took a deep breath. 'I think I have to go back to the monastery, to face my past.'

A hint of the turmoil created at the idea of going back to where her mother and the monks had been slaughtered by the Legion must have shown on her face, as Hannah moved forward to hug her. Justice was grateful for the comfort. The thought of returning, after fifteen years, set her stomach churning with a mixture of dread and sadness. It was the last time she could remember being happy, sheltered by the monks, with her mother's love a constant in her life. As much as she loved Jackson and was happy to be here with Hannah and the rest of the friends she had made, part of her wished life could have been different. That she could have remained with the monks, venturing to the towns with Brother Owen as her guide instead of a succession of men who had tried to kill her before becoming her reluctant bodyguards.

But that was not the way her life had turned out, and wishing for it to be different would not help.

Besides, she was happy now. If she could just fulfil her duty by doing whatever it was Gaea meant for her to do, then that would be enough, a way to honour the memory of those who had fallen.

It was not just her mother and the monks who had paid with their lives. Many people—humans, wardens, and half-breeds—had died because she had not fulfilled her purpose correctly.

Once Jackson returned with blood from the newly cured freaks in Harlington, and plans were underway to cure the infected in the other towns, they could then return to the town where she had been born to complete one last task for Gaea.

No matter what, she would find a way to save them all.

THREE

Rona Maguire glared at the man cowering in front of her, disgusted by his cowardice.

They were all cowards, every single one of the people huddled on the ground in front of her, bodies covered with filth from the sewer system she'd found them hiding in. She turned back to the man who had been their unofficial leader.

'Tell me again how you lot managed to survive, and yet our masters were left behind to be slaughtered by members of the Brimfield Council.'

'There was no time,' Evan Johnson said, a quiver in his voice. 'As soon as Master Callaghan died, and his control of the freaks was broken, the council took their revenge by killing the masters. They came after us, too. We were lucky to escape. The wardens would have killed us for sure, if we hadn't got away.'

Rona kicked him in the ribs, snarling when all he did was roll over and wait for her to do it again. There was no fight left in him, the debacle with the wardens weakening him to the point of ruin. She'd be better off putting him down, but he was the best source of information she had on what she now faced.

'How many of you escaped?'

Evan rolled onto his side and got to his knees, one hand holding his side where she had kicked him. His features were racked with pain, but she had no sympathy for him, for any of them.

'Fifty-seven of us made it out of Brimfield, but we lost eleven of them on the way here when we were attacked by freaks. They couldn't infect us, but they could still kill us.'

Rona lunged forward, nostrils flaring, causing Evan to flinch as if expecting another blow. 'What do you mean, they couldn't infect you?'

'The Brimfield wardens came up with a cure, and the council gave Master Callaghan enough to vaccinate two dozen people so our scientists could test it. He used it on me and then got one of his pet freaks to bite me.'

He held up his arm and pulled back his sleeve to show ragged teeth marks on his wrist. 'When I didn't turn into a freak, he used it on himself and the masters. He kept some for the councillors and used the rest on Karline and some of our people so they could act as guards. Then he used the council's airship to turn every single human in town into a freak, all of them under his control. Until the wardens cured them all.'

Rona frowned. If Karline had been made immune to the freak virus, why was she not with this lot? Not that she would ever be found cowering in a sewer. 'Where is my sister?'

Evan sucked in a deep breath before answering. 'She's dead. The wardens threw her and Callaghan off the roof of the council building.' Voice quavering, he described how he had fled the chaotic battle on the rooftop, finding the broken bodies of her sister and the man who had taken control of the Legion on the ground as the wardens used the airship to spread their cure.

Rona turned away, refusing to let him or the others see the tears glistening in her eyes as he detailed the last moments of her beautiful sister's life. Karline had always been the outgoing one, her personality as vibrant as her flame-coloured hair. She'd been intelligent and strong willed, as well as fiercely loyal to their cause, which is why their grandfather had chosen her to accompany him to the mine compound to compete for the role of successor.

To hear now that Marcus Callaghan had been made heir, only to turn on the masters and then be defeated by the wardens, burned. She would not let them get away with killing her sister.

With justice delivered, the opportunity to bring about the Apocalypse was lost, but that did not mean the plan to rule the masses was dead. She turned back to Evan. 'Tell me about the cure.'

She listened without saying a word as he talked. When he finally fell silent, she subjected him to a barrage of questions to make sure there was nothing else of use he could tell her.

'I swear, I don't know what happened to the half-breed who came up with the cure. She could have died in the battle for all I know. As soon as I could, I rounded up as many of our people as possible and fled. We were lucky to escape as it was.' His head hung low. 'We had no food, no water, and the trucks ran out of petrol halfway here. We had to walk the rest of the way, and couldn't risk entering any of the towns we passed for supplies in case the wardens were warned to look out for us.'

Rona looked over at the group of bedraggled individuals. She and her crew had come across them while completing a check of all the Legion strongholds spread throughout the country. They'd been set up by her ancestors after the prophecy of Gaea's chosen one began to circulate. They'd had no idea where the physical embodiment of Gaea's justice would eventually surface, and had made sure they had bases near most of the major towns so they could be ready for the day of judgement.

When that day came, and the world remained as it was,

Rona had begun a search of all the strongholds in an effort to discover what had gone wrong.

Now she knew. The plan her ancestors had set in motion over five hundred years ago had failed. It was time for a new plan.

First, she had to take out the trash.

'Did any of the scientists make it out of Brimfield?' Rona asked, narrowing her eyes when two men and one woman raised their hands.

'You three, get up. I need to speak to you in private.'

The three exchanged worried glances, but they were too weak and cowed to do anything but obey. Her top lip curled into a sneer as they got to their feet and stumbled to the door.

Once they were outside, Rona nodded toward her second-in-command, Richard Carter, using hand signals to tell him what she wanted done. Then she stepped outside, untroubled by the screams that filled the shed or the horrified looks on the faces of the three whose lives she had spared. She had a use for them.

As for the others, they were all unworthy.

For what was to come, only the strongest could be allowed to take part.

FOUR

Hannah was pleased to see the book had given some zing back to Justice's steps, and hoped her guess about having to return to the monastery was right. Despite her assurance that the vaccine had to be what Gaea had meant about cleansing the sins in blood, a niggling doubt ate away at her. What if she was wrong and there was something else Justice needed to do involving blood? The answers might be contained in the monastery, though she knew it would not be easy for her friend to return there.

But with Jackson by her side, as well as Hannah, Justice would be well cared for as she confronted such dark memories in the flesh. That is, if she could convince Justice to wait until after she had the rest of the vaccine ready to go and they had completed their raid on Brimfield.

Leaving Justice to read, Hannah returned to her microscope and prepared another slide. She was working on a way to boost the antibodies in her blood, in case Jackson was not able to get enough blood from the freaks he was curing at Harlington. There was no guarantee any of them would agree to the request, once they discovered how they had been infected in the first place.

That Randolph—the then leader of the half-breeds—had been aware of the practice had sent a shock wave through the rescued people.

Thoughts of the man who had attacked her, who had been intent on handing her over to General Butcher, made Hannah shudder. He had returned to Harlington, along with most of the half-breeds he had once led and a number from Brimfield as well. With the defeat of Butcher's forces, those with young families and many of the older half-breeds had decided it was safe to return to civilisation. Brimfield was closed to all of them, thanks to Councillor Dillon, but Harlington offered a new life.

Though Hannah had been sad to see them leave, it had made it easier on their meagre supplies and cramped accommodations. All of Hanson's construction crew had remained at the compound, as had Felice and several young, single half-breeds who did not want to return to a life of menial labour for humans who looked down on them and paid them a pittance.

They would need to do a supply run soon—find a town willing to trade the vaccine for food and other supplies, though Hannah did not like the thought of withholding a cure if a town was unwilling or unable to pay for it.

She also didn't like the idea of having to return to Brimfield in the near future. The airship they had used to spray the infected citizens with was the easiest way for them to cure the greatest number of freaks in a short time. But stealing the airship, for a second time, would have to wait until she had the vaccine to use. It would be a couple of days before Jackson and the others would be expected to return with the blood.

It was a surprise when she heard his voice in the corridor outside the lab.

She looked over to Justice, who was still engrossed in her book. 'Jackson's back.'

'He's here?' At first Justice wore a smile, but then her brow creased and she shook her head. 'It's too soon. Something must have gone wrong.'

Justice tossed the book on the table and strode for the door, with Hannah on her heels.

Jackson, talking in a low voice to Hanson, looked up at their arrival and gave them a grim smile. 'We've got a problem.'

He filled them in on what Captain Murphy had revealed. 'I've got Jensen and Carstairs putting together supplies. We'll have to visit Brimfield sooner than planned. Two teams. One to secure the airship and one to get blood.'

Hannah grimaced, knowing it was going to be a nightmare to find people willing to donate enough blood for her to make a sufficient quantity of vaccine. With Councillor Dillon out to kill every single one of them, they would have to dodge his security forces to do it.

As Jackson and the others left the lab to get the incursion organised, Hannah was flooded with dark memories of the battle to get out of Brimfield before the mob caught up with them. Hanson shot, face pale, unconscious in the back of the truck. Body bags lined up, a stark reminder of the cost of their freedom. No one had died when they'd gone back to test her theory about cured freaks being the best candidates for the antibodies she needed to create her vaccine, but it had been clear the people of Brimfield wanted to kill them rather than help them.

That was why Jackson had decided to go to Harlington instead.

With that option lost to them, Brimfield was the last hope she had of making enough of her vaccine to make a difference. Taking a deep breath, she gripped the edge of the bench and closed her eyes, working to block out the memories. This time, it would be different. It had to be.

She opened her eyes and scanned the lab, trying to determine what she would need to take with her to collect and transport the blood safely back. Jackson would want to get going as soon as possible, so there was no time to waste. She went to the storage cupboards lining one wall. Hands shaking, she pulled one open and grabbed out syringes and blood bags, placing them on a nearby bench.

Soon she had a pile of gear and was stuffing it into two backpacks. Her hands had steadied as she worked and by the time she was done, her resolve had strengthened. One way or another, she would get the blood she needed and help cure the world of freaks.

FIVE

Hanson attempted to stare Jackson down. 'You are not coming with us.'

'I'm captain here, Hanson. Not you.'

'Then act like it. You're in no condition to go up against Councillor Dillon. Hannah said you need to take it easy until your blood levels build up. Not go tearing off and starting a war with another township.'

'I'm not starting a war with Brimfield. We just need more resources.' Jackson grimaced. 'I can't sit around and do nothing while you and the others put yourselves in danger.'

'Then go find us some other resources, ones that aren't guarded by angry humans out for your blood. At this stage, you are the only person Hannah can use to make her vaccine. We can't afford for you to get caught, or worse.'

'Hanson is right,' Justice said, putting a hand on Jackson's arm. 'We need you more than we need Hanson.' She shot him a tight smile. 'No offence.'

He grinned back. 'Is all good. I know you love me.'

Justice rolled her eyes and then focused on Jackson once more. 'Besides, there is something I need to tell you.' She led him away, and Hanson let his smile go.

As confident as he sounded, he knew that getting in and out of Brimfield in one piece was not going to be easy. He strode over to the ATV Jackson and Carstairs had taken to Harlington and checked the gear his team had prepared for their mission. Stun guns were in one pile, with the medical equipment beside it.

Hanson looked over at Leon, who was ticking items off a list Felice had given him. 'Which of the medics will be coming with us?'

'That would be me.'

Hanson spun around and faced Hannah. 'No way. You are not coming with us. It's too dangerous.' He didn't need to hear Leon's low whistle to know that delivering an order to the pretty young half-breed was a bad move, but he couldn't help it.

Hannah put her hands on her hips and glared at him. 'You do not get to tell me what I can and cannot do, Hanson Forsythe. And if you think I'm going to let anyone else handle my equipment, you'd be wrong. I am going on this mission whether you like it or not.'

'We'll see about that.' He stormed off, searching for Jackson. Maybe he would have more luck convincing Hannah that she was needed here.

After a short search, he found Jackson and Justice standing with the grim-faced commander of the mercenary unit, the Righteous. Mouth twisted into a wry smirk, he scanned the black-clad man, aware he'd formerly been contracted to kill him and Jackson by Councillor Dillon. It had only been luck, an uprising by humans from Harlington, that had forced the councillor to cancel the contract. The Righteous never gave up on a kill order otherwise.

Even though the mercenaries had helped them to defeat General Butcher and the sadistic Major Templeton, Hanson was glad to know that they were about to leave.

'Are you sure we cannot convince you to stay?' Jackson asked. 'We could use your help in Brimfield again.'

Before Hanson could protest that he was more than capable of seeing his small team victorious, Isaac Smith shook his head.

'I've got bills to pay, men to take care of. If I keep taking on jobs pro bono, the Righteous will fold. As it is, the only reason I helped you in the first place was for Justice's sake.' He gave a grim smile.

'And the vaccine,' Hanson said, crossing his arms in front of his chest as he came to a halt beside Justice. 'It wasn't as if you got paid nothing for your trouble.' A good portion of Hannah's vaccine had been used to inoculate the mercenaries against the freak virus. That vaccine could have been used on the half-breeds the security guards in Harlington had infected to produce more freaks for their training exercises.

Now that Harlington was barred to them, the remaining portion of vaccine was all they had unless he and his team returned from Brimfield with more blood. A team that was not going to include Hannah.

Jiggling from one foot to the other, he waited for the mercenary commander to say his final goodbyes and head for the gate with the rest of his people before rounding on Jackson.

'You need to tell Hannah she can't come with me. She's too valuable to risk.'

Jackson shook his head. 'Sorry, Hanson. I wish I could, but she's as stubborn as you are. She insists on going with you, and nothing I say will change her mind.'

'You're the captain. She has to listen to you.'

'So you'd think, but I'm finding I don't have as much authority as I would like these days.' He leaned in and smiled down at Justice.

The smile she gave him in return was so full of emotion, Hanson had to look away.

He cleared his throat, scuffing his feet in the red dirt. 'What if she gets hurt? What if something goes wrong?'

Jackson clasped him on the shoulder. 'You're a good man, Hanson. She'll be in good hands. I know you won't let anything happen to her, and neither will Carstairs. He'll be in charge of the team to get the airship. Once he has that in the air, he can spirit the rest of you out of Brimfield and away from trouble. Just make sure you don't miss the deadline.'

Hanson grimaced at the mention of the lieutenant from Harlington. He was way too friendly when it came to Hannah. But at least she would be on his team, not Carstairs'. He would only have to put up with him and his overly friendly smiles on the way to and from Brimfield. Maybe he could get Carstairs to drop his team to the ATVs so they could drive back with Barrett.

No, he didn't need Carstairs' help to look after Hannah. His team would watch her back. They all knew how important she was. They'd never let anything happen to her.

Resigned to having Hannah as part of his team, despite his misgivings, Hanson strode back to the ATVs that would take both teams to Brimfield, working on a way to make sure Carstairs travelled in the second ATV.

SIX

Councillor Kelvin Dillon glared at Neil Barrowman, annoyed by his aide's subservient manner. 'What do you mean, he got away?'

'By the time the security guards realised who was at their gates, Captain Kyle had turned around and headed back to wherever it is he and his wardens are hiding out,' said Neil.

'Imbeciles. He should have been arrested before he could turn around.' He ground his teeth; the failure of the Harlington security forces to apprehend Jackson Kyle made him want to hit something. 'You can be sure the Over-Council will be hearing about this. As will Ward High Command. That disgraced captain knew Kyle was wanted by his own people. He should have taken steps to arrange his capture.'

He pushed his chair back and stood up, moving to pace in front of his large wooden desk. 'Kyle will go to ground now, aware all the councils and Wards are on the lookout for him and his renegade wardens.' Not that them being on the lookout had achieved anything at Harlington.

He faced Neil. 'Is there any word yet on where Kyle is hiding out?' That damned mercenary commander had known, but the freaking bastard had sided with Kyle, helping the warden trick him into cancelling the contract on him and Hanson Forsythe. If he ever crossed paths with the mercenary, he would make him pay dearly for that. He'd tried to take out a contract on the commander, but his offer had been knocked back. Supposedly, it was against some kind of mercenary code.

Still, he'd put out the word that the Righteous were not to be trusted. Even if no one took up the offer of a substantial reward for the commander's head, once jobs started to dry up, he'd soon learn that it did not pay to cross Kelvin Dillon.

'I'm afraid not, sir. We know it is somewhere between here and Harlington but have been unable to pinpoint where they have made their base. According to the old maps, there are no ruins big enough or in a stable enough condition to house them between here and there.'

Kelvin thumped his hand down on his desk. 'Damn it. Tell them to keep looking. They're out there somewhere, and we need to find them before they come back and attack us again.'

'Sir, do you really think they would be stupid enough to come back after what happened last time?'

'Not stupid. Desperate.' He gave a cruel smile. 'We have something they need.' He might not know where his foe was hiding, but thanks to communications with High Command and the Over-Council, he knew what Kyle wanted.

'They need more blood to make their vaccine. So far, Kyle has been the only source of the antibodies needed to make the cure. From what I was told, in strict confidence, the wardens believe our people can supply the blood, the ones that were turned into freaks.'

Neil shivered, and Kelvin's smile widened. Neil had been one of those infected by Marcus Callaghan and subsequently cured by the wardens. 'If you want to keep your blood where it is, you need to find out where Kyle and his wardens are hiding out. Then we can take the fight to them, rather than wait for them to realise the only hope they have of spreading their cure is right here in Brimfield.'

Neil's brow creased. 'But don't we want them to spread the cure? After all, if they get rid of the freaks for good, there would be no need for wardens anymore. Life could go back to the way it was before the virus started.'

'Don't be an idiot. Brimfield has a chance to become the premier town in the country. There are no freaks here. No wardens, and no half-breeds. Our original citizens are safe from the virus, and we can make sure people pay dearly to come and live in safety with us.'

'Won't we just end up like before if people find out how good we have it here?'

Kelvin grimaced, aware Neil was referring to the lower-class humans who had fled to Brimfield from Harlington en masse once word got out that the town was freak-free. That had ended with them trying to take over, and Kelvin needing to be rescued by Kyle.

'We will vet people at the gate and impose a hefty tax for entry to Brimfield. Those who cannot pay will be turned away. I will not let our home be overrun by riffraff ever again.' He rubbed his hands together. 'In the meantime, we need to organise a welcoming party for when Kyle realises Brimfield is his last hope of securing the blood he needs.'

He strode to the door, beckoning for Neil to follow him as he headed for the office on the ground floor that housed his top security guard, David Flanders. He would make sure there was no chance of escape for Kyle this time, sure a closed gate wouldn't deter him from making the attempt to get what he needed. He would have people stationed on every street, hidden, watching for the first sign of Kyle and his renegades. Once they were spotted, the rest of his forces would charge in.

Then he would see how smug Kyle was once he had him in chains. Forget about handing him over to the Over-Council for punishment. Kelvin would execute Kyle himself, and the half-breed who had killed his son. No one messed with the Dillon family and got away with it. Before he was finished, Kyle and his renegades would be crushed beneath his feet and Brimfield would become the most prosperous town of all, thanks to him.

SEVEN

Jackson scratched his head as he looked at Justice. 'A supply run?'

'You said sitting around doing nothing is driving you crazy, and we need supplies. Carstairs said there are still more supplies at the Harlington Ward storage shed. Even with Isaac and his mercenaries gone, we are still stretched to the limit. Ward rations may not taste the best, but they are better than going hungry while we wait for Barrett and Trev's garden to produce enough to feed all of us. If we could get some more livestock, that would help too, to keep everyone fed while we go to the monastery.'

'You win,' he said, smiling as he came forward and wrapped an arm around her. 'As long as you come with me.'

She'd been spending so much time with those dusty old books, and it would do her good to get out and about. Maybe it would distract her from the notion she had failed in some way when she'd dispensed Gaea's justice. As much as he would like to journey with her to the place where she was raised, he knew High Command was where he could make the most difference. It was the only way for the wardens to move forward. He would have to go back, plead his case, and hope the colonels were smart enough to listen. But he couldn't leave until Hanson and the others returned from Brimfield, their mission a success.

Hanson was right: as the only currently available source of antibodies needed for the cure, he was too valuable to risk on a trip to Brimfield, much as it would please him to go against Councillor Dillon one more time.

Though a supply run wouldn't be as exciting, they did need more food.

'All right. Let's get going.'

Within minutes, Justice was beside him in the cab of a truck, while Barrett and Trev made themselves comfortable in the back. As the two of them showed an aptitude for cooking, they had become the compound's official chefs. Though Jackson didn't anticipate trouble, he had a stun gun strapped in his holster, while Justice and the half-breeds were also armed.

Not that he hoped for them to have to use their weapons. Especially Justice.

She hadn't said much since shooting General Butcher to save Jackson's life, but he knew it weighed on her. Her nights were restless, and she'd been hesitant to take the gun from him when he handed it to her. But as much as he wished she never needed to fire a weapon again, he knew the odds were she would have to defend herself at some point in the future. Especially if he couldn't talk her out of going to the monastery until after he had sorted out the mess at High Command.

Pushing thoughts of the future out of his head for the moment, he drove out the gate, the tyres squelching in the red mud. The storm had passed as quickly as it had arrived, though heavy skies remained overhead. This time of year was notorious for bad weather, making it hard for the solar panels to gather energy throughout each day. While many industries had recovered in the centuries after the devastation caused when the freak virus first surfaced, solar was still the only viable source of energy. With luck, they would be able to stock up on batteries, fuel for the generators, and oil for the lanterns while at the Harlington storage depot to get them through the coming weeks.

He pushed thoughts of all the things he needed to take care of from his mind, determined to enjoy the reprieve from command. He'd left Lieutenant Jensen in charge of the compound, though he knew the warden would have much preferred to be on the mission to Brimfield with Hanson and Carstairs. Jackson needed someone he could count on to hold down the fort while he was gone, and Jensen had matured a lot since his time as patrol leader in Brimfield. In particular, everything he had done to help Lieutenant Anderson and the others escape from Harlington and to rescue Jackson in High Command showed he had the potential to be a good leader.

A pang went through him at the thought of Geoff Anderson. His old friend should be there with them, fighting to ensure a future free of freaks. Instead, he'd become a victim of General Butcher's determination to stop the Wards from becoming redundant.

Jackson feared that was also the reason High Command was licking its wounds and hunkering down behind their desks. The colonels had spent their entire careers fighting freaks. It was what they were bred for, what they expected to die for. If there were no freaks to fight, they would lose a major part of their identity. But even knowing his time as a warden was coming to an end, Jackson knew he was doing the right thing in pushing for a future not tainted by fear of infection.

Justice was silent beside him as she gazed out the window, and he knew it wasn't the view that occupied her thoughts. There was not much to see beyond the occasional rusted car wreck, sparse trees, and sun baked earth alongside the rutted road. She smiled when he reached over and took her hand and gave it a squeeze.

'Not long now,' he said, not sure if he meant their arrival at the storage depot or for the future where they no longer had a responsibility to others guiding their actions.

When they reached the depot hidden away in a valley created between two low mountain ranges, Jackson got out of the truck and opened the rear to let Trev and Barrett out.

'You keep watch,' he said to Justice.

She gave him a solemn nod and then scanned their surroundings while he and the others headed for the roller door at the front of the depot, using the combination Carstairs had given him to unlock it.

Within an hour, they had loaded the truck with the last of the supplies. Jackson hoped it would be enough to see his people through the storm season. If Murphy couldn't convince Acting-General Stratton and the colonels that he and his wardens were not traitors, it could be a long time before they were welcome in any of the Wards to trade for more goods. Even then, it could be difficult with the Over-Council out to get them as well.

Once they had the cure ready to go, maybe the humans would accept that they were not the enemy Councillor Dillon was making them out to be. It all hinged on getting more blood for the cure and the airship so they could safely deliver it. He only hoped that when they returned to the compound, Hanson or Carstairs had checked in and had been successful in their mission.

EIGHT

ANDY STRODE TOWARD THE FRONT GATE, A FROWN CREASING his brow as he watched the mercenary commander, Isaac Smith, exit his four-wheel-drive.

'What happened?' All the garbled radio communication had said was that the mercenary was returning and that the matter was urgent.

'Where's Justice?' Smith asked. 'I have something for her.'

'She and Captain Kyle are on a supply run. They should return soon.'

Smith grinned. 'Excellent. Then she can make sense of this.' He turned to his vehicle and thumped on the side. The rear door slid open and two mercenaries hopped out. One of them leaned in and helped another person exit the vehicle.

The figure was swathed in a brown robe with the hood up. As one of the mercenaries took his arm and led the newcomer forward, the monk lifted the hood back and revealed a travel-weary face. He sagged and would have fallen if not for the firm grip the mercenary had on his arm.

'Found this guy walking beside the road between here and Harlington,' said Smith. 'He stepped into the middle of the road, right in front of me, and I nearly hit him. When I got out to yell at him, he told me I needed to bring him to Justice.'

Andy's mind whirled. What was a monk doing looking for Justice?

The question must have been in his eyes as Smith shrugged. 'Your guess is as good as mine. Other than demanding I bring him here, the crazy old fool hasn't said a word.'

Not sure what was going on, Andy stared at the monk. 'Who are you? What do you want with Justice?'

'My business is with her, young warden. Not you. Not him.' He indicated toward Smith with a nod of his head. 'Only Justice.' The monk's voice was hoarse, saturated with weariness.

Andy frowned. 'Now listen here—'

'Lieutenant Jensen, shame on you. Can't you see our guest is about dead on his feet. The questions can wait until after he's fed and rested.'

A flush warming his cheeks, Andy spun around to find Felice staring at him, hands on her hips and a wry smirk curving her full lips. There was a challenge in her gaze, one that had him flushing even more.

He crossed his arms and lifted his chin. 'I am in charge of base security while the captain isn't here.'

'I doubt one monk is going to endanger the base, especially when he is surrounded by soldiers.' She gave Andy an arch look before stepping forward and clasping the monk on the arm. 'Let's get you settled in while we wait for Justice and the captain to return.

The monk gave Andy a slight nod, a faint smile curving his lips, before he limped along with Felice and the mercenary. Andy watched them walk away, his gaze on Felice's back, her ponytail swinging with each step she took.

Smith chuckled as he clasped Andy on the shoulder. 'So

much for you being in charge.' Then he strode off after the trio, the remaining mercenary staying with the vehicle.

Andy followed Smith, wondering what this old monk had to do with Justice. If previous events were anything to go by, things were about to get interesting.

NINE

The sky was darkening when one of her men called out to Rona that the scientists were ready.

She turned away from the brown landscape that surrounded the Legion compound she had arrived at two days earlier. It had been an agricultural college before the freak virus had been unleashed on the world. Several years afterward, when the small town nearby had perished in the confusion and flames brought on by mass panic and anger at what the so-called cure for the common cold had wrought, the Legion moved in.

Its location, four hours southwest of High Command and a similar distance to the northwest of Dalwaring, had been an ideal spot at which to observe what the government was up to. No one travelled this way anymore; the land that had been drought-stricken even before the Legion began their assault on the country was not an attractive option for those looking to eke out a living in the new world order.

With residential quarters for staff and students, it offered much in the way of housing, and careful cultivation had brought some of the land back to life, though that was kept hidden in case someone did stumble out this way. For the most part, the surviving towns were located closer to the coastline, centred in land that offered more resources for the people who survived the initial furore.

Now Rona headed for a building that had once housed a state-of-the-art laboratory for the students of centuries ago. The Legion had turned it into biological storage, securing samples of the original freak virus in case they were ever needed.

It had been some time since the college had been used by the Legion, only a token force manning the facility to ensure it remained undetected and its fresh produce harvested and sent on to the other strongholds. The lab had needed cleaning up, grime-covered benches washed, floors and walls scrubbed, so the scientists she had brought with her could work in relative comfort.

Not that she cared about their comfort. After failing in Brimfield, they were lucky she let them live. But she needed them. The old masters had kept the brightest of minds with them.

Karline had been one of those bright disciples destined for greatness, until the wardens dashed her promise on an unforgiving ground. They would pay for that with their lives, but first she would bring them to their knees. They would soon know what it felt like to have their purpose for living taken away, to have the thing you had worked for all your life forever out of reach.

She passed groups of Legion members she had found as she made her way to the college, all working hard to make the place liveable again. It would be their new base of operations, with the stronghold near Brimfield compromised now the wardens were aware it existed. Once the wardens were no more, all the strongholds would be made operational and Rona would see to it that every town knew they owed their lives to the Legion.

Outside the lab, she nodded to the guards stationed on

either side of the entrance and received a steady nod from each in return, with one hurrying to open the door for her. Inside the now pristine space, the three scientists hunched over a table and jabbered excitedly to each other as they stared at their handiwork.

Rona took in the test tubes, beakers, microscopes, and vials of who knew what. She had no idea what it all meant; she cared only about the outcome.

'Will it work?'

The scientists all spun around, one of the men clutching his throat and yelping.

Rona snorted. This lot were not fighters, to be caught so unawares even when they had to be expecting her arrival. Too engrossed in their science to pay attention to their surroundings.

The lead scientist, Bryant Montgomery, a gaunt man whose hair was thinning, pushed back his glasses and gave a wary nod. 'It is as you requested. We believe we have successfully configured the virus to shut off the pain receptors, allowing those infected to fight longer, unhampered by a survival instinct.'

'You haven't tested it?'

'We were waiting for you.'

'Then what are we waiting for?'

With more guards in tow, she led the scientists to the shed where livestock had once been housed. It was beyond the shed where the crops were tilled. The shed had since been filled with garden supplies and farm implements, but the cages for housing cattle remained intact.

Inside the first two cages were a pair of male travellers who had been making their way from Alston to Dalwaring, Rona's group coming across them after their vehicle had suffered a flat tyre. They had initially hidden when Rona and her forces had drawn near, but it had been a simple matter to prise them from their hiding holes and tie them up.

The third cage held a Legion member who had failed in his duty at Brimfield. He had been turned into a freak by Marcus Callaghan and then cured by the wardens. He had fled in a different direction to Johnson's group, taking refuge at the college, thinking he would be safe there.

Now he, like the others, would be a guinea pig for the scientists' modified virus.

Two of Rona's men entered the first cage to subdue the prisoner. He got to his feet and made to escape, but, weakened by lack of food and water, his efforts were ineffectual. Within seconds, he was face down on the ground, his arms twisted behind his back and a foot wedged into the back of his neck.

With an impatient growl, Richard ushered the scientist hovering in the doorway forward, even as the process was repeated in the other two cages.

With a scurry, Bryant entered the first cage and knelt beside the prisoner, hands shaking as he uncapped a syringe and injected the virus into the man's arm. Then he lurched to his feet and bolted out of the cage. Chest heaving, he watched as his colleagues repeated the process in the next two cages. Richard ordered his men to withdraw, and they let the men go and calmly exited the cages, locking the doors behind them.

'How long until the virus takes effect?' Rona asked Bryant.

'We boosted the strength as you requested, but cannot estimate how long until the effects will be felt since this is the initial test of this configuration. With the previous one, the subjects began feeling the effects of the virus within hours. The time to fully infect them depended on their overall health and constitution.'

Rona hadn't taken her eyes off the first prisoner to be injected with the modified virus. When he shot to his feet and launched himself at the bars, hands outstretched for her throat, she gave a delighted laugh.

The whites of his eyes shone, and he showed no sign of being affected by the bright lighting in the shed. Then his eyes began to leak blood. It dripped down his cheeks, but he gave no sign it bothered him as he hurled himself at the bars, desperate to get to her to rend her flesh.

In the other cages, a similar transformation had taken effect, the newly created freaks snarling as they attempted to reach the humans outside the cages. Even the one who had been cured in Brimfield had turned, and within minutes instead of hours. The rattling of the bars filled the shed.

'Get your men ready,' Rona told Richard.

No sooner had she spoken the words than the freak in front of her gave an almighty wrench and tore the hinges off the cage door. In a split second, he bounded through the gap he had made.

Guns fired, and the freak's body was pelted with bullets. He ignored the pain of his injuries as he fought to get to Rona. A shot to his head sent him flying backward to land in a crumpled and bloody position on the ground. On either side of Rona, her men continued to fire at the prisoners in the remaining cages and soon all three freaks were dead.

Rona faced Richard. 'Well?'

'It took four times the firepower it should have to take them down. They're strong. Fast. And they don't give a shit about how much punishment they take. Only way to put them down for good is a headshot.'

'Excellent.' Ignoring the carnage in the cages and on the ground in front of her, Rona turned to the scientists, who were cowering in a group as far away from the dead freaks as possible.

'You have done well. Now, I need you to complete the bloodwork to make sure the next batch of freaks will obey me before we do a field test.'

Bryant unravelled his thin frame as he shook his head. 'The equipment to do that is at the mine stronghold, but it has been compromised.'

Hands on her hips, Rona stared at him. 'Can you or can

you not replicate the gas Marcus Callaghan used to control freaks?'

'Of course, but this lab is not equipped for large-scale production. It would take months to make enough to control the volume of freaks you're talking about.'

'Don't give me excuses. Make it work or you will be one of the next test subjects.'

He blanched and hurriedly nodded. 'I'm sure we can come up with something,' he said, voice quavering as he looked at his fellow scientists.

'Excellent. I'll send my men out to find you more volunteers to test the gas on. As soon as you are ready, we'll head to Dalwaring and see how the wardens stand up against these new freaks.' A smile curved her lips as she left the shed, stepping around the dead body of the initial test subject.

Once her new breed of freaks were unleashed on the world, under her command, the wardens wouldn't stand a chance.

TEN

Callum Murphy met the eyes of the sitting colonels one by one. Then his gaze returned to the man who had taken charge of High Command after the death of General Butcher. 'I am telling you, Acting-General Stratton, you have nothing to fear from Jackson Kyle. He is not out to destroy the Ward. He is merely doing what all wardens have been trained to do: fight freaks.'

'He murdered General Butcher, as well as Major Templeton. He and his renegades are responsible for numerous casualties among our wardens. And you expect us to trust him?' Stratton's gravelly voice echoed through the large chamber where Callum was being interrogated.

He fought a wince at the reminder of the deaths that had occurred during the ill-fated attempt to take the compound where Kyle and his people now lived.

'General Butcher and Major Templeton were casualties of a war of their own making.' It had been Justice who had fired the fatal shot that killed Butcher, while a mercenary had been responsible for Templeton's death, but that did not matter here. All were under Kyle's command at the time, so he was ultimately held responsible.

'As I stated in my report, Kyle ordered his people to use non-lethal force.'

'I'm sure Butcher found it lethal enough,' one of the colonels said with a wry expression.

'Be that as it may,' said Callum, 'our losses would have been far greater if Kyle had not given that order. Unlike us, they sustained significant casualties.' No need to mention that he had also ordered his wardens to use non-lethal force. Those Templeton brought in had shown no hesitation in killing their former allies.

'What occurred at the compound where Kyle is residing was regrettable, an ill-planned endeavour that should never have been carried out,' he said.

'You are questioning General Butcher's orders?' Stratton's brows lowered.

'Yes, and so should you. His actions resulted in a schism within our ranks. He acted without the backing of the sitting colonels.' He let his gaze run over all of them, reminding them they had done nothing to stop Butcher when he had begun his vendetta against Kyle. Even now, they sat silent and allowed Stratton to do all the talking.

Callum shook his head. 'General Butcher should never have ordered the attack. Instead, he should have worked with Kyle to see that the cure was dispersed to each Ward. If he had done so, countless lives would have been saved.'

'Are you willing to stake your career on a cure that has never been properly tested?'

'Yes, sir, I am. You have Captain Landry's testimony that Kyle was not infected, although he had sustained a freak bite when she encountered him in Alston. A fact that the head medic at the Alston Ward has also testified to.'

'The medic was not present during the supposed incident where Kyle was bitten. All he has to go on is what he was told by Major Wallace, who is not here to testify on Kyle's behalf.'

'Because Butcher had him murdered.' A bitter taste filled Callum's mouth.

'Major Wallace was executed for treason. While it is regrettable that he was killed before he could be properly questioned, we must work with what we have.'

'Wallace was not a traitor to the Ward. He was deliberately silenced so he could not counter Butcher's version of events, and you know it.'

Stratton sighed. 'Arguing over what has happened in the past does not help us now. Without proof of wrongdoing on General Butcher's part, we can only look to what facts we have. As it stands, Jackson Kyle is a traitor to the Ward and must be brought to justice for the crimes he has committed against his fellow wardens. That is the law. Even if we were to find proof he acted in good faith and exonerate him, the human Over-Council is also out for his blood. He is a marked man, regardless of the outcome of his trial.'

Callum bit down on an angry retort, taking a deep breath before speaking again. 'If I can show you the cure is real, that we can rid the world of freaks thanks to Jackson Kyle, will you reconsider your stance toward him and his wardens?'

A long silence met his words.

Then Stratton asked, 'How do you propose we test this cure when we do not have any of the vaccine Kyle's half-breed created? Major Templeton destroyed the supplies they took to Harlington.'

'No, he didn't. He had it sent here, to High Command, on General Butcher's orders. It's here somewhere, hidden. Find out where Butcher and that measly aide of his stashed it and you will be able to protect every warden in High Command from infection.'

'Even if what you say is true, finding the vaccine could take days. There are hundreds of places it could be hidden within the citadel itself, let alone the entire town.'

A grin formed on Callum's lips, grateful for the note

slipped into his hands by a helmeted warden when he had first arrived in High Command. 'I already know where the vaccine is hidden.' He pointed in the direction of the old medical facility just outside the citadel. 'Butcher had it taken to the medical centre where Major Wallace was murdered.'

This was where all Butcher's dirty work had been done, where he'd had his scientists working to see if they could replicate Hannah Young's vaccine.

Callum straightened his shoulders. 'I request permission to take a patrol to Dalwaring, where we can prove that the cure works.'

A chorus of voices erupted as the colonels debated his request, but he was confident they would eventually see this made sense. Once he was able to prove to them that the cure worked and that Butcher had lied to them, maybe they would reconsider branding Jackson Kyle a traitor.

Callum couldn't do anything to get the Over-Council off Kyle's back, but if the Ward was willing to reinstate him, it would give him a stronger position to argue in his defence with the humans.

With a cure for freaks as a prize, even they would have to realise that keeping Kyle alive was for the good of all humankind.

ELEVEN

Justice leaned back in her seat and closed her eyes, allowing the rhythmic thump of the tyres to lull her into sleep as Jackson drove them back to the compound, the truck filled with much needed supplies. With everything that had happened lately, she'd had little time to rest. What sleep she had managed to snatch had been filled with darkness and screams, visions of the battle to stop Butcher and Templeton destroying them all.

She swallowed heavily, remembering the way her shot had hit the general right in the chest, how his body had jerked and convulsed as he'd been hit by a lethal amount of electricity. She hadn't meant to kill him, only stop him from hurting Jackson, not realising her weapon had been set to maximum strength.

What was done was done.

She had killed him, and now had to deal with the consequences in nightmares and missed sleep.

But she would not feel guilty for saving Jackson's life.

With him at her side, knowing he would do whatever it took to keep her safe, she dozed off, not stirring until they reached the gates to the mine compound and waited for the gates to open, still not ready to let go of her slumber.

'Your mercenary is back.'

Her eyes shot open and she sat up. 'Isaac is here?'

She'd been sad to see him go, though she'd understood why he couldn't stay. Having him around was almost like having Jonah back. Not that the brothers were alike in personality, but he had been a part of her past, something she was lacking.

She looked ahead and saw Isaac talking to Lieutenant Jensen, just outside the common room. Felice was there as well, in animated conversation with the two men. Then she spotted the truck and waved.

Jackson pulled up in the space outside the common room and cut the engine.

Justice scrambled down and headed toward Isaac. 'What's wrong? Why are you here?' She scanned his face, taking in the tense set to his shoulders and the grim look he shared with Jensen.

Isaac turned to her with an easy smile on his lips, a smile that did not reach his eyes. 'Nothing's wrong, little sister. I just found something that might interest you.'

'Lieutenant Jensen,' said Jackson, 'Trev and Barrett will need help unloading supplies.'

'I'll get people organised with the unpacking,' Felice said, tapping Andy on the arm. Without waiting to see what his response was, she strode off for the building where the single men were quartered.

Jackson, a hand pressing into the small of Justice's back, turned to Isaac. 'What have you got for us, Smith?'

'Nothing for you, Kyle. This particular surprise comes with Justice's name on it.' He opened the door to the common room and gestured for Justice to enter in front of him.

The lights inside were dimmed to conserve energy, and at first Justice couldn't see anything that could be classed as a surprise. Between meals, the room was empty, the tables cleared until the next meal.

No. Not completely empty.

A figure in a brown robe sat with its back to Justice, head bowed.

Heart thudding, Justice stepped closer, recognising the attire as the same worn by the Gaean monks where she had been raised. But they were all dead. Killed by the Legion's men in an attempt to stop her from dispensing justice.

Breathing shallow, not daring to hope, she called out a soft hello.

The figure straightened and stood, pushing the seat back and turning to face her, hands clasped in front of him in a sign of respect that was so familiar it ached.

Justice gasped, stumbled, and would have fallen if not for Jackson's firm hold.

'Brother Owen.' The name came out as a sigh, but he heard, inclining his head and giving her a tentative smile.

'Justice.'

At the sound of his voice, tears streamed down Justice's face. 'How is this possible? I saw you. You were dead.' Her eyes roamed over his face. He looked no older than he did the last time she had seen him. There was no sign of injury though his face was thinner than she remembered it.

'Our Goddess had need of me, and I was recalled from my slumber shortly after the day of Judgement.'

Hand to her mouth, Justice fought back a gasp. He'd been resurrected by Gaea. Just as she had. 'The others, are they …'

Sadness wreathed his features. 'I am afraid not. Merciful as Gaea is, she cannot tear through the veil lightly.'

A sob lodged in Justice's throat as the faint hope that her mother was alive was crushed before it had begun to thrive.

She lowered her head, letting her hair fall forward to shield her face as Jackson took her in his arms. She soaked in his strength for a moment and then pushed away from him to face Brother Owen once more.

'I have to go back to the monastery, don't I?'

He nodded grimly. 'I did not have time to fully prepare you for your purpose. Because of that, your judgement was flawed. That needs to be rectified, and the first step is to return to the monastery so that we can retrieve the implements of your purpose.'

'What implements?' Jackson asked.

'That I cannot say. It is between Gaea and her vessel. All I know is that without the implements of her role, the fate of humankind is doomed. Justice must be at the appointed place with everything she needs to have any hope of saving us all.'

Jackson tightened his grip on Justice.

'Gaea said I needed to look to the past and wash the sins of the fathers clean with blood. I didn't understand what she meant, but you're saying I have to do this at the monastery.' It was the only thing that made sense, though she couldn't think of what sins needed to be cleansed in a place dedicated to the Goddess.

Brother Owen shook his head. 'The monastery is part of your past, but it is not what the Goddess is referring to. We need to find the place where the fate of humankind was doomed, where the men who sought to control the world unleashed their monsters.'

'You don't know where that is?'

'I am afraid not. That will be revealed to you once you have taken charge of the implements of justice. For that, we do need to go to the monastery. The chest is hidden in the catacombs below, in a secret chamber only you can open.'

Justice pulled her shoulders back. 'All right. I'm ready.' She would go to the monastery with Brother Owen and make sure once and for all that Jackson and those she loved would have a future.

TWELVE

Under the cover of darkness, Hanson surveyed the wall that shielded the western side of Brimfield through infrared binoculars. He was looking for the small gap he and Ben had found when they were children roaming around on the outskirts of the half-breed zone. As in Harlington, the Brimfield zone had once been a school. The administration block at the front had been turned into an orphanage, while most of the classrooms were converted into homes for half-breed families. Single half-breeds had been housed in the two dormitories that backed up to the wall. When they were dodging lessons in how to become perfect servants for some human, he and Ben had retreated to the shadows at the rear of the male dormitory and played imaginary games where they performed amazing feats that had the humans cowering at their feet and begging to work for them.

He clenched his fists. Ben would never receive the recognition he deserved for his part in freeing the citizens of Brimfield from the Legion, thanks to Cole Dillon. Now, because of Cole's father, he and the others had to steal into Brimfield the back way and try to find a human willing to give them the blood Hannah needed.

Hanson no longer cared about having the humans bow down before him, as he had as a kid, but the thought that any of them would say no to Hannah made him want to smash something. One way or another, he would make sure she got her blood, even if he had to sit on the first human they came across to get it done.

A darker shadow at the base of the wall caught his attention, and he adjusted the focus of the binoculars.

There. That was the crack he and Ben had found all those years ago.

He strode back to the ATV and tossed the binoculars on the front seat, then reached in to grab a backpack full of supplies.

He turned to Hannah, who stood beside the ATV with a bulging pack. Even muffled with rags, the contents tinkled slightly with each movement she made.

'It's not too late to change your mind,' he said. 'You can wait here with the ATVs while Carstairs and I—'

'Not happening, Hanson. I am doing this whether you like it or not.'

'Not that I don't think you won't be an asset on this mission,' Carstairs called out from where he stood beside the second ATV, 'but he does have a point. We can get the blood you need without you having to set foot in Brimfield.'

While he appreciated the support, Hanson wished it came from anyone other than Carstairs, though he didn't mind the way Hannah shifted her glare from him to the warden.

'You take care of your mission, and we'll take care of ours,' she said, gripping the straps. Then she fixed her gaze on Hanson. 'We're wasting time. Let's go.'

Sure that this was a bad idea, he indicated for Leon and the others to follow as he led them to the crack in the wall. It was smaller than he remembered, and they had to take their packs off to squeeze through, making him glad for the Ward body armour he wore to protect his skin.

Once through, he took a moment to reorient himself. It felt like a lifetime had passed since he'd been in the half-breed zone. He'd been dumped outside the zone's orphanage as a newborn, never leaving until he turned twelve and was assigned to a construction crew. He'd spent the next sixteen years living in the male dormitory, working from dawn to dusk, returning to the zone each afternoon before darkness fell and the freaks came aboveground to hunt. If not for the freaks, he was sure the humans would have insisted he and the half-breeds work even longer hours.

Still, as hard as life had been, there had been many good memories made in the zone. He'd got to work with his best friend, and if not for the trouble Cole Dillon and his group liked to cause, he'd had no real complaints.

But now, now he was a warden. Under Kyle's leadership, he and his friends had been given a chance to take their lives in a new direction, to make something of themselves, and he was not going to waste any of his new life dwelling on the past. Without sparing a glance at the dormitory where he and Ben had spent many of their off-duty hours, he led Hannah and the others through the zone.

Unlike in Harlington, the zone was not fenced off and there were no guards waiting to check them in or out. But there was movement in the buildings he passed. There may no longer be any half-breeds in Brimfield, but it seemed someone was making use of the place where they had once lived.

Cautioning for quiet, he wove his way between the buildings to the street that led into the city centre. There, at the edge of the closed shops, streetlights still shining bright despite the fact there were no freaks left in Brimfield to deter, he called his troops to muster around.

'Town council is that way, three blocks over,' he said to Carstairs. Though the warden had studied a map one of the Brimfield wardens had drawn from memory, it wasn't the same as actual knowledge of the area. He had Michaelson and Dale with him. Both wardens had taken part in the battle to steal the airship the first time around. They would make sure the lieutenant from Harlington didn't get lost.

Carstairs looked at his watch. 'See you back at base in twelve hours. Good luck.' The lieutenant leaned in close to Hannah. 'Be careful out there. Just because there are no freaks doesn't make it safe.'

Hanson gritted his teeth as she gave him a quick smile.

He turned away as the lieutenant and the others headed off and scanned the street ahead of him. 'Any idea where we might find ourselves a human who doesn't mind being turned into a pincushion?' he asked Hannah.

Before she could answer him, shouts came from the direction Carstairs had taken.

'Damn it,' Hanson said, spinning around at the unmistakable sound of gunfire. He started to run in the direction of the fighting.

A squad of guards spilled out of a store on his left, with a second squad emerging from a laneway on the right.

Hanson grabbed Hannah's hand as he ran, calling out for Leon and the others to follow. Blood thumping in his ears, curses flying from his mouth, he sought to put distance between them and the guards, darting into a street on the left. If they could make it to the construction area he and the guys had been working on before they'd been forced to take refuge with the wardens, they had a chance of losing their pursuers. He knew that section of town better than any other. They'd be safe there.

Well, as safe as they could be in a town where everyone was out to get them.

A sharp tug on the arm holding Hannah spun him around, and he lost his grip on her hand. It took a moment before he could halt his forward momentum and turn back. She was on her hands and knees, chest heaving, the guards closing in on her. Leon was at her side, pulling her to her feet.

Hanson raced back to help.

A shot rang out, skimming past his head and hitting the building beside him.

He cursed and ducked down as more shots rang out.

He heard Hannah cry out, followed by the sound of Leon and the others yelling, and then someone latched on to his arm and he was wrenched around, slamming into a storefront.

He lashed back with his fist, hearing a loud groan as he connected with the soft belly of whoever was behind him.

The weight on his back shifted, and he straightened in time to see Hannah and the others being surrounded by guards with guns drawn.

The guard who had sucker-punched Hanson was bent over, sucking in air.

Hanson clocked him in the chin and then darted into the street he'd been aiming for, guilt tearing through him as he ran as fast as he could for the next intersection.

He couldn't help Hannah if he was captured along with her. He had to stay free, to figure out a way to rescue her and the others. Councillor Dillon wanted him dead, but he had no reason to kill Hannah.

Acid churning in his gut, he cursed the councillor with every swear word he knew as he looped around the streets, trying to keep up with the guards and their captives. Hannah and the others just had to hang on long enough for him to figure out what to do.

THIRTEEN

STANDING IN THE SHADOWS CREATED BY A STAND OF TREES, Rona stared at the canister containing the gas the scientists assured her would put any freaks sprayed with it under her control. Now it was time to find suitable candidates to test it on. Dalwaring was teeming with people: human, half-breed, and warden. Not that she was ready to take on the Ward yet. Instead, she had watched as a group of young men finished work for the day and returned to the houses where they resided. Four of them clearly lived together, single men from the looks of it. They would be perfect test subjects.

When the noise in the streets subsided, people locking themselves in against the advent of night, Rona made her move.

She left the shadows cast by the trees and strode around to the back of the house. With the amount of firepower her team was carrying, any number of freaks would be easy prey if the test failed. She had her marksmen take up positions on the roofs of the neighbouring houses. Then, when everyone was in place, she gave the order to move in.

One of her men smashed through the back door as another took the front, cutting off the means of retreat for those inside. Rona entered with four more men. The young occupants of the house were in the dining room and panicked at the arrival of the Legion. They fought to escape, but were no match for seasoned soldiers.

Within moments, they were trussed up and lying on the lounge room floor with a soldier standing beside each of them.

'Ready?' Rona asked.

She received four grim nods in return.

'Do it.'

In a synchronised motion, the four soldiers injected the virus into the prone men and stepped back. As the bodies on the ground began to writhe, the virus taking effect, Rona stepped forward and sprayed each of them in the face.

'Freeze,' she said, eyeing them carefully.

The result was instantaneous. All movement stopped and the four men's eyes, whites shining, trained on her.

Warmth flooded Rona's body. It worked. These men, these freaks, were now hers to command.

In simple terms, she gave her orders. Then, without a backward glance, Rona led her team outside to where the marksmen held out rope ladders for them to scale. From the safety of the roof, she watched the back door of the house they had just exited.

Her men had tied the ropes in such a way that it would not take the young men long to break free.

Sure enough, within moments, a figure appeared in the doorway, blood pouring from his eyes as he gazed about, showing no sign he was affected by the bright lighting shining down on him. He loped off into the darkness and was soon followed by the other three.

Minutes later, the sounds of shattered glass came from the house behind. Then came the screaming.

A fierce exultation filled Rona as she indicated for her men that it was time to leave before the wardens came to investigate. She'd find out soon enough how they would fare against her new freaks.

Besides, she had more important matters to attend to.

Back at the agricultural college, Rona stood with arms folded in front of her chest as she watched the scientists hand out packs containing the new version of the virus to the teams she had selected. Each team leader held a canister of gas that had been created with their blood to allow them to control the freaks.

'I really think you should reconsider,' Bryant said as he stood beside her, nervously eyeing the gun in her holster. 'These new freaks of yours—they are going to be hard to kill. You are making the same mistake our forefathers made, and it cost them dearly.'

Rona stiffened as she faced him. 'I am nothing like the forefathers. I know exactly what I'm doing.' With the Legion's plan to bring about the Apocalypse in ruins, it was time for a new plan. Rona and her people would never be safe, not with wardens in the world.

She was well aware of damage her freaks could do. That was the point. The wardens would find them a much harder adversary than those they had fought for the last five hundred years. That would keep them busy and help to reduce their numbers while she took care of the wardens responsible for her sister's death.

She would not stop until she had eradicated the Wards completely.

When only humans were left, the Legion would be free to take control of the rest of the world.

'Master Maguire, I beg you to—'

'Don't call me that.' Hands bunched into fists, she took a step toward the scientist.

He recoiled, head ducking down. 'My apologies.'

'I am no master. I am just doing what needs to be done to keep our people safe.' If she hadn't taken steps, the wardens would have been able to roll out their cure and rid the world of freaks completely. And once they had, she was sure they would turn their attention to the group that had been responsible for the deaths of many wardens in Brimfield. No, she had to stop them before they destroyed everything she stood for.

Her earliest memories were of sitting beside Karline as their father explained why it was so important that the Legion gained control. He told of a time when the world's resources were stretched thin, children Rona's age and younger starving because they had nothing to eat, while the governments ensured the wealthy remained fat and well fed. The Legion had created the original freak virus to bring down the corrupt governments, to do away with the excesses, and to make sure all humans had access to the same quality of living.

Over the years, the masters had lost sight of that goal, seeing themselves more as gods than a group working for the good of the people. That was why it had been so important for Karline to be named heir. As the elder child, Rona's father had been grooming her sister from birth to take over the Legion. He'd said it was the only way to get them back on the right path, one that led to equality and freedom for all.

Equality that could not be possible with the wardens, with their enhanced strength, intelligence, and other abilities.

Rona had to make sure the future her father had been grooming Karline for came to pass. She was supposed to be at her sister's side right now, acting as her second-in-command to make sure the days after Judgement were handled with minimal loss of life. To see the Legion through the Apocalypse so they could emerge from their strongholds and help the towns and cities find their way back to the light.

But Marcus Callaghan had been named as the heir, leading the Legion on a deadly path that had resulted in Karline's death at the hands of the wardens. Even if she didn't need to wipe them out to ensure an equal future for all humankind, Rona would have hated them for that alone. For that reason, she would make sure not a single Brimfield warden survived. She would wipe Brimfield off the map— raze the town and everyone who dwelled there to the ground.

Even then, that would not be enough to assuage the rage she felt over her sister's death.

Karline was everything she was not.

She would have been a fantastic leader. The Legion would have fallen to their knees before her, and the rest of the humans would have followed suit.

In honour of her memory, Rona would do what must be done. Maybe then she would be able to stop seeing Karline's final moments every time she closed her eyes. She wasn't there, only had Evan Johnson's account to go on, but the image of her sister being tossed from the roof of the Brimfield Town Council by a faceless warden came to her with such immediacy she felt it was true. Her sister had died an agonising death, plummeting several floors to slam into the ground. She would have been aware of what was happening, known there was no escape for her, and yet Rona could imagine Karline blaming her for not being there, for failing to protect her as their father had told her she must.

Instead, the masters had ordered her to do a sweep of all the strongholds, to make sure they were ready for the Legion's people to ride out the initial confusion of the Apocalypse.

She had not been there to protect her sister.

But she would protect the rest of the Legion if it was the last thing she did.

As the last box of supplies was loaded into the trucks, she strode forward and addressed the teams of men assembled in front of her.

'You all have your directions. I want you to get as close to each half-breed zone as you can before you release the virus. Make sure your freaks know that wardens are their targets. Then get out of town as fast as you can. I don't want any of you getting caught up in the chaos as the new freaks begin to emerge from the zone and the wardens are alerted.'

Half-breeds were stronger than humans and their tainted blood would make even stronger freaks. She was targeting every town that had a Ward garrison. When the half-breeds emerged from their zones and attacked the wardens, it would create confusion and carnage. There was a chance many humans would die as a result of her actions, but that was a price Rona was willing to pay to ensure a future for her people. They would remain safe within the strongholds, while she and her soldiers began the final task of eliminating the wardens once and for all.

As the teams armed with the virus left the old college, Rona organised the rest of her troops into two teams. One was to take the scientists to the mine compound to create more of the gas.

The other team, led by Rona, would head straight to Brimfield to destroy the people responsible for Karline's death.

And she would not stop until every single one of them was dead.

FOURTEEN

Kelvin Dillon stood up so fast the chair toppled over behind him. He ignored the crash as it hit the ground, focused on the captain of the Brimfield Security Guard. 'How many did you get?'

'We captured eleven of Kyle's people,' David Flanders said. 'Most of them appear to be half-breeds, with only a few wardens. My men are taking them to the detention centre as we speak.'

Kelvin stiffened. 'Kyle wasn't among them? What about the bastard half-breed that murdered my son?'

'There was no sign of Kyle. As for Hanson Forsythe …' David winced. 'He was with this group, but he got away.'

Heat suffused Kelvin's face, hands clenching into fists as he shouted, 'You let him get away? That man killed my son in cold blood, and you let him escape?'

David stiffened. 'He has nowhere to run. We have every possible exit locked up. Soon as he surfaces, my men will get him.'

Anger making his movements jerky, Kelvin smoothed down his silk shirt and moved to the coat stand to retrieve his jacket. He thrust his arms into the sleeves and slipped the jacket onto his shoulders, grimacing when he could not make the sides meet to do the button up. The damn woman Neil had hired as his housekeeper after all the half-breeds had deserted must have shrunk it in the wash. He'd get his assistant to find another housekeeper from the Harlington people he had magnanimously allowed to stay in Brimfield after the lout who'd previously led them had been vanquished.

He took the jacket off and threw it on the floor before storming out of the office with David at his heels. The scum who followed Jackson freaking Kyle would be more concerned about their own fates than the fact that he wasn't wearing a jacket.

There would be no waiting for David's men to capture Forsythe.

When he reached the ground floor, he strode over to Neil's desk. 'Get on the broadcast system. I want an announcement ready to go in five minutes. Either Hanson Forsythe hands himself in or I start executing the prisoners—one every hour until either he surrenders or they're all dead.'

His assistant blanched. 'Sir, we don't even know who the prisoners are. Shouldn't we wait—'

'I don't give a shit who they are. They're scum and they all deserve to die. One way or another, I will end the Brimfield Ward.'

After making sure Neil was hurrying off to do his bidding, Kelvin indicated for David to take the lead, a smile forming on his face at the thought of finally getting his hands on the half-breed who had murdered his son. The half-breeds were all the same, too stupid and sentimental to let others die in their place. Hanson Forsythe would hand himself in.

Smug anticipation filled him as he followed David to the detention centre, and he mentally composed the words he would use to advise the half-breeds and wardens of their fate.

He was almost there when the announcement came over the town-wide broadcast system, and his smile widened as he thought of the horror it would instil in his captives.

That horror would grow when they realised he had no intention of sparing their lives.

FIFTEEN

A HARD SHOVE IN THE MIDDLE OF HER BACK SENT HANNAH stumbling, and she fought the urge to turn and punch the guard behind her. This was the third time he'd pushed her, even though she was complying with the orders she'd been given once the guards had surrounded them.

A shout rang out in front of her, and she saw Leon spin. He looked as if he was going to punch the guard giving him grief. Three more guards shouted for him to turn around, their guns waving in the air, grim expressions on their faces.

'Leon, let it go,' she called out. They did not need to set the guards off. Their fingers appeared twitchy enough as they scanned the shadow-strewn streets while they marched Hannah and her companions onward. She had rarely been in the streets of Brimfield so had no idea where they were taking them, but she didn't think it was anywhere good. She fought the urge to look at the shadows too deeply herself, or to look behind her.

Hanson was not among the group of captives, meaning he was still free.

Much good that would do him. He was one against many.

'It will be all right,' Carstairs said from beside her.

Blood trickled down his face from a cut on his left brow. With his hands tied behind his back, he couldn't wipe the blood away from his eye, making it run down the side of his handsome features and giving him a ghoulish cast. His grey eyes were sombre as he gazed at Hannah.

Despite the optimism of his words, she could see he didn't think it was going to be all right at all.

The guards had been waiting for them, capturing both parties with relative ease, outnumbering them five-to-one. Luckily, cuts and bruises were the worst they had suffered before they'd been disarmed and bound.

Hannah looked over to the guard carrying her backpack of supplies. He'd rummaged in it after ripping it from her back, and she only hoped he hadn't broken any of the equipment. She would need it to collect blood from some of the town citizens, and she played with the idea of having that particular guard strapped to a table while she forcibly extracted his blood to make her vaccine. While she was at it, she'd be sure to do the same to the guard who kept pushing her in the back.

After tramping a number of blocks, the guards led them to a squat brick building. It was utilitarian, with barred windows and a heavy door at the front. A large sign above the door proclaimed: 'Brimfield Detention Centre'.

Hannah swallowed heavily. She had heard about this place. It was where half-breeds who displeased the humans were brought for punishment, many of them never seen again. Some of the wardens who had hated that she lived at the Ward had taken pleasure in taunting her about it, saying this was where she would end up one day. Turns out they were right, but she bet they would never have expected wardens would be her fellow prisoners.

Not that she could summon up a sense of satisfaction to know wardens would share the same fate as the half-breeds. With everything that had happened since Justice had entered

Jackson's life, the enmity most wardens felt toward half-breeds had faded away. Now they were all working together for the greater good.

Even the guards who were marching them to their prison.

At least, she hoped it was just to the prison they were being marched, and not to their deaths.

But with Councillor Dillon out to get revenge for the death of his son Cole, she knew all their lives hung in the balance. She couldn't wait for Hanson to figure out a way to save them. She and the others would have to figure out a way to escape on their own. Though that would have to wait until they weren't surrounded by guards.

The lead guard called a halt as he went to the door and pressed an intercom button. A short conversation followed, though Hannah was too far away to hear it.

The door opened and he stepped inside, beckoning for the guards to follow with their prisoners. Conscious of the hard eyes and many weapons trained on them, Hannah moved forward when she received another shove in the centre of her back. She would surely be bruised in that spot for days to come.

Inside, she scanned her surroundings, finding the interior to be just as utilitarian as the outside. It seemed the council did not find it necessary to make the working environment for their guards comfortable.

The front of the building was one large space filled with grey desks and grey cabinets. Five doors were set in the back wall. Two of the doors were marked as amenities. One had a sign indicating it was the office of the commander of the guard, and the other had a large window that looked through to a small dining area.

The fifth door, set in the middle of the wall, was made of a dull black metal, with a barred window in the top section. A guard strode forward to unlock the door. It opened with an ear-piercing squeak that had Hannah wincing. A dim corridor was visible on the other side of the door and she could see the bars of what had to be a number of cells, far more than they'd had at Brimfield Ward Headquarters.

With a deep breath, she stepped through the doorway and allowed herself to be shoved into one of the cells. With a rough grip, the guard unbound her hands and pushed her forward, the clang of the cell door closing behind him before she had even turned around.

The clanging of more doors shutting came as her companions were shown to their own cells. A couple of wardens and half-breeds ended up together, but Hannah had a cell to herself, as did the two female wardens who had accompanied Carstairs.

He was in the cell directly across from Hannah, using the small basin set in the corner to wash the blood from his face and hands. Hannah rubbed at her wrists, not willing to speak while the guards were still in the cellblock. Even when they left, she was still reluctant to voice her concerns aloud. Who knew what kind of surveillance they had? They could be sitting outside the main door, just waiting for Hannah or the others to start talking.

Not that they had appeared interested in talking to their captives. Other than confiscating their weapons and gear, they had asked no questions about why they were in Brimfield.

That lack of interest made Hannah wonder if they already knew the reason.

After the main door locked behind the guards, silence reigned in the cellblock. Carstairs crossed to the door of his cell and beckoned Hannah closer. His hair was wet from his drenching, and the cut on his brow still bled, making a watery red mess on one side of his face. But he showed no sign it affected him.

'Hanson will come for you. You know that, right?'

Hannah looked at the main door, not sure if it was safe to talk. Councillor Dillon wanted Hanson dead, along with Jackson. If he found out the young half-breed was in town, he would stop at nothing to find and kill him.

That fact was borne out a moment later when a crackle of static came and a shaky voice followed. As the words sank in, Hannah's horror grew. They had to get out of there before Hanson did something crazy. She had to stop him from turning himself in to Councillor Dillon.

Her hands as shaky as the voice on the broadcast, she reached into her hair and pulled out the hairpins keeping her ponytail smooth. It was not that she had been worried about her looks for this mission, but, after everything that had happened, she had known it paid to be prepared for any eventuality.

She twisted the two pins and knelt down to work on the lock. 'Let me know if anyone's watching.' She nodded toward the barred window in the door. From his cell, Carstairs should have a clear view of anyone standing on the other side.

The others came to the doors of their cells, and Hannah was grateful to see that she wasn't the only one to have some form of lock pick. But they would need to work fast to have any hope of getting out before the guards figured out what they were doing, and also to prevent Hanson from doing anything stupid.

It didn't take long for Hannah to get the lock on her door open. She silently slid the padlock aside and opened the door. Then she moved across the corridor to start on the lock on Carstairs' cell. She was conscious of time passing, sweat beading on her brow as more of their people lined up behind her in the corridor.

The lock on Carstairs' cell was dirtier than hers had been, and it took her a while to get it open. Eventually he was free, and she twisted her hairpins back into shape and slid them into her hair once more. They might come in handy again before they were out of Brimfield.

She scanned the others, all out of their cells and milling in the corridor. She looked to Leon, who worked his way through them to reach her and Carstairs.

'There's no back door, or any windows big enough to crawl through even if we could take out the bars. The only way out of here is through that door.' Leon pointed back into the main room, which would no doubt be filled with guards.

Carstairs carefully approached the window set in the door and looked through, his expression grim as he turned to face Hannah. 'I count at least ten guards in the main room, with no way of knowing how many more are in the building,' he said in a low voice. 'They appear to all be armed, so going through them will need an element of surprise.'

Hannah winced, remembering how badly the door had squeaked when it was opened to let them in. That would signal to the entire building that the prisoners were free.

'Or you could skip the door and use my way.'

Hannah gasped at hearing Hanson, spinning to look where his voice had come from.

Above her.

Relief that Hanson hadn't tried to turn himself in surged through her as she tilted her head back and found him smiling down at her from a manhole in the ceiling.

'Why am I not surprised to see you lot out of your cells already?' he asked.

Hannah shook her head, fighting back a hysterical laugh.

Within moments they had it arranged, with Carstairs and Leon remaining on the ground to boost each person up into the ceiling cavity. Hannah went first, feeling warm with Hanson's firm grip on her hands as he helped to pull her up. When she was kneeling beside him, perched on a wooden beam that traversed the length of the large building, he leaned in and wrapped his arms around her.

'I was so worried.'

Hannah hugged him back, moulding her body to his hard planes, before reluctantly detaching herself and moving aside so the others could be lifted up. Hanson directed them to the end of the building, to the hole he had made in the back roof to gain access, and they threaded their way through the ceiling space slowly, careful not to make any noise.

Hannah waited beside Hanson until all of their people were out.

Carstairs came last, closing the manhole behind him, teeth gleaming in the light of the torch Hanson had set on the next beam over. 'I locked all the padlocks. Figured it might slow them down if they couldn't figure out how we escaped.'

Hannah gave him a pat on the arm, and was surprised when he leaned in close and gave her a hug. Over his head, she saw Hanson frown and carefully disengaged herself. Then, with the two men behind her, she made her way to the hole and let Leon help her down the side of the building.

They gathered in a huddle, still keeping their voices low as they tried to figure out what to do next.

'They have my equipment,' Hannah said, nibbling at her bottom lip. 'I can't get the blood I need without it.'

'Getting blood is the least of our problems,' said Hanson. 'It won't take them long to discover you've escaped, and they'll be after us. They obviously knew we were coming, so going for the airship would be a suicide mission. We have to leave Brim-field altogether. We'll have to get the blood another time.'

Hannah didn't want to give up. They needed that blood to make more vaccine. But she knew Hanson was making sense.

Still. If they came across a medical facility on the way out of Brimfield, she might be able to find what she needed, assuming they could waylay one of the humans to get the blood.

But when they tried to retrace their steps, they found the way that led to the half-breed zone was blocked off. There was no way out.

SIXTEEN

The warden beside Callum shifted uneasily as he approached the house from which screams had erupted just moments ago. Now all was silent. Checking his surroundings, he noted the position of the wardens that had come with him from High Command, where he had ordered them to deploy. He held two stun guns, one of which had been modified to shoot the dart containing a dose of the cure.

A way back, another ring of wardens watched on. Some of them were there on behalf of High Command to bear witness. The others were from the Dalwaring Ward, with standard stun guns at the ready in case the trial went wrong. But it wouldn't go wrong. Callum had faith in the cure devised by Captain Kyle's half-breed. He just had to show the others and then they would know the renegades were working for the good of the Ward and all humankind.

Still, an edge of concern fluttered at his awareness.

The lights were on in the house from which the screams had come, but if there were freaks inside, they would be unable to fight because of the punishing glare affecting their hypersensitivity to light. They could be facing a human intruder instead of a freak.

They would find out soon enough.

He gave the order to his small team of wardens, volunteers who had agreed to help him test the cure. A patrol from Dalwaring stood ready with bright lights, currently muted.

Callum took the lead, and was metres away from the door when it burst open.

A woman, blood streaming from her eyes, launched forward, racing toward Callum. He fired his standard stun gun first, then followed with the dart laced with the cure.

Neither hit appeared to have any effect. The woman kept coming, and he had to stun her twice more before she stumbled and fell to her knees, still trying to get to him. Rage filled her bloodied eyes as she snarled, reaching for him with hands formed into claws.

Another hit from the stun gun and she toppled sideways, bloody smears on her face as she finally lay still.

Callum sucked in a breath. With her body weight, it should not have taken four hits to bring her down. He checked his gun to make sure it was set at the optimum level. A big man would take more than one shot, but a woman who was barely five feet tall and looked to weigh little more than a child? Impossible. His gun must be malfunctioning.

He turned to see about getting a replacement.

'Look out!'

The yell came from one of the wardens watching from the sidelines.

Callum spun around to see four more freaks emerging from the doorway. Three men and a teenage girl. All of them had blood streaming from their eyes, snarling and growling as they launched themselves at Callum.

He fired automatically at the closest one, even as more shots were fired by the wardens either side of him.

The teenager stumbled, but the three men kept coming. One latched on to the warden beside Callum, bringing her down and smashing against her helmet with brutal blows.

Callum dodged the teenager and fired at the freak on top of the downed warden, hitting him again and again.

The man slumped on top of the warden and, after a quick glance to see that the other freaks had been taken care of, Callum moved to free the warden trapped beneath the unconscious body. He pulled the freak aside, wincing when he saw the bloody crack in the faceplate of the warden's helmet.

He hit the freak with a dart laced with the cure and then held out a hand to help the warden to her feet.

The warden staggered once she was upright, then wrenched off her helmet and tossed it aside. Blood coated her face, smearing her mouth, and a shard of glass was embedded in a wound on her cheek. She plucked the glass out and dropped it to the ground, disgust rippling over her features.

Then her eyes widened. 'Captain Murphy, I don't feel so good.' She placed both hands on the sides of her head and gave a low moan, swaying in place.

He scanned her body, searching for signs of another wound, but could see nothing.

Her eyes rolled back in her head and her body began to shake, her low moan becoming a growl. The whites of her eyes began to shine, bloody tears falling as she stiffened and locked her gaze on Callum.

Horror engulfing him, Callum was too slow to react when she reached for him.

The other wardens did not hesitate. Her body convulsed as she was hit by multiple stuns before collapsing on the ground at his feet. Callum stared down at her, focusing on the blood around her mouth. It must have been the freak's blood, not from the wound on her cheek. Infection never occurred so quickly. But there was no denying she was now a freak. Still wrapped in horror, he lifted his stun gun and darted her with the cure, relieved she would not need to be put down as would normally happen in this case. With her having ingested the virus, there was no way to cut out the infection, even if she hadn't turned so fast.

Dimly aware of shouts, he pulled his gaze from her prone body and looked up to see the wardens from High Command shouting at each other, while the Dalwaring wardens kept a close watch on the unconscious freaks spread in front of the house.

'What the hell happened, Murphy?' Acting-General Stratton stepped toward him, chest puffed out. 'No one turns that fast.'

Callum shook his head. 'I don't understand it either. It shouldn't be possible.'

'It took dozens of hits to bring them down,' said the captain of the Dalwaring Ward.

Callum frowned. So, it wasn't just his gun that had been malfunctioning. Had someone rigged them to make sure he failed the test?

Before he could voice his suspicions, shouts of alarm rang out as the supine freaks began to move.

The wardens shone the lights on them, but the freaks gave no sign it affected them as they got to their feet and charged toward the gathered wardens.

Further screams sounded in the distance and Callum could see even more freaks racing toward them, drawn by the sounds of violence. They closed in fast, launching at the nearest wardens and bearing them to the ground, body armour and helmets offering limited protection in the face of this stronger freak. Within moments, some of the wardens turned and attacked their former comrades, adding to the chaos and confusion.

The wardens around Callum fired their stun guns over and over again, but the freaks did not stop.

'Switch your guns to lethal dose,' Stratton called out, firing at the freaks surrounding them.

'But they can be cured,' Callum protested.

'We don't have time for the cure to take effect, if it even will. These freaks are stronger than any we've ever encountered before, and they're not affected by the light. Our wardens are being slaughtered. We have to end this now.'

With the decision taken out of his hands, he could only watch on as one after the other, the freaks were put down. It took considerably more firepower than it should have to do the job. Soon, the only freak left alive was the warden whom Callum had injected with the cure. She began to stir, but the whites of her eyes still shone. The cure had not taken effect.

As she was stunned into unconsciousness again, Callum had a horrible feeling that she might never be cured.

Horror swelled within him as he surveyed the dead scattered over the road.

Was he right? Had someone sabotaged the cure, as Templeton had done in Harlington?

Eventually, as dawn cast its wan light over the blood-splattered streets of Dalwaring, and the infected warden was stunned for the fourth time, Stratton called an end to the campaign. Callum stood, arms limp at his sides, as the warden was put down like the rest of the freaks.

The cure hadn't worked, and as much as he wanted to believe it was due to sabotage, the nature of this new kind of freak had him thinking something else was in play—something that would adversely affect all humankind before long.

SEVENTEEN

In the room he shared with Justice, Jackson packed the items he would need for the trip to the monastery with her and the monk. His plan to put this off until after he had sorted out the mess at High Command had been shot to pieces by the arrival of Brother Owen. There was no way Justice would want to delay this trip, and he didn't want her to go without him.

Even so, misgiving sat heavily in his stomach as he contemplated the coming journey. Justice had told him about her time living with the monks. The monastery was the last place she had been happy. It was also the place where her mother and everyone she cared about had been murdered by the Legion. It was sure to dredge up bad memories to return there. But he had to hope the good ones would outweigh the bad.

Still, he would be there with her, to help her deal with the pain of facing her past and coming to terms with the future. It had to hurt to know that Gaea had brought Brother Owen back to life, but not her mother.

'Are you sure you can spare the time to come with me?'

He put down the backpack he was stuffing with clothes and took Justice's hand. 'I am not letting you go without me.'

'But what about the wardens? Don't they need you here to lead them? And what about High Command?'

'Lieutenant Jensen is more than capable of running things here while we're gone. And I'm sure Murphy can handle things at High Command until I get there. It won't take us that long to get to Shelton. You and your bodyguards may have had to visit each town in the country before arriving in Brimfield, but we can take a more direct route.'

Justice gave him a tremulous smile. 'Thank you.' She leaned in and kissed him, melding her body to his.

He wrapped his arms around her, losing himself in the feel and taste of her.

Too soon, a knock at the door pulled them apart.

'Yes, what is it?' Jackson called out.

'Captain Kyle,' Jensen said, his voice tight. 'We've just received a message from High Command. Captain Murphy needs to talk to you. He says it's urgent.'

Letting his arms fall away from Justice, he stepped to the door and wrenched it open. 'Any idea what's going on, Lieutenant?'

Jensen shook his head. 'All I know is that he sounds real shaken up.'

Conscious of Justice following, Jackson fought the urge to run. Murphy was a capable captain; if something had him riled up it did not bode well.

In the room the Legion had used for communicating with the outside world, Jackson took a seat at the radio console and spoke into the mic. 'This is Kyle.'

Static flowed through the speakers for a moment before Murphy's voice came over the waves. 'It's a freaking mess, Kyle. Someone has cooked up a new batch of freaks, and they're impervious to your cure.'

'What the hell?' Jackson listened in horror as Murphy detailed what had happened at Dalwaring.

'If you want to have any hope of salvaging your reputation, and your career, you need to find out who's behind this and stop them.'

'You think it's some of Butcher's supporters?'

'Who else could it be? They've been out to discredit your vaccine from the minute you showed up with it. They have to be behind it.' Murphy was silent for a moment. 'Wardens died, Kyle, and those that were infected turned within minutes. It was a bloodbath. Acting-General Stratton has called for a vote to recall all wardens to High Command. If the vote passes, humans will be left unprotected. They won't stand a chance. You need to get here and make sure that doesn't happen.'

Jackson rubbed at his eyes and then pulled the mic closer. 'I'll be there as soon as I can.'

Murphy signed off and Jackson turned to Justice.

She wore a troubled expression, but still managed a smile. 'It's okay. I know you need to do this.'

'Will you wait for me to return from High Command before you leave?' Even as he asked, he knew the answer.

'I wish I could, but I have a feeling that things with these new freaks are going to get worse before they get better. Maybe this is what Gaea was referring to, about the imminent destruction of humankind. If we don't find a way to reverse our fate soon, all could be lost.'

Jackson gave a grim nod. Then he turned to Jensen. 'Any word from Brimfield?' If Hanson and Carstairs returned soon, they could go with Justice to the monastery in his stead.

Jensen's expression darkened. 'Both teams missed their check-ins. There has been no communication from them since they let us know they were in position and about to enter the town, and they have not responded to our calls.'

'Damn it.' He ran a hand through his hair. Everything was going to shit.

'Prepare a team to go to Brimfield. We need to find out what has happened to Hanson and the others. I'll also need a patrol to go with Justice and the monk.'

'No need. My men and I will escort Justice to Shelton.'

Jackson turned to see Smith in the doorway to the communications room. The mercenary bristled with weapons. After having fought him, Jackson knew he would be a formidable ally. 'Are you sure?'

'It looks as though you'll need all your men here.'

Jackson turned to Justice, and she gave him a tremulous smile. 'It's okay. I know you have to go. Isaac will look after me. The wardens need you more than I do.'

Hating that he was being torn in different directions, Jackson gave a nod and faced Smith. 'Anything happens to her, I will hunt you down.'

'No need for hunting—I'd hand myself in. But I promise you, no harm will come to Justice while she is in my care.'

Jackson wished he could take that assurance at face value. While he knew the mercenary commander meant what he said, there were no guarantees in this world. Especially now. But it would have to do.

EIGHTEEN

Justice fought the urge to look behind her as the four-wheel-drive drove through the gates of the mine compound, not wanting to ruin her composure by taking one last look at Jackson. They had said their goodbyes in private.

It wouldn't be a last look, anyway. They'd be reunited soon, after she had finished her task and he had sorted out the mess the wardens at High Command had got themselves in.

'Cheer up, little sister. Your man is more than capable of taking care of himself.'

'I know,' she said, giving Isaac a smile. 'It's not him I'm worried about. It's the idiots in charge of the wardens that need watching. That lot wouldn't know how to lead themselves out of a one-way street.' Anger burned at the memory of how Jackson had been treated by Butcher last time he'd gone to High Command. At least he had a patrol of loyal wardens from Brimfield with him this time.

But she'd seen how many they would face. High Command teemed with wardens. If the colonels turned against Jackson, if he and Captain Murphy couldn't convince them someone else was behind the new freaks discovered at Dalwaring and the attempt to sabotage

Hannah's cure again, then she feared he was walking into a trap.

Still, she had found him last time. If anything went wrong, she would track him down again.

First, she had to find out what Gaea had left for her at the monastery.

It would take them two days of travelling, only stopping to switch drivers, before they would arrive at the small town where she had been born. Two days to come to terms with the memories the homecoming would trigger.

Part of her hoped Brother Owen was wrong, and that when she arrived, she would find that her mother and the other monks had all been resurrected. But she knew it was wishful thinking. For all her willingness to give humankind a chance to stave off their own destruction, Gaea was not the type to do anything that would upset the balance. She had brought Justice back because she had only half completed her purpose. She had then resurrected Brother Owen so he could help her finish what she had started on the day of Judgement. As much as Justice would love to think her mother and the dead monks were necessary to her task, she knew it was love that made her wish them returned to her. Their purpose in raising her, nurturing her early years, was done, as with all the bodyguards who had died protecting her so she could make it to her twenty-fifth birthday. They were not needed to take this final step.

What that final step was, Justice still had no clue. Other than telling her there was something at the monastery she needed, Brother Owen had been tight-lipped. She turned to survey him where he was sitting in a meditative pose in the backseat of the four-wheel-drive, eyes closed, showing no sign he was aware of the two big, burly mercenaries on either side of him.

As if he felt her gaze upon him, he opened his eyes and smiled at Justice. 'You have many questions, but I am afraid I do not have the answers you seek. The Book of Gaea that my brethren and I follow is a guide only. It does not list the steps you must take to fulfil your purpose in detail.'

'How can that be? You are Gaea's monk, dedicated to her worship. Why would she keep anything from you?'

'As we have seen, there is much opposition to Gaea's role in shaping the Earth. Were her instructions written down for all to read, it would be easier for them to find ways to impede our purpose. And while we monks may be accustomed to deprivation in our pursuit of holiness, no man is immune to torture. It is inevitable that we would be made to reveal our secrets if pressed. It is the way of humankind to rationalise the giving of secrets in order to stop the pain.'

A haunted look in his eyes suggested he was talking from experience, and Justice swallowed heavily. How much had this monk, and the others, sacrificed because of Gaea? Because of her?

'Gaea's secrets will be revealed to you, now that you are of age,' said Brother Owen. 'When we reach the monastery, I will take you to the secret chamber where you will place your hand against the scales on the altar. Then Gaea will reveal her next set of instructions to you.' He gave a rueful chuckle. 'This is what I would have done before your twenty-fifth birthday, after we had completed our pilgrimage to visit each of the towns and cities that remain. But it seems fate had other plans.'

Not fate. The Legion. They had torn her from her home, from her mother's dying arms, and away from the knowledge that could have saved so much pain and heartache. But then, if she had been guided by Brother Owen, she would never have arrived in Brimfield at the right time to ensnare Jackson in the bond, helping him to stave off the freak virus that burned through his veins.

She would not have channelled the power of her judgement through his body, starting the chain of events that led to

Hannah's cure, a cure someone out there seemed determined to render obsolete before it had a chance to change the shape of the Earth.

Brother Owen waved a hand in front of him. 'What we have now is a temporary state of affairs. A state of limbo, if you will. Certain conditions were not met, and Gaea has given us another chance to get it right. If we fail …'

Justice didn't need him to complete his sentence.

There would be no second chances.

She faced forward, accepted a travel ration from Isaac, and peered ahead. They had the road to themselves, and no sign of habitation nearby. The land to either side of the road was empty, though the recent storm had given some life back to the sunbaked grasses and trees. In the distance, she could see a low range of mountains, while birds wheeled in the air. It was a beautiful if harsh landscape, a reminder of what it was she was fighting for.

She had to plan for the now to make sure they all had a future to look forward to.

NINETEEN

Hanson kept a firm hold on Hannah's hand as they ran down the street and took refuge in a dark alley, Leon and the others close at their heels. They all squeezed in behind a large truck, gasping for breath after their madcap run through countless streets since they had escaped the detention centre. There had been no thought given to their route, just the need to put as much distance as possible between them and the guards.

The sound of booted feet rang out in the distance and Hanson waved a hand to get the attention of the others. They were making too much noise. The guards would hear them for sure. He held his breath as a large group of guards ran past the alley opening, weapons at the ready.

He let out his breath slowly, sagging with relief that the guards hadn't stopped to search the alley. But he couldn't rely on all of them being sloppy.

They had to find somewhere better to hide, fast.

The half-breed zone was out. The guards would expect them to make for the gap in the wall they had used to enter Brimfield. It would be well guarded for sure.

Think, Hanson. Think.

Where could they go that the guards wouldn't think to look for them?

He was tempted to make for the construction site again, but though he knew the area well, it didn't offer much in the way of security. Besides, with the entire Brimfield security force after them, they'd never make it that far.

'We have to get underground.'

Hanson swung his head around to face Hannah, her whispered suggestion making him smile. 'You're a genius.'

Humans were terrified of the dark. After generations of fear, they would be hesitant to go underground to search for them, even if Brimfield was now freak-free. Hell, even Hanson inwardly winced at the thought of using the tunnels as their refuge. But going underground was better than winding up in the guards' hands. He'd been lucky to escape their clutches last time, but with Councillor Dillon determined to see him dead, he'd be more likely to wind up being shot on sight than being locked up with the others in the detention centre.

In low whispers, he detailed his plan, relying on Leon and the other members of his old crew to show the wardens the way.

Giving Hannah's hand a quick squeeze, he moved out from behind the truck and they made their way to the opposite end of the alley. Three streets stood between them and the culvert near the council building that Jackson had led them out of the night they'd liberated Brimfield from the Legion's clutches. They would use it to get to the tunnels and hide out in the underground carpark until they could figure out what to do next.

One way or the other, he was going to make sure Hannah got out of Brimfield safely, with the blood she needed to make more of the vaccine. No way was he going to let Councillor bloody Dillon ruin life for the rest of humankind.

As images of besting the vindictive and conniving councillor fuelled his fire, Hanson led his people out of the alley.

There was no sign of the guards, for the moment, and he quickly made for the end of the street.

The way was clear, and he felt hope buoy him up as he ran as quietly as he could for the next cross street. Two more turns and they would reach the alley that led to the culvert. Two more turns and they were home free.

He turned the next corner and hurried Hannah along to the alley entrance.

A soft cry came up behind them and he stiffened, sure the guards had found them.

Instead, it was one of the wardens, hobbling along. Hanson hurried over to him.

'What's wrong?'

'Twisted my freaking ankle as I took the corner,' he hissed in a low whisper.

'Let me check it.' Hannah pulled free of Hanson and knelt down, hands reaching for the warden's leg.

'There's no time,' Hanson said, gripping Hannah's arm and pulling her to her feet. 'You can check it once we're underground.' He turned to the warden. 'Can you make it?'

Indignation coloured the warden's voice. 'Of course, I can. Just caught me by surprise.'

Hanson waved Leon over. 'Help him get into the culvert.'

Leon slung the warden's arm over his shoulder, even as Carstairs moved in and did the same on the other side. Then they set off with the others in tow.

After a quick head count to make sure they hadn't lost anyone, Hanson made to move after them with Hannah, but a shout froze him where he stood.

The sound of running feet came from close by.

He looked to the other end of the alley, to where the others were rapidly disappearing. He and Hannah were too far away. They would never make it.

He scanned the alley and settled on a recessed doorway. It would have to do. He sprinted for the doorway, pulling

Hannah along with him and pressing her into the alcove. He followed her a split second before a bunch of guards entered the alley and spotted Leon and the others.

A shout went up, and the guards raced after his friends. All Hanson could do was stand there and hope none of them noticed him and Hannah.

TWENTY

The thick pall of smoke in the distance sent tension writhing its way through Jackson's body.

'That doesn't look good,' said Corporal Irvine. She sat in the passenger seat, while the rest of her patrol were in the back of the ATV.

'No, not good at all.' Jackson pressed down on the accelerator, gritting his teeth against the bumps and jolts from the increased speed. Taking the inland route from the mine compound to High Command meant a far less comfortable drive than when using the main road. The old inland route hadn't been used in decades. The bitumen was cracked and pitted, many of the potholes big enough to cripple less sturdy vehicles than an ATV. In some places the road was impassable, with trees fallen across it, forcing them off road. But even then it was still faster than taking the much longer coastal road, and speed was of the essence, if what Captain Murphy had said about the new kind of freaks was true.

Freaks impervious to pain, who could come out in daylight. Were they the cause of the fire up ahead? A large fire blazed out of control—if the black smoke clouds were anything to go by.

'Check the map, Irvine. Are there any towns near here?'

The corporal spread out the map and ran a hand over the squiggling lines, checking her compass for verification.

'Washbourne is straight ahead, just over that hill.'

Jackson slowed the speed of the ATV as it crested the rise, and he got his first glimpse of Washbourne, a town built on both sides of a small lake. Flames had already destroyed the watch tower on this side of town. From his vantage point, he could see the timber bridge that crossed the lake had collapsed, and the fire was quickly spreading to the buildings on the other side. Misgiving sitting heavy in his stomach, he headed down the hill.

Caution would suggest they steer well clear, that stopping to investigate would take time they could not spare. But gut instinct said this fire was connected to the new freaks. The road curved around the town and Jackson's tension ratcheted up a notch when there was no sign of anyone attempting to put out the blaze. If left unchecked, the entire town would soon be engulfed.

Many buildings still stood, untouched, but it would not remain that way for long. As Jackson watched, flames leapt from one building to the next and another inferno began. But it was the dark shapes on the ground that concerned him more than the fires.

The shapes were ominously still, a number of them wearing black body armour. Other civilians were scattered among the bodies, many of them recipients of extreme violence. He winced at the carnage perpetrated here. These people had been slaughtered, ripped apart by a foe not even wardens had been proof against. Even children were counted among the dead, but there was no sign of who or what had killed these people and for that Jackson was grateful.

He and the half dozen wardens with him would be no match for this foe, with only a handful of weapons between them.

But Jackson would do whatever he could to make sure this never happened again. He had to stop High Command from recalling all the wardens. With sufficient firepower, and if they all banded together, they would see this threat through. If the new freaks were not stopped, this could signal the end of humankind.

He had to hold the tide, to give Justice time.

She would come through. He knew she would. He just wished he knew where she was and how far away she was from fulfilling Gaea's final mission.

TWENTY-ONE

After his third circuit of the compound in as many hours, Andy returned to the communications room.

'Any word from Captain Kyle?'

'No, sir. There has been no word from Brimfield or Sergeant Saunders either. But there's a fresh storm brewing, so that could be causing interference.'

Andy nodded. 'Keep trying to raise them,' he said as he clasped the warden on the shoulder. He hoped the storm would blow over fast and their communications would be back up and running soon. In the meantime, he would keep busy as best as he could.

With quick strides, he made his way to the main gate, climbed the guard post, and scanned the barren ground spread out in front of the compound, looking for anything out of place.

Nothing.

The same as every other time he'd looked.

He should be out there, leading the new team that had gone to Brimfield to find out what had happened to Hanson and the others. Instead, he'd had to send Casey Saunders and the remainder of his old patrol. While he was thrilled Captain Kyle considered him up to the task of commanding the compound in his absence, standing around doing nothing was going to drive him crazy.

Hell, he'd even be happy to travel to an old monastery with Justice and the mercenary commander. Anything would be better than being left behind. At least when they'd been in charge of the Brimfield Ward, he'd had regular patrols to do, freaks to catch, humans to protect. Here, even though he was supposed to be in command, he had nothing to do, not with Felice being so efficient. Anytime there was a problem, she took care of it before he even had a chance to think up a solution.

Not that he begrudged her organisational skills. She did a damn good job. She was intelligent, a fierce fighter and friend, and had a habit of showing up whenever she was needed. He was long past the days when he saw her as a half-breed. She was a warden, just like him, determined to see an end to the freak virus and make the world a better place for all.

She was currently doing a full stocktake, and had asked him to dine with her that evening, so they could figure out what they would need to make living at the mine more sustainable in the long term. He was looking forward to spending time with her, even if it was work related. But that was hours away, and he had to keep busy until then.

He shook his head, ready to climb down the ladder and do another sweep of the compound.

As he turned away, a dust cloud in the distance caught his eyes. He grabbed a pair of binoculars from the warden on duty and trained them on the cloud.

'Incoming vehicles,' he called out, spotting the shape of at least two vehicles at the base of the cloud.

'Think it's the captain returning?' the warden on guard duty asked.

'No way to tell at this range,' Andy said, sure that if it had been Kyle or the others returning, they would have radioed ahead. He sent one of the wardens on duty to the communications room.

She returned soon after to say that no communications had been received from the team in Brimfield or the follow-up team. There was also no incoming hail from the approaching vehicles.

Though the sky overhead was overcast and the wind had picked up, the storm had not yet eventuated. But there was a chance it was causing interference as the communications officer had suggested, and perhaps this was their people returning and their radio calls were not getting through. Still, it paid to be cautious.

'I want all available wardens on alert until we figure out who this is,' said Andy.

The warden beside him called out a warning to those below, and soon more of them had clambered up to the wall to look out over the barren landscape. Andy swiftly gave orders for two patrols to take up positions in the rocky areas either side of the gate. The gate was locked behind them, with the rest of the wardens posted to the wall and the occupants of the compound ordered to remain silent. Andy didn't want any noise rising to signal that the compound was occupied.

Soon, the vehicles were visible without the use of the binoculars. Andy frowned. They weren't ATVs. These were old four-wheel-drives, travelling slowly on the bumpy road heading to the mine complex.

Andy waved his wardens down into a crouch. He hunched over and made his way to a slit in the wall that allowed him to see out without being spotted, his gut clenching as the lead vehicle got close enough that he could see the occupants in the front.

They were strangers.

The lead vehicle pulled to a stop in front of the camouflaged gate set into the rocks, and Andy narrowed his eyes as two men bristling with weapons got out of the back. One of them waved to the vehicle behind them and it stopped a short distance back. Then the two men, weapons at the ready, scanned the gate.

Silence filled the air while Andy waited to see what the men would do next.

They must have known this place existed. There'd been no hesitation in their approach.

They weren't wardens. Their stance, though it suggested some kind of training, was not military. As far as Andy knew, the only people who knew this place even existed, other than the wardens, was the Legion.

That clenching in his gut tightened at the thought.

The Legion had done everything they could to wipe out the Brimfield wardens. Did they know they had fled here, after being chased out of Brimfield, and had come to finish the job?

No, that didn't make sense. They were making no effort to hide, and two vehicle loads of people would not be enough to take on the Brimfield Ward. Unless this was just a diversion.

The mercenary commander had gained access to the compound via the tunnels when he'd first attempted to carry out a kill order on Captain Kyle. Maybe this lot had been sent to the front gate to distract from a second force creeping their way in through the back door.

The mine was locked up, the tunnel the mercenary had used also secured, but Andy quietly gave the order for two patrols to go and check out the other means of access, just in case.

As he continued to watch, one man stood back with his gun ready as the other approached the gate.

'It's locked,' he called out in a low voice to his companion. 'From the inside.'

The second man whipped up his gun and aimed it at the

gate as he retreated to stand beside the open door of his vehicle.

Andy gave the signal for his guards outside the gate to move in.

Within moments, the two vehicles were surrounded, and the two men from the lead vehicle disarmed. The remaining occupants of both vehicles exited and joined them as they knelt with their hands behind their heads.

Once the wardens were assured the vehicles were now empty, Andy climbed down from the wall and strode to the gate. 'Open it up,' he said.

A short time later, he stood outside the gate surveying the ten people lined up by his wardens.

Four were clearly guards, their demeanour suggesting they were capable of extreme violence. The others were a mixed bag of men and women, none looking as if they knew which end of a weapon to hold, let alone what to do with it.

'Who are you?' Andy directed his question to the man who had approached the gate.

The man glared up at him, but didn't say a word. Andy raised his stun gun and shot him in the chest, stepping back as he pitched over face first in the dirt.

Then he pointed his gun at one of the others in the group, a thin man who looked about to pee his pants. 'Who are you?'

The man's face was ashen, his lips quivering and tears rolling down his face. 'I'm sorry. We didn't know anyone was living here. Please don't kill me.'

'Shut up, Bryant.'

Andy quickly stunned the man who had spoken before turning back to Bryant, not bothering to inform him the guns were set to stun and not kill.

'I'm going to ask one last time, who are you?'

In a stammer, he said, 'Bryant Montgomery. I'm a scientist. We came here to make gas for—'

The two remaining guards jumped to their feet and tackled Bryant.

Andy fired at their backs, even as his wardens leapt in to pull them off. The scientist's face was bloodied, dirt clinging to the mess on his face, a wheeze coming from his mouth as he hunched over himself.

As Bryant fought to regain his breath and composure, Andy turned to the woman next to him. 'Why are you here?'

With the four guards down for the count and Bryant incapable of answering, she didn't take long to reply, but from the hard look she gave him, she was not intimidated by being outnumbered.

'This is one of our strongholds, and Master Maguire will not be happy to find wardens trespassing.'

'Master Maguire?' Andy's stomach plummeted at having his fear confirmed. 'You're from the Legion.'

It wasn't a question, but she nodded, her cold gaze fixed on his. 'You need to leave, before our master returns from Brimfield and finds you here.'

'What did you say?' He lunged forward, and for the first time, her composure broke.

She flinched and ducked her head as if expecting him to hit her. Andy had no time for that. He spun around and ran for the gate.

'Get on the radio. Our people need to know the Legion are on the way to Brimfield. We'll send them more information as we have it.'

Hoping that the radio transmissions would go through, he returned to the woman and helped her to stand, pulling her toward the gate. 'You need to tell me everything you know.'

She cast him another cold glance and tossed her head. 'I don't have to tell you anything.'

'If you won't, I'm sure he will,' Andy said, indicating to where one of his wardens was helping Bryant along.

Her eyes narrowed. 'You're making a mistake. You really do not want to go up against the Legion.'

'We already have,' Andy said with a grim smile as he led her inside. He heard her take a startled breath as she looked ahead and saw a sea of wardens and half-breeds waiting inside the gate.

Her shoulders slumped. Then she straightened them and tugged her arm free. 'Fine, you have the upper hand for now. But that will change once Rona takes care of the rest of your people. After what you did to her sister, she is going to wipe every single warden off the map.'

'Her sister?' Andy shook his head. He thought all the masters had been men. Old men, who had been killed by the councillors back in Brimfield after the debacle with Marcus Callaghan.

She gave a disgusted huff. 'You wardens think you're so special, but you're no better than thugs. You and your wardens threw Master Callaghan and Karline Maguire off the roof of the Brimfield council chambers. You murdered them.'

'Hang on a minute. Your people were attacking us. You killed innocent people. And we did not throw anyone off the roof. The woman did that to herself, taking your Master Callaghan with her.'

'What?' For the first time, her voice shook. 'That's impossible. Evan Johnson was there. He said the captain of the Brimfield Ward threw them off the roof.'

'He's lying. Captain Kyle would never do that. That woman, Karline, she'd been abused by Marcus. She sacrificed her own life to kill him.'

She bit her bottom lip. 'That's not possible.'

'It's the truth.' Andy had heard enough from Hanson and the others to know the woman who had killed Marcus Callaghan had been in a bad way, her body showing signs of physical abuse and trauma when she'd let them in to see the man who had abused her.

'It's true,' said a new voice.

Andy looked behind him to see Bryant being propped up by one of his wardens.

'Master Callaghan took pleasure in hurting her. He made it clear she was his property, his to do with as he willed. I wasn't there when he fell from the roof, but after what he put her through, I'm sure she welcomed death.'

'But Evan said—'

'He wasn't there. He was running for his life, like the rest of us. All we saw were the bodies on the ground as we escaped. The only ones on the roof were the freaks and the wardens.'

The woman scowled at Bryant. 'Why didn't you tell Master Maguire the truth about what Marcus had done to Karline?'

He winced, red suffusing his face. 'Would you want to tell Rona Maguire what was happening to her sister before she died? Do you think she would care that we'd had no choice but to follow Marcus, or would she have expected us to risk our own lives to save her sister?'

It was her turn to wince. Whoever this Rona was, clearly her determination to protect her sister was legendary among the Legion.

'Better for her to blame the wardens than to take it out on us,' said Bryant.

His words pulled Andy from his thoughts. 'What is she planning to do?'

The woman grimaced as she looked over at Andy, all her anger gone. 'She is marching on Brimfield now, with the bulk of our people, and she plans to kill everyone in the town, starting with the wardens.'

Andy shook his head. 'We left Brimfield not long after your people did. There are only humans left there now.' Humans and the two teams of people who had gone to Brimfield to get blood and the airship. And a third team on its way to find out what had happened to them.

After ascertaining that there had still been no communication from Hanson or the others, Andy called for guards to take care of the prisoners, ordering them to be locked up in the mine compound as he set about organising another team to Brimfield. He had to warn his people about this Rona and what she had planned. And this time, there was no way Andy was staying behind.

TWENTY-TWO

A jolt shook Justice awake and she sat up. She was still in the front seat of the four-wheel-drive, with Isaac at the wheel.

He glanced over at her. 'Sorry. This stretch is bumpy. Lots of holes. Hard to avoid them all.'

She smiled at him. 'It's fine, I've slept long enough.'

'Wish I could say the same for the rest of them.' He indicated in the back seat where a sonorous snore was coming from either Brother Owen or the two mercenaries. All three were fast asleep, the jolting of the vehicle showing no signs of waking them soon.

Justice could understand Brother Owen needing to sleep, to recover after the punishing journey he had undertaken on foot to find her. The mercenaries, well, they had fallen asleep almost before the vehicle had left the compound.

She looked ahead, narrowing her gaze as the glare from grey clouds pierced her eyes. The sky had been cloud-free when she'd succumbed to the monotony of the drive and the unchanging scenery.

'Where are we?'

'About five hours out from Cadel. But we won't make it there today.'

'Why not?'

'Storm's about to hit. It's been chasing us for the last two hours and will catch us soon.'

Justice turned to look past the men sleeping in the rear of the four-wheel-drive. A swirling mass of black clouds filled the sky behind them, jagged flashes of lightning flaring in the midst with increasing frequency. The space between the clouds and the ground was covered in sheets of rain.

A heavy gust of wind buffeted the vehicle, and Isaac cursed as it forced them sideways. They hit another hole in the deserted road before he straightened their course.

'The wind's picking up. There's an old town up ahead. Most of it is in ruins, but one of the buildings was still intact last time I came this way. We'll hole up there until the storm passes, and continue on to Cadel in the morning.'

Justice nodded, watching in the side mirror as the storm drew closer, the flashes of lightning coming so close together it kept the sky lit up behind them even as the clouds in front of them began to darken.

There was a heaviness to the air, a feeling of a great weight pressing down on them as Isaac drove onward. The wind gusts grew stronger, and the muscles in his arms bunched as he fought to keep them on the road, such as it was. The trees and grasses beside the road bent over in the wind, and a loud rushing filled the air as the first raindrops began to fall.

It started light, a few spits, but almost immediately it became a wall of water thumping onto the vehicle, the windscreen wipers ineffectual as they fought to clear the way.

Isaac cursed, hunching forward, peering into the growing darkness.

'How far away is this place?' Justice had to raise her voice to be heard above the torrential rain, gripping the side rest to stop herself from being banged around as the vehicle skidded on the slick mud.

'Too far,' Isaac said, strain in his voice. 'Renfield, wake up.'

In the back, Renfield's eyes snapped open. 'What's the situation, Commander?' There was no sign of drowsiness in his voice.

'Wake Sutherland. Break out the weapons and watch our rear.'

Visibility had reduced to almost nil, Isaac having to slow the vehicle to keep on the road and stop it from sliding in the now muddy surface.

As Renfield woke Sutherland, Brother Owen asked, 'Do you believe someone is following us?' His voice was weak with fatigue, but steady.

'No way of knowing in this mess, but I like to be prepared. Captain Kyle will kick my arse if I let anything happen to Justice.' He shot her a quick grin. 'I can take him, of course, but wouldn't want to upset my little sister here.'

While she appreciated his attempt to lighten the moment, Justice did not return his smile.

'It is good that you are vigilant. Justice will need your keen eye and support in the days to come.'

Justice twisted to look at Brother Owen. There had been something in his voice, a sense of finality that hinted at dark times ahead. Before she could ask him what he meant, Isaac called out that they had reached the spot where they were to take shelter through the storm.

Justice faced the front but couldn't see anything through the blinding rain, the drumming on the roof drowning out sounds from outside the vehicle as well as visibility. She peered ahead, catching a glimpse of a large white shape a short distance ahead. Isaac was headed straight for it, turning the vehicle to the side at the last minute to avoid hitting it.

There was a lessening in the sound of the rain hitting the

roof. They had to be under some form of cover, though it didn't shut out the roar of the wind.

'Grab the gear,' Isaac said to Renfield and Sutherland. Then he pinned his gaze on Justice. 'You wait there until they make sure it's safe.'

Then he was gone, his mercenaries exiting along with him, leaving her and Brother Owen alone in the vehicle. Her old mentor was slumped in his seat, chin down.

Though reluctant to disturb him, Justice wanted to ask him what he'd meant earlier. Before she had a chance, her door opened and Isaac appeared in the gap.

'Hurry up and get inside. This storm is going to get worse before it gets better.'

Justice unbuckled her seat belt and climbed out of the car, grateful for Isaac's support as the wind pushed and pulled at her from all directions. He wrapped an arm around her back and guided her toward a door in the front of the building. Rain pelted diagonally under the rusted awning above their heads and she was soaked before taking a few steps, relief swamping her as she stepped fully inside the building and moved from the doorway to allow Renfield to usher Brother Owen inside.

Once they were all inside, Isaac set a lantern burning before he rummaged in a bag and handed Justice a towel, raising his voice to be heard above the thunderous pelting of the rain on the metal roof and the roar of the wind outside.

'Dry off as best you can. We don't want you catching a chill.'

He lit another lantern and strode away to confer with Renfield, making no effort to dry himself. Justice did the best she could with the towel and then handed it to Brother Owen, whose brown robes were sodden. She had no idea what he wore underneath, having never seen one of the monks who'd raised her without their robes. She and her mother had worn simple shift dresses under their robes, as the rough spun material had been scratchy against their bare skin, but the monks had never seemed to care about their physical comfort, only with their spiritual role as followers of Gaea.

She was not surprised when all Brother Owen did was dry his face before wringing out his robe as best he could.

Justice turned in a circle, the light of the lantern allowing her to see the warehouse was empty of any machinery or shelves. It was about the size of the warehouse she and Hannah had spent the night in when they were refused entry to the half-breed zone in Harlington. They'd had nowhere else to go. There were no windows that she could see, though there were skylights in the roof that lit up with each flash of lightning.

The flashes were coming farther apart now, and Justice hoped that meant the storm was easing or moving off.

Down the far end, a section was walled off, perhaps as storage or office space. As she watched, a light appeared in that area and she stiffened, only relaxing when she realised it was Sutherland.

'We'll bunk down here for the night.'

Justice, still watching Sutherland, jumped when Isaac spoke, not realising he had returned to her side.

He gave her a wry grin. 'It won't be comfortable, but it is better than the five of us trying to sleep crammed inside the four-wheel-drive.'

Justice smiled. 'I'm sure it will be fine. I've slept in worse places.'

His brow creased. 'Of course, you were on the run for fifteen years. I'm betting you're more used to roughing it than me and my men. If any of them whinge about how hard done by they are, you have my permission to slap them.'

Justice shook her head at the thought of slapping one of the hulking mercenaries. Sutherland was walking toward them, a torch in one hand and his rifle in the other. His gait was purposeful, his expression firm.

'There's another door back there.' He indicated over his shoulder. 'I've blocked it as best I could, but it wouldn't take much for anyone to prise it open.'

Isaac nodded sharply. 'Renfield will watch the front. I'll need you to take the back.'

Sutherland grinned. 'Good thing I slept the bulk of the way here. Wouldn't want to miss out on my beauty sleep.' He saluted and then scooped up a backpack and headed back to the rear of the building, disappearing into the office space.

Isaac then called to Renfield, who was in the process of putting on a coat made of a rubbery material. 'I'll relieve you in four hours.'

Renfield nodded and then made for the front door. A whoosh of cold wind whipped through the building when he opened the door, the roar of the wind and rain intensifying, before the door closed behind him.

Then Isaac turned to Justice and Brother Owen. 'Who's hungry?' He bent down and pulled packages of food out of a backpack. Thanks to Trev and Barrett, they were well supplied for the trip to Shelton.

Isaac spread the damp towel on the ground and gestured for Justice to sit. Brother Owen gave no sign he was disturbed by the grimy concrete floor as he sat beside her, remaining quiet as Isaac handed them a small parcel of food and a water canteen each.

'It's not much,' Isaac said, 'but I'd rather not use up all our supplies in one meal. I'm hoping the storm will blow over by morning. We need to eat and drink sparingly in case it doesn't. Sutherland said there are amenities back that way, but they aren't the cleanest. Still, it's better than having to go outside in this kind of weather.'

Weather conditions that Renfield and Sutherland were currently outside in, standing guard, Justice recalled.

'Do you really think it's necessary to keep watch? People would be crazy to be out in this weather.'

'We were out in it, and this is the only decent shelter this side of Cadel. Anyone who travels this route regularly would know this place was here and head for it. Better to be alert for any fellow travellers than have them stumble upon us in the middle of the night.'

Justice nodded, the thought of strangers barging in while they were asleep not appealing, though she wouldn't begrudge shelter to anyone caught unawares by the ferocious storm. She took small bites of her sandwich, washing it down with sips of water, while Brother Owen did the same.

Isaac demolished his sandwich in three bites, before grabbing two more out of his pack, along with two bottles of water. 'I'll take these to the men. You two should rest up while you can. If the storm lets up, we'll be leaving as soon as it is safe to do so.'

Justice, remembering a time when she had to do this with Jackson, made up a bed for herself on the hard floor. It wouldn't be as comfortable as the time she'd spent in the maintenance room under Brimfield, and she wouldn't have his arms around her as she slept, but it would have to do.

Brother Owen was already curled up within his brown robe, using his pack for a pillow, and appeared to be asleep within minutes.

After braving the dark and dank amenities, Justice lay down on her back, also using her pack as a pillow. She was cold, damp, and after sleeping in the vehicle most of the way there she was not all that tired, but she closed her eyes and tried to still her mind.

So many questions chased their way through her head.

What was it that Gaea needed her to do? What were the tools she needed to collect from the monastery?

Brother Owen had been no help, saying he didn't know how it would be revealed to her when they reached the monastery, but that didn't stop her from wondering.

Despite not being tired, the sound of the rain drumming

on the roof eased her into a semi-somnolent state. She was half aware of Isaac returning and making a bed for himself nearby, but she didn't move or speak.

Eventually she drifted off, her dreams a confusing mix of storms and shadows that alternately concealed and revealed the rooms of the monastery. Bodies were strewn everywhere, just as they'd been when she'd been dragged away by her first bodyguard, but now she was alone as she hunted through shadows for her mother's body. It was not there.

Instead, a soft whisper filled the monastery, her mother's voice, urging her to be careful.

Justice woke with a start, something pressing on her face.

She tried to sit up, hands reaching for whatever covered her mouth, finding a muscular arm.

'It's me,' Isaac whispered. 'We have a problem.'

Her initial panic at being held down had dissipated at the sound of Isaac's voice, only to return when she realised what he'd said.

She tapped his arm to let him know she understood, and he released her. She sat up, peering into the darkness, the lantern that had been on when she'd lain down now off. The interior of the warehouse was almost completely black, only a faint light coming through the skylights in the roof.

It was still raining, but she could no longer hear the roar of the wind and the flashes of lightning had stopped. The storm was losing strength, but that was a good thing, not the problem to which Isaac referred.

Isaac moved over to Brother Owen's side, repeating the process he had used to wake Justice. There was no sign of Renfield or Sutherland, and Justice guessed they were both still stationed at the doors. She had no idea how long they had slept for, or if the other mercenaries had been given a chance to rest.

A clatter came from the rear of the warehouse, and she spun to look in that direction. She could see a faint glimmer of light on the ground, coming from under the door to the office area. That door also led to the exit, the one Sutherland was supposed to be guarding.

Had he made that noise, or was someone else out there?

Isaac grabbed her arm, pulling her to her feet and along with him as he headed for the side of the building. In the dim light, she could see his head swivelling from side to side even as he gestured for Brother Owen to follow them.

They had just reached the wall, and he was directing them along it toward the storage space when the front door was wrenched open. Dark shapes filled the entrance, too many to be Renfield and Sutherland.

Lights switched on, panning over the centre of the warehouse, fixing on the bundle of packs and improvised bedding. Isaac pushed Justice down into the corner between the wall and the storage room, standing in front of her as the light panned over the rest of the large space. They were far enough away that shadows around them remained to obscure their presence, their dark clothing helping to hide them.

Brother Owen had not yet reached the corner. He'd pressed himself against the wall and crouched, and she hoped he was out of sight. But they would not stay hidden for long as the newcomers stepped farther into the warehouse, more lights being turned on.

'Search the place,' a low voice said. 'Their vehicle is still here, so they must be as well. Smith knows better than to head out into the night without protection.'

Justice felt Isaac stiffen, but he made no other move.

What was he waiting for? The newcomers were sure to spot them soon. And what had happened to Renfield and Sutherland?

The door into the office space opened, and more dark figures stepped out.

'All clear back here, sir,' one of them said.

'Spread out. Smith has two of his men with him, as well as

two civilians. They can't be far. Search the building. Find them, fast.'

The speaker headed for the main door just as Isaac let out a low whistle.

Gunfire erupted, coming from above, spraying into the men at both exits.

Shouts and screams rang out as the men fired in the air, trying to hit their attackers.

Isaac pushed Justice down lower and she huddled with her arms over her head, aware that would not stop a bullet, and neither would the body armour Jackson had insisted she wear.

As the newcomers ran for the exits, Renfield and Sutherland dropped from ropes tied to the beams in the roof at either end of the building, cutting off their retreat, still firing.

Bullets slammed into the walls as the newcomers fought back, more screams filling the air, along with the smell of gunpowder. Silence soon returned though, and Justice dared to lift her head. The newcomers were all dead, spread across the floor.

Justice shakily got to her feet, surprised by the carnage and the silence of the aftermath. 'Who were they?'

'A rival company,' Isaac said with a grimace, scanning the mess while Renfield and Sutherland dropped all the way to the ground and came to join him. 'Check outside, make sure we got them all.'

They headed off to follow his orders, but Renfield stopped halfway to the front door and pointed to the wall where Brother Owen was slumped. 'The monk's been hit.' Then he continued on his way.

'Damn it,' Isaac said, striding toward Brother Owen. 'How bad is it?'

Justice hurried over to them as Brother Owen lifted his head and gave a pained sigh. 'Bad enough.'

She knelt beside him, sucking in a gasp when she saw blood on the hand clutching the front of his robe. Isaac grabbed one of their packs and pulled out a first-aid kit, quickly ministering to the wound in Brother Owen's side.

'I've stopped the bleeding for now, but he needs urgent medical attention,' he said as he turned to face Justice. 'Pack up our gear and bring it out to the four-wheel-drive. We can be in Cadel by daybreak.' He leaned down and helped Brother Owen to his feet.

He didn't spare a glance at the dead mercenaries as he made his way to the door, and Justice did her best to do the same. There had been so much blood and death in her life. When would it stop?

She stuffed their belongings into the packs and hurried outside, hoping that the medics in Cadel would be able to help.

She could not lose Brother Owen, not again.

TWENTY-THREE

Hannah aimed her stun gun at the backs of the security guards blocking access to the alley Hanson had been leading her toward, but didn't fire. There were too many of them. Her stun gun would run out of charge long before she and Hanson had fought their way through. Leon and the others had fled into the alley while she and Hanson had covered their rear before being cut off by this new contingent of guards. Luckily for them, the guards had been focused on following the others rather than looking behind them to where she and Hanson were holed up in the doorway of the building opposite the alley.

'It's no good. We'll have to go around,' Hanson whispered in her ear, tugging on her arm and pulling her back the way they had come.

It had been like this since they escaped the cellblock, running into one lot of guards after another. She just hoped Leon and the others had been able to make it to the culvert. The only saving grace was that many of the guards appeared to be new recruits, not as experienced as those who had been working for the council long-term, and thus were easier to avoid. Unfortunately, the last lot had been veteran guards and harder to ditch. It had only been Hanson's knowledge of the streets of Brimfield that had saved them. Hannah would have been lost within one turn if she'd been on her own.

Hanson gripped her hand, tension radiating from him. He scanned their surroundings as they darted away from the alley their friends had fled down. He kept them to the shadows as much as possible, avoiding the bright streetlights. Although Brimfield was now freak-free, the streets were also empty of civilians, making it easy for the guards to spot any fugitives, and they showed no sign of giving up on the search.

Hannah and Hanson had to get off the streets and find a place to hide until daybreak, when they had a better chance of hiding in plain sight and catching up with the others.

Hannah eyed the buildings around them as they left the town centre behind. The lights were off in the empty buildings now that there was no need to ward off freaks, making it easier to spot which ones were occupied. She found a likely store and tugged on Hanson's hand.

'We need to hide.' She used her free hand to point at the building she had picked out. It was a clothing store. 'We can find something to cover our body armour, help us blend in.'

Hanson frowned as he went from scanning the streets to the store. The sound of running footsteps and shouts came from the street they had just left and his lips firmed into a line. 'Fine. Let's see if there's a back entrance.'

They slipped around the edge of the shop, Hanson letting go of her hand as they slid through a small gap between it and the next building. Hannah flexed her fingers, resisting the urge to grab hold of him again as more shouting could be heard nearby. If they were separated, she would be totally lost.

Once they reached the back alley, Hannah grabbed her hairpins out and set to work on the lock securing the door. Within moments, it was open and they entered, closing the door just as light streamed into the laneway. Hannah froze, hand on the lock as she reengaged it, not daring to move as she listened to the searchers running through the laneway. Hanson was pressed into her side, equally still, his warm breath stirring the hair on the side of her head.

'They can't have got far. Keep looking,' a voice called out. 'Councillor Dillon will have our heads if we lose the half-breed again. Unless you want to be the ones swinging on the gallows, find him.'

Hannah felt Hanson stiffen at the mention of the gallows. She'd known it was a common practice in many towns, for half-breeds to be hanged when they were deemed criminal by the town councils, but to hear that this was the fate awaiting Hanson if he was captured was worse than hearing about some unknown half-breed being treated so callously.

They had to find a way to get underground, to get out of Brimfield before their luck run out. They had been short of luck on this entire mission. They'd been ambushed from the start, locked up and barely escaped, with no way of getting the blood she needed to make more vaccine, and now they were stuck playing a cat-and-mouse game with hundreds of guards eager to hand Hanson over to the council to be executed.

This was not how it was supposed to go. They were supposed to sneak into Brimfield, get the blood and the airship, and get back to the compound.

As the sound of the searching guards retreated, Hannah slumped down and rested her forehead on the smooth wood of the door.

Hanson shifted position, an arm coming around her back and squeezing her close. 'Hey, it will be okay. We'll find the others. We're going to be fine.' His other arm wrapped around her. 'You'll see.'

Hannah twisted to face him, placing her hands on his chest and gazing up at him. 'Councillor Dillon plans to hang you. Nothing about this is fine.'

He'd been right. She should never have come on this

mission. She was no warden. The training Daniel had given her had not prepared her for this.

'If it wasn't for me slowing you down, you wouldn't have been separated from the others. You'd be safe now, not stuck in the back of some store hiding from council guards.'

Hanson gazed down at her, the light coming in through the store's front windows allowing her to see his handsome features as he lowered his head to whisper in her ear. 'Trust me, I'd much rather be stuck here with you than crawling around in the tunnels with Leon and Carstairs.' He gave a low chuckle that set butterflies flying in her stomach. Then he said, 'And you smell heaps better than they do.'

'This is not funny, Hanson. We're in real trouble here.' She banged on his chest. 'Can't you be serious for once?'

His arms tightened around her, the humour in his clear green gaze replaced by an intense look. 'I won't let anything happen to you, Hannah. I promise. I'll get you out of here if it's the last thing I do.'

'We are all getting out of here.' Moment of self-pity over, she glared at him. 'No one is staying behind. No one is having last moments. We're in this together.'

A loud bang came from the laneway and they both jumped. Still cradled in Hanson's arms, Hannah's heart raced, and not just from the fright. He was so close, his body pressed up against hers, the scent of him teasing her nostrils, the very maleness of him impinging on all her senses and setting a smouldering fire burning in her core. This wasn't right. This was Hanson. Her friend. She cared about him, sure, but that was it. Wasn't it?

But as much as she knew she should pull away, leave the safety of his arms, part of her didn't want to move. Part of her wanted to get even closer, to run her hands over the hard planes of his chest, to explore the skin so tantalisingly close to her own.

She gazed up at him, lips parting as she saw the way his

head was cocked to the side, listening intently. When nothing came, he shifted to look down at her once more, and her eyes widened when his gaze focused on her mouth. He let out a low groan, the sound of it sending a shiver racing down her spine even as parts of her began to tingle. His arms tightened around her and his head lowered.

'Hannah,' he said, voice husky, gaze never leaving hers.

Another bang came from the alley and a harsh whisper quickly followed.

'Are you sure they came this way, Leon?'

'Carstairs?' Hanson's head flung back, and he released Hannah so suddenly she would have fallen if she wasn't so close to the wall.

Hanson reached for the handle and wrenched the door open, striding out into the laneway and causing a string of strangled curses from both Leon and Carstairs.

'What are you two doing here?' Hanson asked.

'Looking for you two,' Carstairs said, his head swinging around as Hannah stepped out of the store.

His eyes narrowed speculatively as he looked her up and down, and she was sure her cheeks were flushing and that he was aware of what had happened in the store with Hanson. Well, what had almost happened. Her experience with men was limited, but she was sure he had been about to kiss her.

'You're not hurt?' Carstairs stepped closer and placed a hand on Hannah's shoulder.

'She's fine,' Hanson said, pushing between them and forcing the warden to let go. 'We're both fine. Thanks for asking. But that will change if we stand around here yapping all night. Did you find the culvert?'

'Sure did,' Leon said, a wide smirk on his face. 'Everyone else is already underground, heading for the carpark. We just came back to see if you two needed help remembering the way. Though from the looks of it, you found yourselves a cosy place to hole up.'

'Nothing cosy about it,' Hanson said, his tone rough as he strode for the end of the laneway. 'Let's get out of here before any more guards show up.'

Hannah bit her bottom lip as she followed him. He didn't look at her or even acknowledge her presence as the four of them made their way to the culvert and quickly moved underground. Maybe she was wrong. Maybe he hadn't been about to kiss her and she'd misunderstood his intentions.

As for her, what had she been thinking? Had she really wanted him to kiss her or was it all some kind of reaction to being in danger and proximity?

As they journeyed through the tunnel system, she took no notice of where they were going, only dimly registering when they reached the underground carpark and were reunited with the others. It was time to make plans for what to do next. She had to focus, stop thinking about Hanson and what might or might not have been going on back in the store.

But when she looked up, she caught Hanson watching her, an unreadable expression on his face as he moved closer. None of the others were near, standing in the middle of the carpark going over what supplies they had between them. Though she did notice Carstairs looking her way every now and then.

She held her breath when Hanson reached her side, sure he was going to say something about what had happened in the store.

'We forgot to grab clothes for our disguises,' he said.

Relief swamped her, swiftly followed by a pang of disappointment. She took a shaky breath and focused on the problem at hand. 'The shopkeeper would probably have noticed any missing items and reported it anyway. We'll have to come up with another way to get disguises for when we go back aboveground.' They couldn't stay down there for long. The supplies they had brought was only intended to cover a short mission to get blood and steal the airship.

'I'll get Leon on it. He'll come up with something.'

Hannah nodded, swallowing a lump in her throat. 'It will be dangerous. With the guards still looking for us.'

Hanson shot her a grin. 'He'll be fine. This is exactly the kind of challenge he likes.' His grin faded. 'I meant what I said before. I will get you out of here. We need you back at the compound mixing up more vaccine for us. The Ward medics are good for taking care of injuries and stuff, but they don't know half what you do when it comes to curing freaks.' Then he nodded and walked back to the main group, leaving her to stare after him in puzzlement.

Was that all he cared about, keeping her safe for the sake of the vaccine?

And what was it she cared about?

TWENTY-FOUR

Callum paced in front of the tavern on the outskirts of High Command, stopping every now and then to look in the direction of Dalwaring. There was still no sign of a vehicle.

Where was Kyle? The last radio transmission he'd received said he was close. He should have been there by now. Unless he'd met up with some of the new freaks. Reports had come in of more tangles with them, with many wardens killed or injured and infected during the fighting. The sitting colonels were about to go into a meeting to elect the next general and to vote on removing all wardens and having them return to High Command. He needed Kyle to help talk them out of it.

Despite everything that had happened with General Butcher, Jackson Kyle had a good reputation among the colonels. If anyone could make them see reason, it would be him.

Finally, a dust cloud sprang into the air, signalling a vehicle was approaching, but not from the road. It came at a forty-degree angle from the road, and as he squinted, Callum realised it was almost in a direct line to the mine compound. It had to be Kyle.

It had better be, if the wardens were to keep their charter with the humans.

The vehicle materialised through the dust cloud, an ATV, though it was too far away for Callum to see who was driving it. Still, it was a Ward ATV and Kyle was the only warden he could think of who wouldn't use the main road. A crackle came from the hand-held radio in Callum's hand before Kyle's voice sounded through the earpiece.

'I hope those wardens with you are a welcoming committee and not there to throw me in another cell.'

Callum looked behind him to the group of wardens he had arranged to accompany him as he waited for Kyle before toggling the button on the radio. 'They're here to ensure you make it to the citadel.'

At least he hoped that's why they had agreed to accompany him. As much as he would like to think all wardens felt it imperative to uphold the charter to protect humans from freaks, the recent events had sent a shock wave rippling through their ranks.

The fight at Kyle's compound had also caused some animosity, though that was mostly directed at Major Templeton and General Butcher, rather than Kyle and his people. Still, he had done his best to find wardens who were not involved in that battle and who appeared to believe as he did that removing wardens from the human towns would end in disaster.

Humans had no hope of defeating these new freaks. If they were abandoned by the Wards, soon there would be no humans left and the wardens would face a country full of freaks out for their blood.

'Glad to hear that,' said Kyle. 'The colonels need to hear what I have to say.'

But would they listen?

Callum pushed his doubts down. Kyle was almost there, and he would take on the role of convincing the colonels.

What had happened in Dalwaring, even though the new freaks had been destroyed, had dented the colonels' faith in him and Captain Landry.

Kyle's ATV slowed as it approached the tavern, coming to a stop in front of Callum.

Kyle climbed out of the vehicle and moved over to shake Callum's hand. 'It is good to see you again, Captain Murphy, though I wish it were under better circumstances.' His expression was grim, and he shook his head. 'These new freaks need to be stopped.'

'You had trouble?'

'Not us,' Kyle said, waving a hand toward the wardens who had accompanied him, 'but we saw enough to know these new freaks are bad news. Washbourne is gone. There's no one left alive, human or warden.'

'Shit.' Callum ran a hand through his hair. Washbourne was only a small town, but any loss of life due to these new freaks was one too many, and to have wardens numbered among the dead was catastrophic. Once the colonels heard about it, they would be even more determined to recall the wardens from the other towns and cities.

'This is a hell of a mess, Kyle. It's going to take some major firepower and strategic planning to sort it all out.'

Kyle gave a grim nod. 'We need a coordinated effort, sweeping from town to town until we eradicate these new freaks. You said you got all the ones in Dalwaring?'

'Yeah.' He grimaced. 'Acting-General Stratton has ordered wardens to kill all freaks on sight. I know you were hoping they could be cured, but he wants to take no chances with one of them mutating and infecting others with this new virus strain.'

'Any word yet about how the new strain came about? It's been five hundred years without a change. Seems suspicious for it to mutate now, after all this time, without some sort of catalyst.'

'I was hoping you'd have an answer for that. Or that Hannah Young would. She was the one who came up with the first cure. Any chance she can whip up another one?'

Kyle grimaced. 'Right now, she's in Brimfield with a bunch of my people, attempting to get more blood so we can make and distribute more of the original vaccine. We lost contact with them shortly before your message came and I've sent a fresh team in to help locate and extract them if necessary.'

'Well, let's hope they're successful because we could sure use her help on this.'

'My team will come through. They won't let anything happen to Hannah, and if anyone can come up with a second cure, it's her.'

For all the confidence of Kyle's words, Callum could tell from the tightness around his eyes that he knew creating a new cure was going to be easier said than done. But that was a problem for another time. Right now, he had to sneak Kyle into the citadel so they could confront the colonels and stop them from leaving the humans unprotected.

They had to make them see that breaking the Ward charter would be a disaster for all humankind.

TWENTY-FIVE

Jackson's grip tightened on the edge of the desk as he listened to Captain Murphy describing the terrifying attacks by vaccine-resistant freaks in three other towns, as well as Dalwaring.

'This new virus is spreading too fast for us to contain it. We've had unconfirmed reports that it's in six other towns and we've lost contact with the Wards in four more. It's a blood-bath. Humans and wardens are getting slaughtered and High Command is convinced someone is behind it.'

'For the virus to spread that fast, it has to be man-made,' said Murphy. 'Do you think the Legion could be behind it again? You said that guy who was leading them in Brimfield admitted his ancestors created the first virus five hundred years ago.'

Jackson tensed. 'He's dead, along with his old masters, and we have control of the compound with their lab.'

'They could have more than one lab. Besides, who else would want to unleash stronger and more resistant freaks? Though I would have thought they'd target you and Justice, seeing as you are the ones who defeated them last time.'

Acid churned in Jackson's gut at the thought of the Legion

going after Justice again. He'd had no contact with her since she'd left the mine with the mercenary commander. What if all this was a way to weaken the wardens so they could get to her? She believed her purpose had not yet been fulfilled, and that was why Gaea had brought her back from the dead.

Did the Legion know that as well? Was that what the new virus was all about? Their bloody Apocalypse?

'Regardless of what their goal is, we need to find a way to stop these freaks before there are no humans left to protect or wardens to fight them,' Murphy said, dragging Jackson's attention away from thoughts of where Justice was and if she was okay.

'You're right. We need to find the source of the virus and stamp it out, stop them infecting more people.'

The door to the small office opened and Captain Landry burst in. 'You need to get to the main chamber. The colonels have already started to vote on whether to recall all wardens to High Command.'

'What the hell? They said they would hold off on the vote until after I talked to them.'

Jackson jumped to his feet and raced for the door, Murphy on his heels as Landry led the way.

The noise in the room was silenced as the three of them burst in.

'You can't recall our people. The humans will be slaughtered without wardens to protect them,' Jackson called out as heads swung their way.

'Our wardens are being slaughtered alongside the humans,' said Acting-General Stratton. 'These new freaks don't care about getting hurt. They don't seem to feel pain, and light isn't stopping them. We can't fight them, not effectively. We have to withdraw before there are none of us left.'

'The Ward charter states we must protect the humans. It's our sole reason for existing,' said Jackson.

'You yourself said the world is changing and that it was

time for wardens to embrace a future without Wards,' said Stratton. 'This may not be ideal, but we need to safeguard our own people first. If we withdraw our wardens and make High Command secure, we will prevail. We stay out there, fighting a losing battle while waiting on your half-breed to come up with another cure, and soon there will be no one left on this godforsaken Earth except for freaks.'

It was a bleak image of a possible future, one Jackson was grimly aware could come true. As much as he wanted to wait for Hannah to come up with another miracle cure, he didn't think it was going to be possible. Not without Gaea's intervention. It was time to cut their losses, but that did not have to mean abandoning the humans.

'Have the wardens evacuate all humans to their Wards. They'll have a much easier time of protecting them from within the garrisons. We already know a kill shot is the only way to take down these new freaks. Have our people switch to live ammunition. It's the best way to contain the spread of the virus.'

The colonels stared down at him, all of them silent as they considered his words.

Murphy stepped up to Jackson's side. 'It could work. Our garrisons and the headquarters in each town are heavily fortified, many of them increasing their protection after what happened in Brimfield. It will be cramped, and the supplies will have to be stretched to make them last as long as possible, but it can be done.'

Stratton conferred with the colonels for a moment, and then faced Jackson. 'You're asking our people to put themselves in siege situations, to lock them away and let the freaks have free rein. And that's only if the human councils agree to this plan.'

Jackson let some of the tension leach from his body now that the colonels were considering his idea. 'Better a siege than to be left to fend for themselves. And if any council chooses not to take refuge within the Ward, that is on their head. But we must make the offer to all humans and half-breeds. To do anything less is to break the charter. And as soon as we do have a cure or come up with a way to stop these new freaks, then the humans can leave.'

Stratton frowned. 'What about the towns that are too small or have refused to allow a Ward to be set up within their perimeter? Your plan leaves them undefended.'

'We put out a call to them, that if they can make it to a town that has a Ward, they would be welcomed. But we have to do it now before the freaks get so far entrenched that travel is impossible.'

Another long silence fell, and then Stratton said, 'It's too risky. Our wardens must be our first priority. To keep opening the garrisons to allow humans to enter would risk the virus affecting all our people. I'm afraid I cannot condone it. We must break the charter and leave the humans and half-breeds to fend for themselves.'

An uproar greeted his words, with many of the sitting colonels agreeing with him and others arguing against it. Jackson shook his head, horrified to think that all the humans he and the others had spent their lives to protect could be abandoned so easily.

Murphy stepped forward and let out a shrill whistle that caused a sudden silence. 'I call for a vote,' he said, voice steady.

'You are not a member of the council,' said Stratton. 'You do not get to have a say in our decision. That is for the general and the colonels to decide.'

Murphy ran his gaze around the room. 'Then one of you needs to call a vote. A vote to remove Acting-General Stratton from his post and to name Captain Jackson Kyle as the new Acting-General.'

An even louder uproar sounded while Stratton glared

down at Murphy. 'A captain, especially a disgraced one, cannot become general, acting or otherwise.'

'Yes, they can. In times of war and when the colonels have placed a vote of no confidence in their current leadership, a new leader can be elected from any able-bodied warden. If we want the Wards to survive, if we want our people to have any hope of a future, then I believe Kyle is the man to lead us.' He turned to Jackson and gave a grave nod.

'Captain Kyle, what say you? For the good of the Ward, are you willing to take command and lead our wardens to victory?'

TWENTY-SIX

Justice knelt in the back of the four-wheel-drive, wincing each time it went over a bump, striving to keep Brother Owen still.

'Sorry,' Isaac called out from the driver's seat as the vehicle slid sideways before righting itself. The torrential rain had stopped, but the slick mud it left on the badly maintained road made it difficult to navigate.

'How much longer?' Justice asked, eyeing the monk's pale face. Eyes closed, breathing laboured, he'd given no indication he'd felt the bumps and jars of the trip.

'We're almost there. Just a bit farther.'

Justice wanted to be relieved, but with Brother Owen losing so much blood, any delay was too long. She only hoped the medics in Cadel were equipped to deal with this kind of injury. The wardens and most town security guards used stun guns instead of live ammunition, so they might not be used to dealing with a gunshot wound. Though they had to be practised at dealing with freak attacks, many of them resulted in the victim being euthanised to stop the infection turning them into freaks if the area where the infection occurred couldn't be cut away in time.

That was another reason Hannah's vaccine was so important: to stop people dying when their injury could be treated successfully.

But that was a problem for another time, one she hoped Hannah and the others were already working on. Justice looked ahead, through the windscreen, nerves singing as the town gates of Cadel appeared in the distance. She had been here before, in the presence of one of her earlier bodyguards, and they had been attacked by members of the Legion. Her memories of the town were a confusing mix of fear and anger as she had run for her life with a man who would not hesitate to kill her if not for the bond. It had been here that she had ended up with Marcus Callaghan's father Luke as her bodyguard. The following year had been a nightmare. She only hoped this visit would not cause even worse memories.

Once he pulled off the dirt road shortcut and onto the slightly better road that led to the next town, Isaac increased the speed of the vehicle. Within minutes, they were pulled up in front of the closed gates, engine still running. He tooted the horn. No one came out of the guard post to investigate and the gate remained closed.

'Boss, shouldn't the gate be open by now?' Renfield, sitting in the back seat, leaned forward. 'Dawn was half an hour ago.'

'Something's wrong,' Isaac said as he gestured for Sutherland. 'Go check it out. Renfield, watch his back.'

As Sutherland got out of the vehicle, Renfield picked up his rifle from the seat beside him and wound down the window. He leaned the barrel on the edge, facing the gate, head down as he scanned the area Sutherland approached.

Sutherland's head was swivelling from side to side as he walked to the guard post and banged on the door. After a long moment, when nothing happened, he lifted a booted foot and slammed it into the door below the handle, forcing it open. He entered the guard post and returned moments later, bending down to Isaac's window even as he kept his gaze on the gate.

'Guard post is empty, but I can hear people on the other side of the gate.'

Isaac gestured for Sutherland to step back and he got out of the car. Renfield did the same, and all three men strode to the closed gate. In the cramped boot of the vehicle, it was awkward for Justice to move to keep sight of them while keeping pressure on Brother Owen's wound. She crouched as low as she could to peer out the windscreen.

'Open the gate,' Isaac called out in a booming voice. 'We have a wounded man who needs immediate medical attention.' He used the butt of his pistol to clang on the metal gate and then called out again.

He kept it up until a loud voice came from up high.

Isaac moved back, Renfield and Sutherland flanking him, head craned to look up.

Justice couldn't see who had spoken, but it sounded as if they had a megaphone, as she had no trouble hearing his words.

'The town of Cadel is closed. There will be no entry to your kind. You need to move along, now, or you will be shot.'

'You may not like mercenaries, but the injured man is a monk,' said Isaac. 'Do you want to be responsible for letting a man of the cloth die when you could have done something to prevent it?'

'Doesn't matter what kind of man he is. He's not coming in, and these gates aren't opening. We're under quarantine.'

Quarantine?

Was there an unknown illness lurking behind these walls? Or was it the freaks causing trouble?

For the hundredth time, Justice wished they had been able to make as much of the vaccine as they needed and spread it around the country. But if it was freaks, they were all vaccinated and would not pose a further risk to the town's citizens.

'What kind of quarantine?' Isaac asked.

For a long moment, the man with the megaphone didn't speak. Then his voice came, lower than before. 'There's a new breed of freak on the loose. Three towns that we know of have been destroyed. Even if I wanted to let you in, I couldn't do it. The council has ordered the gates be chained until the wardens can guarantee all these new freaks are taken care of. But from what I hear, they're just as out-manned as us humans. You want to live? I'd suggest finding yourself a place to hole up with as many supplies as you can gather until this blows over. Forget about your monk. Save yourselves.'

His words sent a shiver over Justice's entire body. The new freaks—that was what Captain Murphy had called Jackson to help with. Was the man right? Were the wardens unable to control them?

She pushed the worry aside and focused on Brother Owen. He needed help now. Isaac was calling up to the man, still trying to get them inside. He got nowhere.

Justice slid around Brother Owen and opened the rear door of the four-wheel-drive, slipping outside and making her way to Isaac's side.

She stared at the top of the gate, to where a man stood looking down at them.

'Please help us,' she said, voice breaking as she held up hands coated in Brother Owen's blood. 'He'll die if you don't.'

For a long moment, the man gazed back at her, and then he disappeared from view. Justice's shoulders slumped, tears stinging her eyes.

Isaac leaned in and gave her a one-armed hug. 'You did your best.' He turned her around and she slowly walked back toward the four-wheel-drive, only to stop when a package landed on the ground in front of her.

She spun and peered up at the wall to see a second man had joined the first. The megaphone obscured his features as he told her what to do to take care of Brother Owen's wound.

He had barely finished speaking when the first man ripped the megaphone out of his hands.

'Take the medical supplies and go,' he said. 'If you're not back in your vehicle and turned around within one minute, I have orders to shoot you.'

With that, there was nothing left for Justice to do but grab the medical supplies and stride back to the car. Beside her, Isaac's expression was grim, but he said nothing as they reached the four-wheel-drive and climbed inside. Justice immediately opened the package as Isaac put the vehicle in reverse and they took off, going off-road soon after and skirting around the town.

Surveying the contents of the package, Justice wished she had more experience with first aid. Brother Owen needed more than just first aid, he needed surgery. But it was clear he was not going to get any help from the people in Cadel. Isaac vetoed Sutherland's suggestion of heading to the next town and trying their luck there.

'Now that word has got out about this new breed of freaks, more towns will be following Cadel's lead. We head straight for the monastery. It's his best chance.'

What if they got to Shelton and the guards wouldn't let them enter either? What would they do then?

That was also a problem for another time. For now, she did her best to make Brother Owen comfortable, finding the painkiller the doctor had mentioned and injecting him with it. The lines on his face eased as she then set about changing the makeshift dressing for a more substantial one. The wound was still seeping blood, but not as badly as it had been earlier. She covered the wound and tried to bind the bandage in place without causing Brother Owen more pain. Whatever was in the syringe worked to ease him into sleep, though it increased the difficulty of Justice's efforts to lift him to secure the bandage properly. She persevered in silence, leaning back and resting against the rear of the back seat once she was done, exhausted both emotionally and physically.

Only time would tell if Brother Owen was going to be okay, and Jackson as well. All she could do was conserve her strength so that when the time came, she was ready to act to save humankind from destruction.

TWENTY-SEVEN

With Hanson and the others well known to many of the humans living in Brimfield, Hannah knew she was the logical choice to go aboveground and gather more supplies. Convincing the stubborn half-breed who had designated himself as leader of their small group was easier said than done.

'You can't go,' she said to Hanson. 'Councillor Dillon has your face plastered on every street corner, and Leon and the rest of the guys all have the tattoos that mark them as half-breeds. I don't have a tattoo, and no one in Brimfield knows what I look like.' She had spent the first twenty-six years of her life sequestered away in the Brimfield Ward. Since then, she had been to Harlington, and then the mine compound, but no one from Brimfield had ever seen her face.

'It's too dangerous. Some of the humans who left Harlington to come here are living in the half-breed zone. You said you confronted their ringleaders in the streets after we got separated. One of them could recognise you.'

'Councillor Dillon got rid of the ones who tried to take over after Jackson saved his life. No one is going to recognise me, and we need more supplies desperately.' Some of them had been injured during their escape and the fight to get to the tunnels.

'But you can't go alone. Someone has to go with you.'

'Many of the humans know what our wardens look like. They can't go aboveground during daylight any more than you can.'

'I can,' Lieutenant Carstairs said as he walked over to join them. 'This is my first time in Brimfield. Other than the guards who arrested us, no one here knows my face. Same as with Hannah.'

Hanson pushed forward, chin jutting out. 'Those guards are still up there searching for us. One of them catches sight of you or Hannah and that's it. You'll be locked up quicker than you can spit.'

Hannah smiled as she leaned in and placed a hand on Hanson's arm. 'Then you will just have to come and rescue us again.'

He crossed his arms in front of his chest and glared at her. 'I do not want you going up there. It's too dangerous.'

'Tough. I'm going whether you like it or not.'

His expression softened. 'Hannah, if anything happens to you … Justice and Jackson will kick my arse. Please, think about this.'

She gave a soft sigh. 'I have thought about it, and I need to do this. If we don't get more medical supplies, Corporal Torres' wound could become infected. And we need more food and water.' She stuffed the money they had pooled together into the back pocket of the jeans the half-breeds had pilfered from someone's clothesline the night before. 'I'll be back as soon as I can.'

'We'll both be back,' said Carstairs.

'You can't go looking like that,' Hanson said, indicating the body armour the lieutenant still wore. 'Leon,' he called over his shoulder, 'find some clothes for the lieutenant to wear.'

Within minutes, Carstairs was dressed in clothes Leon and the others had stolen. Hannah felt guilty for taking someone's stuff, but consoled herself with the thought that they were only borrowing it and it was for a good cause. They needed to spread the cure, to make other towns freak-free so people no longer had to be scared of the dark.

There had been minimal use of the streets at night, even though Brimfield was freak-free. It appeared old habits were hard to break, and after five hundred years of it being too dangerous to venture outside at night, most of the people in Brimfield kept to their old routines. Some had been out when Leon and the others had been scrounging for supplies the night before, but a lot of what they needed could only be bought from the stores, which opened during the day.

With Carstairs at her side, Hannah made her way to the exit leading to the street. Hanson and Leon were with them, and helped to move aside the makeshift barricade they used to camouflage the fact that the entrance to the carpark had been reopened. They would put the barricade back in place once Hannah and Carstairs had gone through.

The warden went first, but before Hannah could follow him, Hanson grabbed her arm and pulled her back. He wrapped his arms around her and hugged her tight. His breath was warm on her ear as he leaned in and whispered for her to be careful. The feel of his hard body pressed up against hers set a flush sweeping over her. She kept her gaze averted when he let go and stepped back. With a slight smile and a wave, she slipped through the opening and caught up with Carstairs.

'So, where to from here?'

Hannah thought over the plan Hanson had scratched out on the concrete floor of the carpark, orienting herself. One disadvantage of having always lived within Ward headquarters was that she had no experience with the town itself. She had to rely on Hanson's memory map.

She pointed to the left. 'It's this way.' At least, she hoped it was.

The streets were quiet, empty, though Hannah could glimpse people moving inside the houses they passed. She was conscious of some of them coming to the windows to watch them and she glanced over at her companion.

'Do you think you could walk less like a warden and more like a human?' His back was straight, his carriage erect, a sign of the training he had received since he could walk, like all wardens. 'Try slouching your shoulders and hang your head a bit.'

He did as she asked, making a reasonable approximation. Not that Hannah had much experience with humans, but at least he looked less like a warden now.

The streets got busier as they neared the merchant district, and Hannah was concerned by the looks they received from those they passed. She had hoped they would be seen as innocuous, but if Councillor Dillon had limited the number of people who could enter Brimfield, any strangers would stand out. She knew some people from Harlington had been allowed to stay and hoped she and Carstairs would be mistaken for them. That was the cover story they had prepared in case they were asked.

No one spoke to them. In fact, no one appeared to be speaking at all. Hannah's limited experience couldn't tell her if this was a new thing or the way life had always been in Brimfield. When she saw people casting suspicious looks at everyone they passed, and the nervous twitches they made at any loud noise, she began to think the citizens of Brimfield were on edge and not just suspicious of strangers.

They reached the start of the shopping district and Hannah handed half of the money to Carstairs. 'This will go faster if we split up.'

'I don't think that's a good idea.' He cast a dark gaze around the street. 'Something is not right in this town.'

'All the more reason for us to get our shopping done and get out of here as fast as we can.' Hannah would never have believed it before, but she would feel much safer to be back underground than aboveground right now. She went over the list of supplies, sending Carstairs in search of food, water, and a blanket so she could make Torres more comfortable. Hannah would take care of the medical supplies, being more familiar with what they needed.

She headed for a large building with a sign that said it was a medical dispensary, mentally preparing her story as she pushed open the door and stepped into the cool interior. Lights blazed down on shelves packed with all kinds of medical supplies, and she grabbed a basket and loaded it with most of what they needed. The antibiotics, however, were not kept on the main shelves. According to Hanson, those were in locked cabinets behind the counter and you had to request them from the dispensary staff.

Hannah approached the staff member behind the counter, taking in the severe hairstyle and the immaculate white coat.

'Ah, hello, my father has cut his leg on some roofing iron while fixing damage caused by the storm. I have cleaned the wound but need some antibiotics to make sure it doesn't become infected, as well as something for the pain.'

The woman's brows lowered. 'I've never seen you in here before. You're one of that lot from Harlington, aren't you? Why don't you go back there and get what you need? We don't want your kind here, stirring up the council and causing trouble.'

Hannah attempted a conciliatory smile. 'I'm not with that lot. They've all gone back to Harlington. Those of us who are left don't want any trouble. We just want a safe place to live. Please, my father is in a lot of pain. He really needs that medicine to help him get better, so he can get back to work helping your council repair the rest of the storm damage.'

The woman gave no sign that Hannah's plea, or mention

of the work the humans from Harlington were undertaking, had swayed her thinking. Just when Hannah thought for sure that she was going to be kicked out of the store, another voice spoke up.

'Give her what she needs.'

Hannah spun around and found a short man with brown wavy hair and wearing a crumpled grey suit standing to the left of the counter. He gave her a weary smile and rubbed at his eyes.

'But, Neil, she's one of the Harlington scum, and I don't think Councillor Dillon would like me to be serving her kind.'

'I'm well aware of where she is from,' said Neil, 'but not all people from Harlington are scum. Many of them are just looking for a better, safer place to live, and for some reason they chose Brimfield.' He had a wry twist to his mouth as he spoke.

He nodded in Hannah's direction. 'I guess having the privilege of being the only town to be free of freaks outside of Ward High Command has its attractions. We have had a constant stream of people looking to relocate to our fair town, not all of them as well intentioned as we would like. But that is our problem. You need antibiotics and painkillers, is that correct?'

Hannah nodded, watching as Neil firmly but politely persuaded the shopkeeper to give her what she had asked for. When she went to hand over the money to pay for the items, Neil placed a hand on her arm.

'That is not necessary. The council will pay for your supplies.'

As the shopkeeper moved away to mark the items down on the council bill, along with a number of supplies Neil had placed on the counter, he leaned in close to Hannah.

'After everything you have done for us, Miss Young, the least the town can do is pay for your medicine. I only hope the wardens or half-breeds you are getting them for are not seriously injured. Councillor Dillon will stop at nothing to capture every last one of you, and I know he means to make an example to ensure no warden or half-breed will ever set foot in his town again.'

Hannah had frozen at his use of her surname, the import of his words taking a moment to sink in.

He spoke again before she could respond. 'You all need to get out of Brimfield as quickly as possible. He has guessed you are hiding underground and is preparing an assault team as we speak. We owe our lives to you for coming up with the vaccine. I would hate for that to be repaid with violence.'

The shock falling away at his words, Hannah shook her head. 'I need more blood from someone who was infected and then cured, so I can make more of the vaccine. People in the other towns and cities are still being infected. They're dying and I need your help to save them.'

He wore a thoughtful expression as he digested her words. Then he gave a rueful sigh. 'Very well, if you will wait outside for a moment while I finish my business here, I will accompany you to somewhere you can draw my blood. I was one of those you cured with your vaccine, and I would be honoured to provide my blood to enable you to cure others.'

The shopkeeper returned to the counter, cutting off further chance of talk, so Hannah simply gave Neil a nod, holding the bag of medicine tightly as she left the shop, and found Carstairs waiting on the sidewalk for her.

In a low voice, conscious of the wary looks they received from people passing by, she filled him in on the encounter.

'Do you trust him?'

Hannah considered her impression of Neil. There had been an air about him, of a man determined to do the right thing even though he knew it would be unpopular. He had been putting his purchases, and hers, on the council tab, so he must work for them. He'd known who she was, and that she had been responsible for creating the vaccine, and yet he had let the shopkeeper believe she was from Harlington.

She nodded. 'I trust him.' But that didn't mean she would be taking him back to their hideout without taking precautions.

When Neil emerged from the shop with a small brown bag tucked under his arm, he eyed Carstairs. 'You're not a Brimfield warden. You must be Lieutenant Carstairs, the warden who deserted from the Harlington Ward.'

Carstairs stiffened, but his voice was even when he said, 'I prefer to think of it as choosing the right side, rather than desertion. There comes a time when a man needs to stand up for what is right rather than blindly following orders that make no sense or are downright immoral.'

Neil's expression was grim. 'You speak the truth, Lieutenant, so perhaps I can trust your promise.'

'What promise?'

'That once I have donated my blood to Miss Young, you will get her as far from Brimfield as possible. My employer has made it his mission to destroy all wardens and half-breeds who once lived in Brimfield. It is not safe for her here, or for any of the others.'

Carstairs gave a low bow. 'I give you my word, I will make sure Hannah gets clear.'

'Very well then, I suggest we get moving. We have attracted too much attention as it is and I would like to get this done before the council finds out. There is an empty doctor's surgery two blocks away. I trust it will have everything Miss Young will need.'

He set off at a fast pace and Hannah hurried to catch up with him, conscious of Carstairs bringing up the rear. If he was leading them to a surgery, that was a much better option than taking him to their hideout. Unless he was leading them into a trap.

She didn't believe so, and was relieved her perception of

him proved to be true when he did take them to a surgery with a closed sign out the front.

The reason it was closed was soon clear; it had recently sustained damage, glass strewn all over the floor and a board replacing the window.

'Dr Aubury objected to serving one of the newcomers from Harlington after the man could not pay. In the ensuing altercation, he was killed and his surgery damaged. Council guards arrived before the surgery could be looted so everything should still be intact.' Neil led the way through the debris of smashed chairs and down a narrow corridor.

'Dr Aubury's receptionist gave me the combination for his medicine safe. If there is anything else on your shopping list that the shopkeeper could not supply you with, I am sure we can find it here, along with everything you need to draw my blood.'

'Thank you,' Hannah said as he led them into a clean surgical room and sat down in a chair. 'You're risking a lot by helping us.'

'I risk far more by standing by and doing nothing. If Councillor Dillon has his way, this town will become even more of a prison than it already is. Captain Kyle is the only man capable of standing up to him. All I ask is that you tell him what is happening here. People disappear if they dare question Dillon's orders. He is out of control and will take every man, woman, and child in this town down with him.'

Sorrow filled his eyes. 'We lost too many people when that man infected us with his freak virus. We can't afford to lose more innocent lives. We need the wardens to come back, to restore order. You tell Captain Kyle I said that, and that there are those who will help him reclaim his Ward.'

'I'll tell him,' Hannah said, internally wincing at laying another burden on Jackson's shoulders. Maybe after he had sorted out the mess High Command had made of things since General Butcher's death, and he'd helped Justice with her mission, and all the freaks had been cured, there would be a way to help the people of Brimfield escape the lock Councillor Dillon had around their throats.

In short order, she had collected a suitable amount of Neil's blood and applied a bandage to the crook of his arm. 'No heavy lifting or strenuous activity for the next few hours, and make sure you drink something sweet and have something to eat as soon as you can to replenish your body's stores.'

He gave a faint smile as he put his jacket back on. 'Thank you for your concern, Miss Young, but it is you who needs to be careful. You have what you came here for. Now you must return to your people and find a way out of Brimfield before the council guards trap you here for good.'

She and Carstairs hurried away from the doctor's surgery, Neil going in the other direction. There were fewer people on the streets now and those remaining walked with more urgency than before, all of them casting scurrying glances around them. Muttered comments from those they passed revealed that the council had called a curfew and the guards were authorised to use force to clear the streets.

As an alarm sounded in the distance, while she and Carstairs made their way underground, Hannah hoped Neil's warning to get out of town had not come too late.

TWENTY-EIGHT

Councillor Kelvin Dillon stormed down the stairs behind David Flanders.

'I'm going to kill every single one of these wardens with my bare hands,' he growled, rubbing at a stitch in his side as he raced to the front door. Here he was forced to stop, to lean over and catch his breath after his mad dash to the ground floor. Then, rage still burning through his body, he forced himself to straighten.

'Sir, I don't believe the wardens are responsible,' David said, not looking at all out of breath after tackling the stairs two at a time. Curse him.

'Don't be stupid. Of course, it's the wardens. Who else would try to rescue the ones you captured last night? Not that you managed to hold on to them for long.' He shot the leader of his security forces a black look, voice hard at the memory of reaching the detention centre only to find out the prisoners had escaped.

'The army outside the gate are not wardens, I'm sure of it,' David said, his tone calm and considered. 'They're humans, perhaps a mercenary company.'

More rage swelled through Kelvin. 'The Righteous?' He

would welcome the opportunity to pound that arrogant commander's face into the dirt as much as executing Jackson Kyle. How dare he renege on a contract? He'd made sure the world knew the man had failed to follow through on a kill order, guaranteeing his reputation would plummet and jobs dry up. If it was the Righteous at the gates, he was no doubt out for Kelvin's blood in an effort to get revenge on having his career ruined.

Well, no matter. He had more than a few tricks up his sleeve. He had not been idle in the past week, and was confident the new people he had hired were more than enough to take care of both wardens and mercenaries.

'No, they do not bear the standard for the Righteous. They bear no standard at all. Whoever they are, they are playing it low-key. Well, except for blocking the gate and demanding we hand over the wardens to them or risk death.' A grim smile played over David's lips as he recounted the threat.

Kelvin frowned. 'It has to be wardens then. Maybe they are in disguise.' They were so arrogant, disguises weren't their style. But he would show them. He climbed into David's vehicle and planned what he would say to the wardens when he reached the gate, leaving them in no doubt that he was in charge. Not them. The days of the wardens lording over the citizens of Brimfield were well past.

But when he got to the gate and made his way laboriously to the guard post, he agreed with the assessment that the force arrayed against them was not wardens. They lacked the clean lines and discipline he would expect to see from the wardens in all encounters. Kyle may have gone renegade, but he was still a warden and would not let his men lounge around if they were supposed to be attacking a town.

Maybe there was a different mercenary company, either with a contract out on the wardens or hired by them to attempt the rescue. Not that it would make any difference. He would not give them up once he recaptured them. They would be the bait to lead Kyle and the half-breed into his trap. David had been sure he'd spotted Hanson Forsythe among the group to enter the town. He was yet to be found, but he would be hunted down soon enough. There was nowhere they could hide, not with the entire town turned against them for their part in the debacle with the Legion.

Before the alarm had signalled an enemy at the gate, David had been preparing a team to infiltrate the underground tunnels to smoke out the wardens and half-breeds once and for all. Now, that would have to wait until after he got rid of this lot.

He grabbed a megaphone from a guard and called out to the force below. 'This is Councillor Kelvin Dillon. You are trespassing on council land and I order you to leave immediately.'

The town fields were spread out on either side of the wide road leading up to the town gates. Kelvin was most put out to see some of the mercenaries had stomped through the carefully tended fields. Whoever this group belonged to would be receiving a bill for damages incurred.

A tall woman stepped to the front of the group arrayed near the gate, her red hair tied back in a braid. She wore a deep red-coloured armour, not what he was used to seeing on a mercenary or warden. The men and women with her were dressed in a mix of old-style army camouflage, body armour, or jeans and shirts. Very odd.

The woman stared up at Kelvin, her gaze unwavering as she called out. 'You will hand over all wardens to me, or I will raze your town to the ground.'

She did not need a megaphone to make her threat heard, the chill in her voice sending a shiver down his spine. She waved a hand and two of the vehicles trampling the edge of his crops moved forward, flame shooting out of spouts at the front.

'We'll start with your food supplies, and then we'll move on to you.'

Anger had Kelvin speechless for a moment, as she got her people to sear the first row of crops to ash.

Then he recovered. 'I will not give in to threats. Any wardens in my town are fugitives, and as soon as I recapture them, they will be executed.'

She took a step back. 'Executed?'

As he watched, a slow smile spread across her face. 'Well now, that changes things.' She waved her hand again, and the flames were cut off.

She gazed up at Kelvin. 'My name is Rona Maguire, and I have a proposition for you. Why don't you open the gate and we can discuss it in a more private setting?'

He curled up his lip. 'We have nothing to discuss.' As if he would be stupid enough to open the gate while an enemy force was waiting on the other side.

'So, I'm wrong in guessing that you hate the wardens just as much as I do?'

Hate the wardens?

He shook his head. 'You're not here to rescue them?'

She gave a low, husky laugh filled with menace. 'I'm here to kill them. All of them.'

TWENTY-NINE

Hanson's mood grew grimmer as Hannah shared what Neil had told her. If what he said was true, they needed to get out of Brimfield, fast. Now that Hannah had the blood she needed, and there was no chance of them getting hold of the airship, there was no reason for them to stick around.

He gathered his people together, arranging for the able-bodied to help the wounded. Once everyone was ready, they ventured aboveground. The half-breed zone would be too well guarded, so they looped around the city centre and made for the wall with the front gate, hoping they would be able to overpower the guards on duty and get the gate open before they were discovered.

The alarm Hannah had mentioned was still ringing, and he hoped it was drawing the attention of any guards on duty.

When he and the others neared the gate, Hanson stifled a curse at the sight of a large contingent of guards lining the wall. Only, these guards weren't facing into town, they were looking outward.

Hanson could hear the sound of engines and a large gathering of people on the other side of the wall.

Was it Jackson, come to rescue them?

Then Councillor Dillon's amplified voice rang out on the other side of the gate. As Hanson listened to the conversation with the woman, who called herself Rona Maguire, his faint hope that this was some kind of rescue attempt faded. He spun and grabbed Hannah's arm, pulling her with him as they made their way back to where the others waited. He didn't spare a glance for Carstairs who, as usual, was right on Hannah's heels. He didn't have time to worry about the warden making moves on his friend. From the sound of things, that Rona woman and Councillor freaking Dillon were soon going to be best buds if she had it in for the wardens that bad. He didn't know who she was, and he didn't want to wait to find out.

He urged his people along to a deserted area on the outskirts of Brimfield, in what had once been a thriving industrial district.

'We need a plan,' he said, scanning Leon and the others. 'Any ideas on how we're going to get out of here now?' Even as he asked the question, his mind was racing, tossing up and discarding one scenario after another.

The means they had used to flee Brimfield last time was not an option.

Even if they could get hold of a couple of vehicles and lure the council guards away from the gate long enough for them to get it open, they would still have to contend with the force waiting on the other side. A force that was out to kill wardens. With the councillor after his head, the fact he was a half-breed wouldn't save him. Or Hannah and the others.

'Is there anywhere we could scale the wall, if we can get hold of ladders?' Carstairs' voice was even, despite the situation they were in.

Hanson shook his head. 'There is barbed wire and other nasty tricks waiting for those who try to get into town that way.' He had been part of the crew that had done repairs on one section of the wall and had seen how deadly the deterrents were for anyone trying to get into town without using the front gate. It had been meant to keep people out, not in, but would have the same effect.

'Then our only option is the same way we came in.'

Hanson nodded, having come to the same conclusion. 'You're right. We don't have any other choice.' His stomach plummeted at the thought of how many guards they would have to fight their way through. He couldn't count on them being called to help deal with whatever was going on at the front gate.

'We don't have any weapons, either. But I have an idea how we can fix that.' Hanson beckoned to Leon and Carstairs. 'You guys take point.' He directed two of the other wardens to watch the rear, keeping Hannah with him.

As quickly and quietly as they could manage with such a large group, they headed to the construction site where he and his crew had been working before they'd ended up locked away in the Ward. His mouth screwed up in a wry smile at how well that had turned out. Ward headquarters and all four garrisons had been razed to the ground by Councillor Dillon in his anger over his son's death at Hanson's hands.

Still, being part of Jackson's new Ward, living in the Legion's mine compound, and even skulking through the streets of Brimfield looking for a means of escape—it was all better than being a slave to humans who could order their deaths for any perceived crime.

At least this way he was a free man, free to choose what he wanted to do with his life. He just hoped that freedom of choice wouldn't see him leading Hannah and the others to their deaths.

Pushing down his uneasiness over his role as leader of this ragtag group, he reached the construction site and winced. It looked exactly the same as the last time he was here. The gate was pushed over, work halted, and tools tossed every which way after the fight. It looked as though the boss had given up on this particular project, with his workers taken and everything else that had happened since then. He felt a pang of sympathy. The boss hadn't been a bad guy—for a human. He'd treated them a darn sight better than others he'd worked for over the years.

Hanson pushed thoughts of the past aside and began to scoop up tools and hand them out to his companions.

Carstairs hefted a crowbar. 'This isn't going to do much good against guns.'

Hanson gave him a grim nod. 'I know. But it's all we've got.' It had to be enough. He had to get Hannah out of Brimfield.

The sky was starting to lighten as they set out for the half-breed zone. They needed to get out of there before the councillor and the force at the gates finished their negotiations. The distraction of the guards, not sure what was happening outside their town, worked to their advantage as they drew closer to their objective.

Finally, they were in position at the edge of the zone, still a couple of blocks away from the gap in the wall, looking out for guards. They had to get out of there fast, or they would lose the only chance they had.

'We need to split up,' Hanson said in a low voice. 'We'll go in groups of three.'

He sent Hannah off with Leon and one of the wardens first. Once they had slipped around the edge of the orphanage, he indicated for the next group to go. Followed by a third. Soon there was only him, Carstairs, and one of his crew left.

Hanson urged them forward, shoulders hunched, expecting an outcry at any moment, but they reached the row of classrooms and slipped behind them without incident. He found the others waiting in a huddle, worried expressions on their faces, especially Hannah's.

She met his eyes and let out a soft sigh, relief in the brief gaze she shared with him.

He nodded, then indicated for Leon to take the next step. This would be the most dangerous, with no cover between here and the male dormitory that edged up against the wall. They would go as a group this time.

Together, they would either succeed or fail.

He grabbed Hannah's hand and took the lead.

The first shot rang out after they made it halfway to the dormitory, but Hanson kept going, pulling Hannah in a zigzag pattern as more shots were fired. Then guards spilled out of the nearby classrooms.

There were too many of them. Armed only with tools, it was hopeless.

Hanson called out for his people to retreat, to get back to their original hiding place. Even as he gave the command, he spun on his heel and ran back the way they had come, pulling Hannah along with him.

A tug on his arm and Hannah was no longer holding onto his hand. He stopped running and found her lying on the ground, body twitching from a stun shot. She was barely conscious. He picked her up and ran for the side of the orphanage as the others crowded around them. The pounding footsteps of the guards in pursuit came from behind them, though mercifully they had stopped firing.

Adrenaline put a burst of speed into his steps.

He was dizzy with relief when he rounded the corner to find the others were there to help him with Hannah.

They raced for the culvert and were back underground, their escape attempt a failure. But at least they were still alive. At least they still had Hannah.

Bleakness threatened to overwhelm him after he laid her unconscious form on a blanket Carstairs grabbed from his pack and hastily spread out on the ground. Hanson held her hand and waited for the stun to wear off, staring at the concrete wall on the other side of the underground carpark.

He had failed her.

He'd failed them all.

He hung his head and fought the urge to weep.

THIRTY

THE VOLUME OF NOISE IN THE ROOM ROSE CONSIDERABLY after Murphy's suggestion to make Jackson acting-general, and from the sound of it, most of the colonels were not happy at the idea of a mere captain being put in charge. Not that Jackson was thrilled about the idea either. It was hard enough running a Ward. To be placed in charge of all wardens, deciding who fought and where, putting lives at risk—it was a daunting task.

'I wish you'd run that by me first,' he said to Murphy, sure the warden's enhanced hearing would pick it up despite the din.

Murphy snorted. 'You'd have said no. Besides, who else is there to lead us? You're the only warden with the guts to stand up for what's right, even if it costs you dearly.'

'You're standing here too.'

Murphy gave a sad smile. 'Too little, too late. I should have acted sooner, back when Major Templeton stormed into my Ward and started throwing out orders that were against the Ward charter. We could have done something then, stopped General Butcher before he pitted warden against warden in that needless battle at your new Ward. Major

Wallace might still be alive, and countless others, if I'd listened to my gut back then instead of trusting my superiors knew what they were doing.'

'You were following orders.'

'Bad orders. It shouldn't have taken the deaths of wardens, good and bad, to make me question the chain of command. Getting you instated as acting-general will go a small way toward rectifying my lapse in judgement.'

'It's not your judgement that was bad. You knew what Butcher and Templeton were doing was wrong.'

'Then trust my judgement now. You need to take charge or there will be no saving the Wards.'

Jackson grimaced. 'If we stop these freaks, find a way to cure them as well as the others, there will be no need for the Wards. Are you sure you're ready for that?'

'With the mess this lot have made, I'm thinking a world where wardens are no longer needed is a good thing. It's time to get everyone back on equal footing. You were right. Human, half-breed, warden—we're all the same. It's time we started acting like it.'

With a determined expression, Murphy stepped away from Jackson, closer to the sitting colonels. 'Enough!'

His roar stunned them into silence, and he immediately took advantage. 'If you do not recognise Jackson Kyle as acting-general then you will lose the wardens' faith in this committee. We were born to fight freaks, and he is the man to lead us in that fight.' Murphy spun around and pointed at Jackson, but before any of the colonels had a chance to respond, a loud boom sounded outside.

Jackson was closest to the door, and he sprinted to it and wrenched it open, eyes narrowed as he took in the sounds of fighting nearby as another boom came.

'Those are the main guns on the citadel walls,' Murphy said, running to his side. 'Other than for drills, those haven't fired in hundreds of years.'

'This is no drill,' Jackson said as screams and yells assaulted his ears. He turned in the direction of the noise. His stomach clenched as he realised it was coming from the section of the wall near the old medical centre, where General Butcher had ordered the execution of Major Wallace and for Jackson to be drained of blood.

When he and Murphy reached the adjourning corridor and burst into the open, he grimaced at the sight of four freaks with blood streaming from their eyes. Wardens were fighting them, but as he watched, one of the wardens turned and attacked the warden beside him. None of the wardens wore body armour, since no freaks had ever infiltrated High Command, let alone the citadel itself. As the newly made freak latched on to the warden and bit savagely into his exposed neck, Jackson knew the rate of infection was only going to get worse.

The citadel gun boomed again, and both warden and freak disappeared in an instant, blood and gore raining down on the rest of the combatants.

'Idiots,' Jackson shouted as he grabbed a fallen weapon and trained it on one of the freaks still standing. 'The blood will infect anyone it touches.' He fired a head shot and took down the freak, then sought out his next target, wanting to get the situation under control before the citadel gun fired again and spread more of the highly infectious blood and matter over the wardens.

Murphy found a gun and took aim beside him, and between them they were able to take down all the freaks.

'Stand back,' Jackson yelled as other wardens rushed into the area. 'Do not touch the blood unless you want to be the next infected.'

At his roar, everyone froze, making the groans of an injured warden on the ground clearly audible. As Jackson carefully made his way closer, the warden's eyes began to bleed. In a split second he was on his feet, injury forgotten as he launched at Jackson. Regret coursing through his veins, Jackson fired, hitting the freak between the eyes.

Sadness engulfed him as the body dropped to the ground. What a waste.

He turned to Murphy. 'How the hell did this happen?'

Murphy shook his head, sorrow in his gaze as he eyed the dead bodies. 'I don't know.'

'Captain Murphy.' One of the wardens in the area came to stand in front of him and saluted. 'Acting-General Stratton ordered the medics to take samples from the wardens who were infected in Dalwaring. Something went wrong. The medic was infected and turned on the rest of the medical staff.'

Jackson shared a grim glance with Murphy and then handed his weapon to the warden. 'Make sure no one touches the dead bodies or comes into contact with the blood. Shoot anyone who tries.'

Then he stormed back inside the citadel and to the room where the acting-general and the sitting colonels were clustered around his desk.

Jackson stalked up to the acting-general. 'You just got over a dozen wardens killed because you do not know what you are dealing with. Either you step down or I will see that you are court-martialled over their deaths.' He tersely explained what had happened and Stratton's face blanched.

'But that's impossible. The medics were ordered to take all precautions with their experiments.' As Stratton spoke, the colonels stepped back, disassociating themselves from their former leader. At this, his shoulders slumped. 'Very well, I concede. It is up to the sitting colonels to decide my replacement.'

Within moments it was official.

Murphy clasped Jackson on the shoulder. 'Congratulations, Acting-General Kyle. What's your first order?'

Jackson scanned the room, meeting the eyes of each

colonel in turn. 'If we don't act now, we face the extinction of mankind. You need to notify the Over-Council that all humans and half-breeds are welcome to take shelter in the Wards. Wardens are to switch to live ammunition, and do their best to hold out until we can get to them.'

He swiftly outlined his plan to mobilise every able-bodied warden at High Command. 'Once they are assembled, I want them to go town by town to help clear out these new freaks.'

It would take time he feared they did not have, not with how fast this new strain was spreading, but there was no other way.

He turned to Murphy. 'I'm putting you in charge.'

'You're not coming with us?'

Jackson shook his head. 'I'll meet up with you as soon as I can.' He had to get back to the mine, to find out if Justice had returned and what had happened to the teams he had sent to Brimfield.

For the coming fight, he needed all of his people on board to have any hope of making it through the days ahead.

THIRTY-ONE

Brother Owen had regained consciousness by the time they reached Shelton, and he now sat in the passenger seat beside Isaac to act as guide, calling out directions in a low voice. He had shown a marked improvement since Justice had given him the painkillers and antibiotics from Cadel, and she was hopeful he would make a full recovery once they had a chance to clean and stitch his wound properly.

To her relief, the gates had been open with no guards in sight when they drove through, though she had seen movement inside the guard post. Unlike the ones in the other towns they had passed, this was a rickety shed propped up against the side of a fence that appeared to be only slightly sturdier. It had been years since Justice was last in Shelton, when she had been sequestered away behind the monastery walls, so she had no idea what the town looked like. She had avoided returning with any of her bodyguards, the memories of all she had lost keeping her away.

It was nearing dusk when they navigated the streets Justice as a child wished she could play in. They were empty, lights blazing in the houses and buildings as the citizens prepared for the coming of night. Freaks were still around here, and she hoped they would reach the monastery before night fell. With Brother Owen injured, their small group would be hard pressed to fight off a number of freaks.

Shelton was a small town, too small for a Ward, so it was up to the town guards to protect their citizens. The high walls at the monastery had been all the protection the monks had needed until the Legion had smashed their way in. Justice had no idea what condition her old home would be in after fifteen years. Brother Owen had not been inclined to talk about what it had been like when Gaea had resurrected him and sent him to find Justice, but she could imagine it was not pretty.

When Isaac drove up to the gates at Brother Owen's direction, she was pleased to see they were closed and what she could see of the wall was intact. Maybe they wouldn't face any freaks or squatters when they entered.

'I locked the gates before I left,' Brother Owen said, wincing as he reached inside his robe and pulled out a large brass key.

Isaac took the key and handed it to Renfield. 'We might as well get settled for the night. No medic is going to come out after dark to see to our patient.' He looked to Brother Owen. 'Think you can survive one more night being looked after by Justice?'

Brother Owen smiled. 'It shall be as my Goddess wills. I am her appointed guide. My life is of no consequence compared to assisting Justice with fulfilling her duty.'

It was a duty she had never asked for, but one for which both she and the monk had already died. Surely Gaea wouldn't allow Brother Owen to be sacrificed a second time?

Isaac seemed to be of a similar mind. 'So, you're good to wait until tomorrow to see a medic, then?'

'Yes, Commander Smith. I will survive the night, to do Gaea's will.'

It was not a resounding avowal of health, but it appeared Brother Owen had said all he wanted to. He leaned against the head rest and closed his eyes as Renfield unlocked and opened the gates. Isaac drove the vehicle through the opening and Renfield quickly locked the gates behind them, jogging after them as Isaac headed for the main building.

Heart thudding in her chest, a ringing in her ears, Justice wiped sweaty palms on her legs as Isaac cut the engine.

This was familiar territory, so familiar it ached.

Late afternoon shadows caressed the grey brick facade of the main building. The flowerbeds lining the cobbled paths leading to the smaller outbuildings were overrun, almost obscuring the paths. The monastery had always been in immaculate condition, the monks taking pride in maintaining their home. The evidence of fifteen years of neglect caused a pang in her heart.

Hand shaking, she reached for the door handle.

Before she touched it, Isaac was there to help her. She was grateful for his support as she looked over the silent monastery, picturing it as it had once been, filled with equally silent monks, her mother at her side, secure that she was loved and cherished.

'Renfield and Sutherland, do a reconnaissance. Justice and I will help the monk.'

As his men left to follow their orders, Isaac looked at Justice. 'You doing okay, little sister?'

Not trusting her voice, she gave a short nod. Then she pulled away and moved to the other side of the vehicle to help Brother Owen stand. He paled with the movement, grimacing as a hand went to his injured side, but he still managed a smile for Justice.

'Have faith in our Goddess. Everything happens for a reason.'

Justice bit back a grumpy reply. Brother Owen had chosen to follow Gaea. She had been given no choice, and her destiny had brought a lot of pain and heartache to her life. But it had also brought her the monks, and eventually led her to Jackson and the friends she had made at Brimfield. Isaac would not be here, helping her now, if his brother hadn't been one of those caught in the bond to become her reluctant bodyguard.

But once she finally secured the future for those she cared about, Justice would not be sad to never hear the name Gaea ever again. For now, she had to enter her old home and discover what the monks had been guarding for so many years.

When Renfield and Sutherland returned to advise the main building was clear, the grim expressions on their faces warned her that what she was about to discover would not be pleasant.

'Looks as if no one has been here in well over a decade, probably since Justice left. There are skeletons scattered around the place, but it doesn't look as though anyone else has been here since they died.'

Justice's stomach lurched at finding her fears were true. To enter the building, to find out what Gaea needed her to do, she would have to see the bodies of her mother and all the monks who had helped raise her. With the shadows of dusk deepening around them, and no other safe place to go, she had no choice but to suck it up and head inside.

She kept her focus on Brother Owen, sure that this was just as difficult for him. She may have lived here for ten years, but the monastery and those who resided here had been his life. It had ultimately led to his death, yet he showed no hesitation as she and Isaac assisted him to the main door.

Either Renfield or Sutherland had set up a lantern on a small table against one wall of the foyer, the light casting flickering shadows down the hall that led to the rooms the monks had slept in. On either side were doors leading to the kitchen, prayer rooms, and the library. Isaac took the lantern in his free hand as they headed further in.

'There is an infirmary at the back, near the personal quarters for the monks,' said Justice. The room she had shared with her mother was on the other side behind the kitchens, so they would not disturb the monks in their prayers or salutations.

Justice kept her eyes averted as they passed skeletons clothed in scraps of brown cloth—the monks who had fallen the day the Legion had come for her. She was thankful she did not have to face the common room where her mother had died trying to protect her.

They made it to the monks' quarters and Justice directed Isaac to the room that had been Brother Owen's.

The door was open, dust covering everything, the bed sheets rumpled. It pained Justice to see it like this. The monks were scrupulous about keeping every area of the monastery clean, never leaving a bed unmade or allowing dust to collect on any surface. Her mother, in return for being allowed to stay there with Justice, had worked just as hard to keep the areas she was allowed to access clean.

This sign of abandonment, more than anything, brought home to Justice just how much she had lost. Tears stung her eyes as she led Brother Owen to his bed and helped him to lie down. Then she quickly excused herself to go to the infirmary to see what supplies were useable to change his dressing.

It wasn't until a hand settled on her shoulder that she realised Isaac had followed her.

'Are you okay, little sister?'

Swallowing down a hard lump in her throat, she said, 'I will be.' Then she moved away, quickly completing her search of the infirmary and returning to Brother Owen with fresh bandages. Isaac was there already, with a bowl of water.

'Pump in the kitchen still works. Places like this are built to last.'

Justice gave him a wan smile as she cleaned and dressed Brother Owen's wound by the light of the lantern. As she worked, Isaac left.

Once she was done, Brother Owen reached out and

grabbed her arm. 'Take heart, Justice. You are stronger than you believe. You will fulfil the destiny Gaea set for you before your birth.'

She laid his hand back on his chest. 'Get some rest. I'll return soon with some food.' Not that they had much left, or that he'd had an appetite since being shot, but he needed his strength just as much as she did.

Before she went in search of the others, Justice headed down the hall to the common room, needing to face her past alone, to come to terms with everything she had lost and the pain and anger that roiled inside her.

The bodies lay as she remembered, discarded on the ground. From the decomposition there was no way to identify each set of remains, except for two.

One skeleton was not clad in the remnants of a brown robe. Instead, it was clothed in black, half lying on top of another skeleton. This was the man who had killed her mother, his body falling on top of hers after his colleague had killed him to protect Justice.

Anger filling her, she cast aside her revulsion and pulled his skeleton off her mother. Then she knelt on the cold stone floor of the common room, tears spilling down her cheeks as she beheld her mother's remains.

Head bowed, body shuddering with the force of her sobs, she remained there for many minutes. Then she straightened her shoulders and wiped her tears away with the back of one hand as she got to her feet.

She had said goodbye to her past. Now it was time to face the future.

THIRTY-TWO

'You betrayed me. You knew the girl was Kyle's pet half-breed, yet you said nothing. You even had the gall to put her purchases on the council account. How dare you?' Councillor Kelvin Dillon glared at Neil. The two of them stood on the sidewalk above a culvert near the merchant district.

'She's going to use my blood to make more vaccine,' said Neil. 'People are dying in the other towns without that cure. She just wants to help them.'

'She's lying. They're all liars, the half-breeds and the wardens. They don't want to help us. They want to enslave us. They've always thought they were better than us, and this new freak is just a lie, a way to get us back under their control. They need to be stopped.'

'I'm sorry, sir, but you're wrong. Miss Young said—'

'I don't give a shit what she said, and you're an idiot for believing her. But we can use that to our advantage. She trusts you, and so will the others.' He pointed at a large pipe jutting out of the culvert. 'David Flanders said the half-breed girl is using that to get aboveground. You're going to use it to find them and end this once and for all. Kill the girl and as many of the others as you can, but leave Hanson Forsythe alive. I want to take care of him myself.' He held out his stun gun, making sure it was set to maximum. Half-breeds and wardens would take more than a standard charge to bring them down.

Neil shook his head, holding up his arms in front of his chest. 'We need their help. You read the report from the Over-Council. The new virus is spreading. It's only a matter of time before it reaches Brimfield. We have to be prepared.'

'Either you lure them into my trap or I shoot you now.' Kelvin aimed the gun at his traitorous assistant's head. 'You chose to side with them, so you can die down there with them if that's what it takes. You can consider this your severance pay.'

He fired the trigger, but Neil flung himself backward, the shot only grazing his side as he toppled into the culvert.

Kelvin cursed, sure the amount of charge he would have received would not be enough to kill him. But maybe the fall had? He leaned over the edge and saw Neil had landed on his back. No movement. He watched for a moment, listening intently for a sign the traitor had survived the fall, but nothing came. He looked dead, but Kelvin determined to make sure of it. He took aim again. There was no way he could miss this time.

Neil deserved to die, and who cared if the half-breed couldn't cure any more freaks. Her blasted vaccine hadn't saved his son. The wardens murdered him in cold blood instead of curing him. All the talk about a new kind of freak had just been scaremongering, a way for the wardens to frighten gullible councils into doing what they wanted. He was too smart for that. He knew the truth and would do every-thing he could to stop the wardens, starting with getting rid of Neil and any other traitors, before ensuring the half-breed and her helpers were wiped out.

The tramp of booted feet sounded behind him, signalling the security guards he had ordered to accompany Neil into the underground tunnel system had finally arrived. He tucked the stun gun into the back of his pants and plastered on a concerned expression as he turned to face the newcomers.

'Captain Flanders, Neil was spotted by some of the wardens and they shot him.' He shook his head. 'He was unarmed, and he didn't stand a chance. I tried to stop them, but they were too fast for me. We need to make them pay for what they have done. Neil was a good man, a loyal employee working for the good of the town.' He fought the urge to sneer as he espoused accolades his former assistant did not deserve.

David dropped into the culvert and crouched over Neil's dead body. 'Sir, he's still alive.'

Kelvin gritted his teeth. Damn Neil. He would ruin everything. 'Is he conscious?'

'No, sir. But his heartbeat is strong. I think he's going to make it. I'll get my men to lift him up.'

'Leave him. I have a new plan for how we are going to get our hands on the wardens. I'll take care of Neil, don't you worry about that.' He held up his hand-held radio. 'I'll have someone here to help him within five minutes.'

He outlined the new plan he had devised for finding out where the wardens and half-breeds were hiding underground, one they would not see coming.

He waited until the captain and his men had moved off to follow their new orders, then gave it another couple of minutes before grabbing the stun gun and aiming it down to the culvert, ready to fire as many times as it took to make sure Neil never woke up.

A noise had him turning as two guards approached, a stretcher slung between them.

'Captain Flanders said we have a man down,' one of them said as they trotted over to the edge of the culvert. 'We'll have him out of there in no time.'

Cursing silently, Kelvin put the gun away and stepped back as they worked to get Neil out of the culvert. One way or another, he would make sure Neil did not wake up.

THIRTY-THREE

Andy tensed his grip on the steering wheel as he approached the ATV sitting in the middle of the road ahead of him. The Ward ATV.

All the doors were open, blood strewn on both the ATV and the ground around it. But there was no sign of Sergeant Saunders or the rest of his old patrol.

In the passenger seat beside him, Corporal Kaia Phillips cursed. 'What the hell happened here?'

Andy scanned their surroundings, hoping to spot Saunders and the others. In the distance, beyond the abandoned ATV, was the old ruin they had stopped at in their initial flight from Brimfield. Maybe Saunders was holed up there with the rest of the patrol, injured. Even as he sped up, heading for the ruins, he was aware that the amount of blood spilled was not a good indicator. He would not lose hope until he was sure. The blood could belong to someone other than his missing wardens.

As he drew near the ruins, all hope was lost when Saunders appeared, blood streaming from her eyes as well as from tears in her body armour. At her back were the remainder of Andy's old patrol with dozens of freaks behind them, many of them wearing the uniform of the Brimfield security guards. All of them were in the same condition as Saunders: infected with the new freak virus.

Andy had no time to wonder how they had been infected, for the freaks were closing in. He spun the wheel and accelerated, conscious of his hands shaking as he drove back the way he had come. He would have to find another way to get to Brimfield, to warn Hanson and the others not just about the Legion, but the freaks as well.

But each time he thought he had got clear, more freaks appeared.

Where were they all coming from?

As the hours passed with no clear way out, he grimly headed back to the mine compound.

'What are we going to do now?' Phillips asked.

'We're going to need more people and a lot more firepower to take out these new freaks.' He'd heard enough from Captain Murphy to know it wouldn't be easy taking them down.

He would not entertain the thought that Hanson and the others might have already been caught by one of the freak packs roaming around.

When he reached the compound, he shot out of the car, calling out to every warden he saw to suit up as he made his way toward the entrance to the mine.

Felice ran out of the cafeteria, meeting him halfway to the mine. 'What's wrong?'

Not stopping, he told her what was happening as he headed for the armoury.

Felice blanched at hearing what had happened to Saunders and the others, but she quickly rallied and sped off to ensure the alarm was raised. Within an hour, all the wardens and half-breeds were assembled on the parade ground, armour on and weapons ready as Andy arranged for vehicles to transport them all.

But in the end, they had not been fast enough.

Answering a cry of alarm from the guards at the front gate, Andy headed for the guard post, only to reel in horror at the sight of hundreds of freaks massing on the other side. They bashed against the gate, desperate to kill or infect the people inside the compound.

With a sickening feeling in the pit of his stomach as he spotted Saunders among them, Andy gave the order to fire. They had to clear the way if they had any hope of arriving in Brimfield in time to help the others.

THIRTY-FOUR

HANNAH STOOD AT THE COUNTER OF THE GENERAL SUPPLY store, frowning at the folded piece of paper in her hand. They'd lost the bulk of their supplies in their aborted escape attempt, and would not last much longer without buying more. Thanks to Neil's generosity in putting their medical supplies on the council bill, she still had money left over from her last shopping trip. Before she had a chance to list what she wanted, the dour-faced shopkeeper handed her a note she said was from Neil.

Her frown deepened as she unfolded the piece of paper and scanned the words written in a neat hand.

Dear Miss Young, please meet me at the same place as last time. I have some important information to relay to you.

Her heart beat faster. With Hanson and Leon on a scouting trip for weaknesses in the wall, and none of the others able to come aboveground, it was imperative she got the supplies back to their hideout. Yet Neil had helped her the day before and given her his blood, and whatever information he gave her could be important. He might even know of a way for them to escape the noose tightening around them now that the council had allowed some of the Legion people into

Brimfield to help search for them. Hannah was just lucky she was too short to be mistaken for a warden and that she didn't walk or act like a soldier. Even when they were off duty, the wardens still looked like what they were, just not in body armour.

Hannah quickly made her purchases, stuffing the non-perishable food items into her backpack and carefully adding the oil and wicks for their lanterns. Their solar lights had all run out of charge, and with no way to recharge them underground they were using the lanterns left behind by Marcus Callaghan.

With limited access to water and other amenities, it was rough living, but with luck a quick meeting with Neil would help to solve some of their problems. There could also be supplies she could grab from the surgery while she was there.

Decision made, she shouldered the backpack and left the shop, taking a moment once she was outside to get her bearings. This was only her second time in the merchant district and she hoped she remembered the way to the surgery. To aid her recall, she crossed the street and stood in front of the pharmacy before heading in the direction Neil had taken her last time. Five minutes later, she opened the door of the surgery, pleased her memory had got her here without any side trips.

Silence filled the empty front room, only Hannah's footsteps filling the space as she closed the door behind her.

'Hello?'

Her soft call was answered by an equally faint voice. 'I'm in the back room, Miss Young.'

Hannah moved past the reception desk, past the doctor's office and medical room, and headed for the door at the end of the hall. This door was slightly ajar, and she saw the flicker of shadows as someone moved around inside.

A prickle swept over Hannah's skin, and she stopped walking. The shadows looked too numerous to be made by just one man. It was a trap. Neil had betrayed her.

She turned to look back toward the reception, gasping when the front door opened and four large men barrelled in. They wore the security uniform of the Brimfield guards and they were armed.

She spun around, searching for a back door, but the door at the end of the hall swung wide open and four more guards emerged, trapping her between the two groups.

Hannah ducked into the room she had used last time she was here and closed the door, scrambling to lock it.

Loud thuds sounded as the first of the guards reached the door and tried to force it open, even as Hannah backed away and searched the room for something she could use to defend herself.

There was a small window that let in light, but there was no way she would be able to squeeze through it.

More thuds came from behind her.

The lock wouldn't hold much longer.

Apart from the furniture there wasn't much else in the room, nothing she could use to fight her way free.

The door slammed open, rebounding on the wall behind it, and Hannah whirled to face the guards. She was outnumbered, but she was not going down without a fight.

She kicked and punched out as more of the guards poured through the doorway, using her backpack as a weapon, landing some hits and feeling satisfaction at the grunts and cries of pain her efforts afforded. But it was not enough. They piled on her, grabbing her arms and legs, rendering her immobile. She was forced to her knees, and one of the guards chained her hands behind her back.

Panting, her breath a rasp, she fought down a rising sense of panic. What were they going to do to her?

The Legion leader had said she wanted to kill all the wardens, and these people considered her to be one of them.

Hannah was roughly pulled to her feet, shoulder aching at the strain as she was marched to the door and out onto the street. The sound of hurried footsteps had her turning to see Neil running awkwardly down the street toward her, alarm written all over his face, blood coating the side of his head.

'I'm so sorry,' he gasped when he saw her. 'I tried to get here sooner, to warn you, but I wasn't fast enough. The pharmacist told Councillor Dillon that I helped you and he made notes to give to all the shopkeepers along with your description. I'll do what I can to get you help, I promise.'

His evident distress soothed the feeling of betrayal she'd experienced, not that his apology did anything to help the situation, and she couldn't see what assistance he could provide. At least her instincts had been right to trust him.

His next words made her forget about anything else. 'Councillor Dillon is going to use you to get to Mr Forsythe. If he doesn't turn himself in within twenty-four hours, he is going to have you hanged.'

As she was dragged away down the street, she looked over her shoulder to see two guards grabbing Neil's arms and pulling him in the opposite direction. She hoped he wouldn't get into too much trouble for trying to help her. After that, she had no time to worry about him.

She was taken to the council chambers and locked in a small room with a black-haired security guard, who asked her over and over where the others were hiding. She refused to answer. There was no way she would betray her people. After an hour of questioning, she was dragged from the room and taken upstairs to what appeared to be a storage room.

As the guard handcuffed her to the metal shelving, Councillor Dillon entered, a smug expression on his flushed face. 'You may have got out of my jail, but you won't get out of here. Not with an armed guard watching you. And once you've served your purpose, I can hang you alongside the freaking half-breed that murdered my son.'

Hannah shook her head. 'You're insane. You have no right to do this.'

'I have every right!' Spittle sprayed from his lips. 'You're a half-breed, and we don't want your kind in this town. From now on, any half-breed found within Brimfield will be executed on the spot. The same for any wardens. And don't think I don't know where you lot have been hiding out. My men are gathering as we speak, ready to storm the underground tunnels. Soon you may well be the last member of the Brimfield Ward left alive. But not for long. If Forsythe slips past my men, you're my insurance that he'll come here. And when he does, he is going to die.'

Bile filled Hannah's throat at the thought of what was to come.

Her friends would have no warning, and she was chained to a shelf, surrounded by guards and unable to help anyone.

THIRTY-FIVE

Hanson paced back and forth. Something was wrong. Hannah should have been back by now. He clenched his fists, banging them against his thighs. She should never have been aboveground in the first place. He'd been furious when he and Leon returned to find that she had slipped out on her own to get more supplies. Sure, they were all hungry, but they could have handled a little deprivation. What they couldn't handle was losing Hannah.

He turned to Leon. 'I'm going after her. If they've got her, then there's a good chance they know where we're hiding. You need to get everyone moved. Take them back to the construction zone. There won't be much cover, but it's better than staying here and waiting to be caught.'

He took a deep breath and faced Carstairs. 'If I don't make it back there with Hannah, you do whatever it takes to find her and get her out of Brimfield. I don't care who you have to kill. You save her.'

Carstairs leaned forward and clasped Hanson's hand. 'Don't worry. I'll take care of her.'

A bitter twist to his mouth, Hanson grabbed a hammer in one hand and a crowbar in the other before making for the exit that had been boarded over, shifting aside the barricade. Then he took off in the direction of the detention centre.

Halfway there, a squad of guards stepped out of an alley and he turned around, sprinting for the next street.

A shot took him in the back, and he stumbled. A second shot took him in the shoulder and his right arm went dead. He balled his good hand into a fist as the guards closed in.

A shadow moved on his right, and something slammed into the side of his head. Blackness coated his vision, ears ringing, fighting to remain conscious as arms reached out to grab him.

Soon he was bound, head hanging down, hardly able to open his eyes while being dragged across the ground.

He was tossed down on a hard, cold surface, head connecting painfully as a rumble started beneath him. He was in the back of a truck, no doubt on his way to the detention centre where he'd hoped to find Hannah. No matter what, he'd find a way to get her free so she could join up with the others.

He drifted for a moment, until the rumble suggested the vehicle had stopped, then rough hands grabbed hold of his arms and pulled him upright. He was lifted from the bed of the truck and made to stand on weak legs.

It took a supreme effort to lift his head to scan his surroundings through blurred vision.

He wasn't at the detention centre.

He was standing in front of the razed ground where the headquarters for the Brimfield Ward had once stood. Three large tents were there now, temporary housing for the members of the Legion allowed to enter Brimfield. The rest of their forces remained camped outside the gates.

Councillor Dillon stood beside the leader of the Legion, the woman who had called herself Rona Maguire, both of them wearing smug expressions.

'He doesn't look like a warden,' said the redheaded woman.

'That's because this scum is a half-breed. The one who killed my son. He was also on the roof when your sister died. For all I know, he's the one who killed her too.'

Hanson fought to unscramble his brain. It was no secret that he'd killed Cole Dillon, but he definitely hadn't killed this woman's sister. He didn't even know who she was. Maybe her sister had been one of the town citizens turned into freaks. The town council had placed the blame for those they had been unable to save on Kyle's head.

From the look on the woman's face, she wanted to kill Hanson there and then, regardless of whether he was the one to kill her sister or not. The councillor wore the same expression. In fact, Hanson was surprised he was still alive given how much Dillon hated him. He would take it as he could. Every moment of life was precious.

He struggled to straighten up, lifting his head and eyeing the woman.

'I don't know who you are,' he said, his voice hoarse and shaking, 'but I didn't kill your sister.'

'Liar.' Councillor Dillon moved and landed a weak punch on Hanson's jaw.

He rocked backward, held in place by the guards either side of him.

'You killed her, the same as you killed my son. Now you will pay for both their deaths, but first you will tell me where Jackson Kyle and the rest of his wardens are hiding.'

Ah, so that was why he was still alive.

Hanson gave a bitter laugh. 'As if I would tell you anything, you lying piece of shit.' He spat a wad of blood and saliva onto the ground. 'Your son was a monster. Same as you.'

While the councillor's face went red, Hanson looked at the woman watching on with a calculating expression. 'Don't believe anything he tells you. He'd say anything to get you to do his dirty work for him.'

Blue eyes cold, she gazed back at him. 'So, you don't work for Jackson Kyle, the former captain of the Brimfield Ward?'

'I'd say we have a partnership, more than me working for him.'

'And did you take part in the battle with the Legion's people, in this very town?'

Hanson froze. He was in serious trouble. Still, he forced a smile. 'We freed this town, after they were all turned into freaks. Instead of thanking us for it, this freaking bastard had us run out of town.'

'Well then, it seems Councillor Dillon has told me the truth. You and your wardens killed my sister by throwing her off a roof.' She pulled a gun from a side holster on her hip and pointed it at his head. Unlike Ward and council weapons, this fired live ammunition. 'You are going to tell me where the rest of your people are hiding, and then I'm going to kill you.'

Oh shit.

This was bad. This was very bad.

THIRTY-SIX

'Perhaps I can help you with that.' Jackson stepped out of the shadows cast by a nearby building, stamping down his anger at these people camping on land he and his wardens had fought and died for. He faced the woman who had her gun trained on Hanson.

She turned around to glare at him. 'And who might you be?'

'I'm Jackson Kyle. I hear you've been looking for me.'

Her arm swung around and the gun was now pointed directly at him. Jackson fought to keep his body relaxed, though he could see this weapon was not a stun gun. It would do serious damage if he was hit, but he had to take the risk. He couldn't stand there and watch Hanson be executed.

When he'd left High Command, he'd intended to go to the mine compound first, but had caught a garbled distress call from someone named Neil, who had said wardens were in danger, and so he'd diverted to Brimfield to assess the situation before going for backup.

When he'd found a large force camped outside the gates, he'd taken advantage of a momentary lapse in security to slip through the gap Hanson and the others had used to enter Brimfield.

Now he wished he'd stuck to his original plan and had Lieutenant Jensen and the others at his back.

If he couldn't turn this situation around, he and Hanson were as good as dead.

He raised his hands and put a conciliatory expression on his face. 'Why don't you put the gun down and we can talk about why you think I'm responsible for your sister's death?'

The hand holding the gun shook as a wave of grief washed over the woman's face. 'I'm not here to talk. I'm here to kill you.'

'I get that. I just want to know why you're blaming me and my wardens, when it was your sister's choice to take her own life.' He'd heard enough during his approach to know her sister had to be the woman who had sacrificed herself to kill Marcus Callaghan.

'You're lying. Karline would never commit suicide.' Rage blotted out the grief, her voice hard, and he could see her finger tensing on the trigger.

'She was being abused by the man who took over the Legion, Marcus Callaghan. She tried to stop him, and was close to forcing him over the edge of the roof, when the fire-hose ran out of water. She knew what he'd do to her for trying to kill him and failing, so she threw herself at him, taking them both over the edge of the roof. She saved us all.' Jackson shook his head, remembering how shocked he'd felt at her actions. Life must have been bad being under Marcus' rule for death to be a preferable option.

'No. That's not true. They said you killed her. You and your wardens threw her and Marcus off the roof.'

Jackson sadly shook his head. 'Whoever told you that lied. I was there. Marcus was about to kill me when your sister appeared with the firehose. I'm sorry it got that far, that I couldn't stop him before she took matters into her own hands.'

The hand holding the gun dropped to her side, tears shimmering in her blue eyes as she stared at Jackson. 'Please tell me you're lying. Please.'

Jackson just stood there, waiting for her to come to terms with the truth.

'Don't be ridiculous, Rona. Of course, he's lying,' Councillor Dillon said, blustering forward. 'He'd say anything to get you to let him go. I know the truth. Jackson Kyle and his wardens are murderers. They killed twenty-seven of my citizens, including my son.' His voice broke, the grief he obviously felt for Cole showing through.

Jackson looked to Rona, waiting to see what she would do next.

She shook, seeming to pull her mind from whatever memory had held her in thrall, gaze now steady as she looked to Jackson. 'Is what he's saying true? Did you kill his citizens? His son?'

Jackson gave a deep sigh. 'I'm afraid so. We did everything we could to prevent human casualties after Marcus turned the entire town into freaks, but it wasn't possible to save everyone. Innocent people died, because of the Legion.'

While he was willing to admit his failings where the protection of the humans within his Ward were concerned, the ultimate blame did not belong to him. 'After he failed to prevent Justice from fulfilling the purpose Gaea created her for, Marcus Callaghan brought your people here. He used the freak virus to control the town and set them against us. The twenty-seven humans that died did so because of your people, not mine. You want someone to blame, then go after the masters who wanted to be proclaimed as gods. It is because of them that innocent people died, including your sister.'

She flinched, half turning away from him to stare off into the distance, gaze unfocused as she looked over the tents.

Jackson didn't take his eyes off her. From where he hung

in the arms of Councillor Dillon's guards, Hanson was also keeping a watchful eye on the proceedings.

The councillor strode forward and grabbed the gun out of Rona's hands and pointed it at Jackson. 'If you won't shoot him, I will.'

'Stop.' Rona stepped between them. 'Give me the gun.'

'Get out of my way or I'll shoot you too,' Dillon snarled.

Within seconds, the sound of dozens of guns being cocked rang out as Rona's people trained their weapons on Dillon. His guards moved up to flank him, causing a tense standoff.

Dillon's features twisted into a hateful snarl. 'Why are you protecting him? You said you came here to kill him. So kill him already and be done with it.'

She glared at Dillon. 'Don't tell me what to do. You lied to me.' In a swift move, she wrenched her gun out of Dillon's hand, his face blanching as she pointed it at him.

'No, no,' he stammered. 'You misunderstood me. I never lied. I told the truth.'

'You said he killed innocent people. They were freaks. It's a warden's job to kill freaks. They were just doing their job.'

'You believe him? After he killed your sister? He's lying. You know your sister would never take her own life.'

Jackson could see Dillon's words were getting to her. He scanned the members of the Legion who had come out of the tents and stood watching on. Even more of them were camped outside the town gates.

'Are any of your people here from Brimfield?' Jackson looked back to Rona. 'They may not have been on the roof when your sister sacrificed herself to kill Marcus Callaghan, but they can tell you what life was like for your sister with him in charge.'

Her gaze was shadowed as she looked into the distance. 'The ones who survived are not here. I sent them ahead to the mine compound near here.'

Jackson froze. 'How many people did you send?'

Her gaze narrowed. 'A small group, to assess the damage your wardens did after they forced my people to flee to Brimfield.'

His tension did not abate, not sure if he could trust her word on what Lieutenant Jensen and the others might be now facing. He let none of that show as he inclined his head. 'Then I suggest you get word to them and divert them here, so they can tell you what was really happening before your sister died.'

Some of his tension was relieved when she gave the order for one of her men to contact the group headed to the mine. It ratcheted back up when she was informed that they couldn't be contacted.

What was going on back at the compound?

He needed to get back there, but first he had to free Hanson and find out what had happened to Hannah and the others.

Before he could say anything, Dillon rounded on Rona. 'This is absurd. You said you wanted to kill all the Brimfield wardens. Well, now is your chance to take care of the warden who commands them. Shoot Jackson Kyle. Now.'

Rona narrowed her eyes as she faced the irate councillor.

'I'm not shooting anybody, not until I find out what really went on here.'

'Don't be ridiculous. I told you what happened.'

'And I don't believe you. I'm sending a second group to the mine, and when they get back with the others I'll get to the truth of the matter. Don't worry, I won't be letting the captain of the Brimfield Ward out of my sight, or this half-breed.'

She gave a sharp nod and a group of her men bounded forward and gripped Jackson by the arms, just as another grouped wrestled Hanson clear of Dillon's guards. Ignoring Dillon's blustering, Rona marched toward the tents, while the men holding Hanson and Jackson forced them to follow.

Jackson looked over at Hanson, but now was not the time

to ask where Hannah, Carstairs, and the rest were hiding. Despite Rona's words, he didn't think she would personally watch over them while she waited to hear back from the second group now heading to the mine. He'd wait until they were alone to question his young friend.

Before they reached the first of the tents, a shout came from behind them and someone called out, 'Freak!'

Their group stilled. Jackson was horrified to find two freaks with blood streaming from their eyes loping toward them.

His stomach lurched at this sign the new freak virus had made its way to Brimfield.

'You need to kill them, right now,' he called out to Rona. 'Aim for the head. It's the only way to be sure to take them down.'

She gave a low laugh as she glanced over at him, not seeming to be fazed as the freaks drew closer.

Jackson tensed, ready to rip free from the men holding him and grab one of their weapons. The freaks had to be stopped, before it was too late.

THIRTY-SEVEN

Rona enjoyed the stressed expression on the former Brimfield Ward captain's face as the freaks barrelled down the street toward them. She fingered the gas canister attached to her belt and stepped in front of Jackson Kyle. She still wasn't sure she believed his story that Karline had taken her own life. While she didn't doubt Marcus Callaghan was capable of committing black deeds, the idea he had abused Karline so much that death was preferable didn't seem real.

Still, what to do with Jackson and the half-breed was a matter to be decided at another time. For now, she would show them she was the one with all the power here.

'I'll take care of them,' she said as she unclipped the canister and held it up.

Understanding dawned in Jackson's expression as the first freak launched at them.

Rona didn't hesitate, shooting a steady stream of gas into the freak's face. 'Freeze,' she said, already adjusting her aim to fire at the second freak. She had enough gas in the canister to subdue six freaks. These two would not be a problem.

The first freak didn't stop. She lunged forward, hands outstretched for Rona's throat. A hard jolt on her arm pulled

Rona out of the freak's path as a gun fired. Stumbling when the person who had latched on to her let go, she spun around and saw one of her men had shot the first freak between the eyes and Jackson was grappling with the second one, muscles in his arms straining as he worked to keep the freak at arm's length. He had hold of the freak's wrists, and was doing his best to force him to the ground.

The freak snarled and slavered, blood pouring from his eyes as he strained to pull his arms free, snapping at Jackson's face.

Rona darted in and gassed the freak, again shouting out the command to freeze.

Again, her command was ignored.

With a curse, she dropped the gas canister and pulled her pistol out of the holster, lining up the freak's head over Jackson's shoulder and firing in one smooth motion. The freak dropped, the force of his fall pulling Jackson forward. Rona used her free hand to steady him as she gazed at the two dead freaks. Then she looked at the canister she had dropped.

'Guess that means you only half took care of them,' said the half-breed she had been all set to execute before Jackson had arrived. He gave her a cheeky grin when she glared at him.

Then she holstered her pistol and scooped up the canister to give it a shake. 'I don't understand what went wrong. The gas works.'

'Didn't work on them,' said Hanson.

She cast him another dark glare before striding over to her second-in-command. She handed Richard the canister. 'It must be faulty. Go grab one of the others from the truck and find me another freak to test it on.'

He dutifully strode off, heading for the town gates where the rest of their people were camped.

Jackson came up beside her. 'Where did these two come from?'

They couldn't have come through the front gates. The bulk of her people were camped there, Councillor Dillon only allowing two dozen of them to enter Brimfield to help search for the wardens and half-breeds.

'Have there been any newcomers to town, other than us?' she said to the rotund councillor.

His face was screwed up in a scowl as he glared at Jackson. 'The gates have been closed since this lot sent a bunch of thugs to try to take over for them. We sent that lot on their way, and we'll soon be rid of you too.'

Jackson shook his head. 'We had nothing to do with what those men from Harlington tried to do, and you know it. We were the ones to save your arse when they attempted their takeover.'

'You tricked me. I would never have cancelled the contract on your head if not for them. You must have sent these freaks here. This is all your fault.' The councillor's face was splotched, sweat dripping from his hairline as he raged.

No, these freaks were Rona's doing, though she didn't yet understand what they were doing in Brimfield or why her gas hadn't worked on them.

From what she had seen so far, Councillor Dillon was inclined to blame Jackson and his people for anything that went wrong in his town even if the problem was of his own making. As hard as it was for her to envision Karline ever taking her own life, she had no trouble seeing this man ally himself with Marcus Callaghan if he thought it would lead to an advantage for him.

She swung back to face Jackson, discounting anything the councillor might say. So far, in the limited dealings she'd had with the former captain of the Brimfield Ward, he had kept his word and made no attempt to blame anyone else for any of his shortcomings. He'd been forthright about his involvement in the battle on the roof that had led to her sister's death, regardless of how it might make him look. He'd even apologised for not being able to stop Marcus before her sister had taken such drastic action.

And he'd just helped to save her life.

He was a good man. A good leader.

As that thought percolated through her brain, her shoulders slumped.

It had all been for nothing.

Creating the virus to get revenge on the wardens and the citizens of Brimfield. The man responsible for her sister's death was beyond her grasp. Karline had avenged herself, leaving Rona to pick up the pieces of her growing list of mistakes.

She heaved a sigh. After all her father's teachings, she'd failed the most important lesson of all, creating a better world for the Legion to thrive in.

She could fix this. Once her scientists were able to make more of the gas, she would take control of all the freaks she had unleashed. They could then take care of them. She eyed Jackson. One of his people had come up with a cure once; surely they could do so again. Though it was galling to admit that a half-breed adopted by wardens had done what her people could not, even after five hundred years of trying.

Before she could voice her idea to Jackson, a shout came from the direction her second had taken. Richard was running toward her, a large group of their people at his back. She frowned as she stepped forward to meet him halfway.

'The freaks,' he gasped out when he was in earshot. 'They're at the gates. A whole army of them.'

'What did you say?'

He bent over double, sucking in air, still holding the faulty gas canister. Breath rasping, he straightened up and faced Rona, his eyes wide and alarmed. 'They appeared out of nowhere and attacked our people. If the Brimfield guards hadn't opened the gates so they could get inside, they'd all be dead or infected now.'

'The guards let freaks into my town? I'll have them shot.' Councillor Dillon's hands were balled into fists, face red as he glared at Richard.

Rona wanted to thump him, but kept her focus on her second. 'What about the gas? It should have stopped them.'

He shook his head. 'It didn't work. They tried to stop the freaks entering town, but there were too many of them. Many of our people are dead or infected. They sacrificed their lives to get the gates closed again, but not before dozens of freaks made it in. And there are hundreds more out there.'

Rona reeled, sure the ground was moving under her.

'Steady,' Jackson's low voice came from beside her and she turned to stare at him, shaking her head, unable to believe what Richard had said.

'It's not possible. The gas works. I tested it before unleashing the virus on Dalwaring.'

'You did what?' The half-breed grabbed her shoulder and swung her around to face him. 'You unleashed this virus? You created these freaks? Are you insane?'

Anger swamped her, and she pulled away from him, hand going to the butt of her pistol. 'Don't touch me.'

'I'll more than touch you,' he said. 'You Legion people are evil. Do you know what these freaks have been doing? How many they've killed? The blood of thousands of innocent people is on your hands.'

She shook her head. 'It wasn't meant to be like this. The freaks were only supposed to target wardens, to keep them occupied while I came here to kill …'

Disgust filled his expression as he backed away from her. 'You're as bad as Marcus Callaghan. You don't care who gets hurt, as long as you get what you want.'

Nausea and pain roiled together in her gut at his words. To compare her to the man who had led to her sister's death. No. She was better than Marcus.

She spun to face her people arrayed in the street behind

Richard. 'Get your weapons ready. Make sure you aim for the head. It's the only way to take them down for sure.'

Then she strode off for the gate, her people crowding around her.

They weren't the only ones. Jackson Kyle and Hanson Forsythe, two of the people she had come here to kill, marched beside her.

In the distance, she could hear Councillor Dillon calling for his guards to protect him, and the bitter twist to her lips became one of disgust. The councillor cared more about saving his own skin than protecting his town. Ahead, screams filled the previously silent night. The freaks were doing what they had been created to do: sow carnage and infect as many people as possible.

Her creations.

Now she would be the one to take them down.

The fighting was dirty, the screams mingling with cries of pain and snarls of rage as those who had survived the initial attack turned and became one of the enemy. Rona steeled herself not to see the faces of former comrades as she shot again and again, determined not to stop until every last freak in Brimfield was dead.

This was her fault.

The litany ran over and over in her head.

Her negligence, the haste with which she had conducted her tests of the virus and the gas, had led to the deaths of many of her loyal soldiers.

Maybe the half-breed was right and she really was as bad as Marcus.

Exhaustion swamped her, but she forced herself to keep lifting her arm. Over and over again she shot, always aiming for the head, never missing.

Soon the streets in front of the town gates were littered with dead bodies. Weary beyond measure both in body and spirit, Rona fired and watched the freak who had once been her second-in-command fall to the ground.

She had no tears to shed for Richard or any of the others. They had been brought to this because of her actions, her need for vengeance. She did not deserve to find solace in tears, not until she had made up for the most colossal mistake of her life.

As she raised her gun one more time, looking for her next target, a hand touched her shoulder and she turned to face Jackson. He appeared to be just as weary and horrified as she was, and yet his stance was straight and the look he gave her steady.

'It's over,' he said. 'They're all dead.'

She looked to see the truth of his words.

Bodies were scattered on the road, many sporting injuries inflicted by the first wave of freaks as well as the head wounds that had claimed their lives after they turned. None of the injured had been spared. Her people had relied on Rona to keep them safe, their belief that she could control the freaks ultimately leading them to their deaths.

In the distance, more screams rose as freaks who had made it into the town centre did their grisly work. If the gas no longer worked, she didn't know how she was going to make good on her promise to fix this.

Hanson was right when he'd said she would do whatever it took to get her way. Somehow, she would destroy all the freaks she had created, starting with hunting down each and every freak that had managed to get past them and into Brimfield.

THIRTY-EIGHT

Justice stood in the door of the room she had shared with her mother, casting her eyes over the beds with rumpled sheets and the meagre possessions they had crammed onto the desk between them, tears blurring her vision. At first, she couldn't bring herself to enter the room, to break the silence that enveloped it as memories flooded her. On a shuddering breath, she finally stepped over the threshold and moved to her bed, shaking dust off the covers as she smoothed them into place. She did the same with her mother's bed. The monks had insisted their rooms remain tidy at all times, so nothing else was out of place.

With a shaky hand, she reached out and touched the spine of the book she and her mother had read on her last day here. The yellow was faded, the cover rough against her fingers as she caressed it, but nothing could dim the memories. She plucked the book from the shelf and tucked it under her arm as she turned and left the room, closing the door behind her.

Then she made her way to where Isaac and his merce-naries were set up in the library, none of them wanting to use the monks' rooms or the common room where they had all died. They were packing up the bedrolls they had used the night before. Justice hurried over and packed up her bedroll, slipping the book inside it. Like the mercenaries, she had not been able to bring herself to sleep in her old room, though sleeping in the soft light cast by the lanterns Renfield had set up had not stopped the dark dreams from creeping in.

As she finished stowing her gear, Sutherland entered with a laden tray in his hands. 'It isn't much, but at least it's hot. No coffee, I'm afraid. Seems the monks only liked tea.' He placed the tray on a table and Isaac and Renfield moved in.

'I'll go see if Brother Owen is awake,' Justice said, her stomach roiling at the thought of food.

As if the memories bombarding her ever since she'd returned to the monastery weren't enough, the thought of what was to come caused what little appetite she had to flee.

It was time for Brother Owen to finally show her the final steps she needed to undertake to fulfil her destiny.

He was awake when she reached his room, kneeling beside his neatly made bed, head lowered in prayer. Justice remained silent as he prayed, moving forward to help him to his feet only when he lifted his head.

His hand rested against his injured side as he straightened up. 'Are you ready, my child?'

No.

'Yes,' she said. 'Sutherland has made breakfast.' She waved a hand toward the communal room.

'I will break my fast after you have the implements of justice our Goddess has entrusted my brethren and me to guard for you. Long have we awaited the day when you would become the woman you were destined to be.' Sadness filled his gaze. 'I just wish they were all here to witness the fulfilment of our purpose.'

Justice lowered her gaze. They had served because of her and they had died because of her. She had to make sure no more deaths occurred because of her destiny.

Light spilled through the stained-glass windows in the corridor as Brother Owen took the lead.

'Should we wait for the others?' Justice asked as they entered the common room.

Isaac and his men had moved out all the bodies the night before, placing them in the monastery's crypt, but dark stains remained on the floor where they had lain for fifteen years. Justice had been grateful they had not asked her to help them with the grisly task, the thought of touching the remains of her mother and the monks sending her into a panic.

'This is your destiny, not theirs. Though I am grateful for their assistance in getting us here, this is between you and Gaea.'

Perhaps he was right. She and Brother Owen were the sole survivors of the Legion's attack on the monastery, though they had both been resurrected to enable them to be here. It was fitting that it was just the two of them when Gaea revealed the final pieces to her plan.

Brother Owen, walking slowly, still holding his side, moved to the plain altar carved from a single slab of black marble. Streaks of silver quartz was threaded through it, catching the light of their lantern and throwing it back.

Stained-glass windows, ten times the size of those in the corridor, allowed coloured lights to illuminate the large chapel. Alcoves set in the walls between each window held statues of Gaea carved from the same black marble as the altar. Behind the altar itself was a painting of Gaea, light shining out of her and obscuring her features. One of the monks had been tasked with maintaining the painting so that Gaea's glory could be seen by all. Though the colours were muted after fifteen years of neglect, it brought back vivid memories of when she had appeared to Justice after her death.

She felt the urge to bend her knee, to genuflect to the Goddess who had overseen every part of her life. She resisted the impulse, straightening her spine and keeping her head high.

Brother Owen moved around to the rear of the altar, running his hand over the top as he went, a wistful expression on his face as he surveyed the dust-shrouded candles and other artefacts on top of it.

Then he took a deep breath and looked to Justice. 'It is time,' he said, beckoning for her to join him.

Justice pushed her misgivings aside and moved around the altar. Brother Owen pointed at a set of scales carved into the side. She had never been back here, and gazed at the symbol that matched her birthmark. At his urging, she placed her hands on the scales, and as soon as she did, a loud crack sounded on the other side of the chapel. Justice looked up to see a large section of the stone wall moving. It was a doorway.

Brother Owen headed confidently toward the doorway. Justice followed, scooping up the lantern on her way.

'What's going on?' Isaac appeared in the doorway to the chapel, head swivelling, Renfield at his back. 'We heard …'

His brow furrowed as he eyed the doorway, then gave Justice a quizzical look. 'You planning an adventure without me?'

'There is no danger for Justice here, Commander,' said Brother Owen. 'It is by Gaea's divine will that we are here.'

'You saying she'll be safe is one thing, but I think I'll tag along just in case.' He signalled to Renfield. 'Sutherland is patrolling the perimeter. You stay here and watch our backs and call out if there's any sign of trouble.' He tapped the radio attached to his belt and grinned at Justice. 'A dark and mysterious doorway in a stone wall. What could possibly go wrong?'

Justice managed a weak smile as she drew even with the doorway. It was dark, her lantern barely lighting up what lay beyond. All she could see was a dark aperture that appeared to go on forever. Isaac switched on the flashlight and it did a better job, enough for her to see they were facing a short passageway that followed the length of the chapel wall before turning.

Brother Owen stepped aside, gesturing for Justice to go first.

She took a deep breath and headed into the passageway, shoulders hunched as the oppressive shadows pressed down on her. It was silent, the only sound their footsteps echoing in the small space. She reached the corner and found herself at the top of a narrow set of stairs.

Isaac brushed past her, his flashlight picking up the bottom some distance below them. 'I'll go first, and the monk can bring up the rear.'

He headed down before Justice could say anything, and she carefully started to descend behind him. It was cold in the stairwell, the stone walls rougher than what had been in the passage above. Dank air lifted lazily, disturbed by the motion of their passage. The stairs were narrow, and she took care with each step, feeling her way in the semi-darkness, focused on Isaac's light. Dust and small stones were knocked by her feet as she slowly made her way down.

'We're not going to encounter any freaks down here, are we?' Isaac asked. 'We may be immune, but I'm not liking these tight quarters if we have to fight.'

'The monastery sub levels were sealed off from the rest of the town when it was originally built. There will be no freaks down here.'

'How long ago was that, exactly? And when was the last time you checked the state of these tunnels? Even the most secure barricades will erode over time.'

'No one has been down here since the tunnels were first built, five hundred years ago. Entry was keyed to Justice so there was no way for them to check. Gaea would not allow freaks to gain access.'

'This is the same Gaea that allowed you monks to be

slaughtered and Justice kidnapped. Seems she's not that proactive in protecting what's hers. She may have brought you two back to life to help fulfil her wishes, but I'm guessing she's not going to do the same for a bunch of mercenaries who just got caught up in the flow of things.'

Justice tensed, ears pricked for any sound other than those made by their passage. Isaac was right; anything could have happened to these tunnels over the past five hundred years. He was also right about Gaea resurrecting only those she needed.

'If it is our time to die, then it will be as Gaea wills it,' Brother Owen said, no sign of misgiving in his voice. But he had dedicated his life to this moment. He probably believed that giving up his second chance at life to do Gaea's bidding was perfectly acceptable.

Justice did not want anyone else to die because of her. She sped up, feet skidding in the dust as she reached Isaac's back.

'Let me go first.' If Gaea needed her, then it shouldn't be tempting fate to put herself in the firing line if any freaks did appear in the tunnel system.

'No need,' Isaac said, grinning at her over his shoulder. 'Looks like we're at the end of the line.'

He held his flashlight higher, and she saw the stairway ended with a dead end.

She slipped past him and scanned the wall, finding the scrollwork of scales set in the middle. She placed her hand on it and winced at the grating noise as the wall slid aside.

A waft of stale, dry air reached out of the opening, but all was still and silent.

The only sound was Brother Owen's laboured breathing as he made his way down the last couple of stairs. When he reached them, Justice moved into the room in front of them. An altar, the twin of the one in the chapel above their heads, dominated the small room. Justice moved around it and found scales carved in the exact same place. She reached out a hand and then hesitated, looking to Brother Owen.

He gave an encouraging nod.

She touched her birthmark against the scales, jumping when the middle section in the top of the altar began to rise. A soft light glowed from the space beneath it, and she leaned over to look inside.

A small chest, about as long as her forearm and a hand's width across, nestled in the space.

'Accept your birthright, Justice, so that you may receive Gaea's final instructions.' Brother Owen's voice was solemn.

Hands shaking, she reached in and grabbed the chest, surprised by how heavy it was. The second the chest was clear of the alcove, the lid slid closed, cutting off the light.

Justice placed the chest on top of the altar, looking for a latch.

There was nothing, not even a seam to indicate where it would open. She turned to Brother Owen. 'What do I do now?'

Before he could respond, a crackle came from the radio attached to Isaac's belt, followed with indistinct shouts.

'Sutherland, report.' Isaac's voice was tense as he received only more crackle in response. Then a dim shout sounded back the way they had come.

Isaac turned, racing for the doorway. Justice heard him thundering up the stairs and hurried to follow him, conscious of Brother Owen at her back. As they passed the doorway, the wall slid back and closed off the chamber. She had no time to worry about that. Isaac was already out of sight, having reached the top of the stairs and bolted down the passageway that led to the chapel. The shouts were louder now, accompanied by the sound of gunfire.

Heart pounding, thigh muscles aching, Justice bounded up the stairs, breathing ragged as she entered the final passage and headed for the light that showed the open door into the chapel.

She reached the door and froze on the threshold. There were freaks in the chapel.

That was impossible. It was daylight.

But the three freaks who were fighting to get to Isaac and Renfield where they stood on top of the altar did not seem to feel pain from the light streaming through the windows.

Did they have lenses, like the ones Daniel had made for Jackson so he could act as Justice's bodyguard at all hours and aboveground?

No.

These freaks had blood streaming from their eyes. It appeared the coloured sunlight was causing them damage, but they gave no sign it affected them. Isaac and Renfield were firing into the freaks, yet their bullets appeared to have little effect.

There was no sign of Sutherland at first, and then a savage snarl had Justice looking to the left to see another freak crouched over the top of the mercenary, slashing into his exposed face over and over again.

Sutherland was still. She hoped he was just unconscious and not dead. At least, with the vaccine, he would not turn into a freak if he was still alive. As Justice watched, a bloody hole appeared in the freak's forehead and he slumped over Sutherland's body.

'Aim for the head,' Isaac shouted, and more shots rang out.

She turned as the three freaks trying to get to him and Renfield fell backward, holes in their foreheads. None of them moved after that.

Justice sagged against the doorway as Brother Owen shuffled past her, making his way to Sutherland.

Justice hurried over to help him pull the freak off Sutherland, as Isaac barked orders at Renfield to make sure the area was secure. Then he hurried to Justice's side.

'Is he alive?'

Sutherland gave a faint groan, and relief made Justice's legs weak.

Then the groan changed to a growl.

Sutherland's eyes snapped open, the whites shining even as blood began to spill from them. Justice stumbled backward as he reared up and grabbed for her.

Isaac grabbed her arm and pulled her behind him.

Sutherland instead latched on to Brother Owen, wrenching him forward and wrapping his hands around the monk's throat. Brother Owen gave a garbled shout as he was dragged backward before being thrown against the ground with so much force that a sharp crack reverberated in the cavernous chapel.

Then Sutherland lurched to his feet and sprang toward Justice and Isaac.

Bang

A hole blossomed in the centre of his forehand, the force of the shot sending him flying. Renfield ran back into the chapel, face pale as he took in the bloodied form of his compatriot.

'What the hell was that?' Eyes wide, Isaac turned to Justice, lowering his firearm. 'No one turns that fast, and freaks shouldn't be able to come aboveground in daylight.'

'These people must have been infected with the new strain of the freak virus Captain Murphy told Jackson about,' Justice said, her voice shaking. 'This is what the people in Cadel were afraid of.' And no wonder, if it could turn Sutherland so fast, even though he had been vaccinated. 'But how did it get here? Jackson said the infected were in Dalwaring. That's days away.'

'I don't know, but I sure hope your friend can come up with a new vaccine. I've never seen anything like it. They took dozens of hits and still kept coming until I used a headshot. These freaks were ten times stronger than any I've come across before. With the speed they infected Sutherland, a handful of these could destroy a town this size within hours.'

'I think this town is already lost,' said Renfield. 'Sutherland said he found these four after they scaled the gate, looking for a place to hide, yelling about freaks killing everyone. One of them must have been infected. He turned and attacked the others as Sutherland was leading them inside.'

Isaac received this news in silence, then he moved to one of the stained-glass windows. Whatever he saw out there made his expression even grimmer. He came back to stand beside Justice. 'We need to move, before any of those freaks figure out we're in here. How's your monk?'

Recalling the sickening crack she'd heard as Brother Owen hit the ground, Justice gasped as she ran over to him.

Isaac grabbed her arm. 'Careful. He could be infected.'

'No.' She wrenched her arm free. 'His robe would have protected him.' From the risk of infection at least. As she grasped his shoulder and rolled him over, she saw that nothing had been able to protect him from hitting the ground. Blood pooled under his head, an indent showing where he had struck the stone.

His eyes were closed, a bubble of blood on his lips. Tears stung her eyes as she reached out to touch his cheek. 'Brother Owen.'

His eyes fluttered open. 'Justice, my child,' he said, his voice weak. 'You must find the source of the virus and wash it clean with blood.' His eyes closed again, his last words almost too quiet to hear. 'The two sides must join together to make right the past.'

Then he was still.

Gone.

Isaac reached out and tugged Justice to her feet. 'We have to leave, now. There's nothing you can do for him.'

With the chest she'd taken from the altar clutched in her arms, she allowed him to lead her away from the chapel and the last piece of her past.

She could only hope that what she held would get rid of the freak virus for good, before more people were slaughtered or infected.

THIRTY-NINE

Though devastated by the loss of life, and the thought that this new freak had been a deliberate attempt to wipe out all wardens, Jackson fought side by side with the members of the Legion. Nearby, Rona fought just as fiercely, her skill bringing down many a freak. The freaks kept coming. With the speed at which the infected turned, the Legion were fighting a losing battle.

A freak launched at Jackson and he aimed for the head, a click the only response when he pulled the trigger.

He was out of ammunition.

As he cast around him for another firearm, he knew it would be too late.

The freak was on him, teeth snapping, claws extended.

Jackson gripped the freak's forearms, doing his best to keep him away from his flesh. But the freak was relentless, blood pouring from its eyes.

Bang!

A hole appeared in the side of the freak's head and he slumped to the ground, nearly pulling Jackson down with him. He let go and straightened, looking around for who had saved his life.

A grin formed as he spotted Carstairs. Behind him were Dale, Michaelson, Leon, and the others, each quickly snatching up firearms dropped by the fallen and joining the fight. Jackson found himself a new firearm, and together they pushed back against the horde of freaks.

He lost track of time, his arm tiring as he faced freak after freak, but he forced himself to keep going. They had to stop this, now, before the entire town was lost, like Washbourne. The memory of the dead bodies littering the wreckage spurred him on. The knowledge there were hundreds more freaks outside the gates was a growing concern. If they found a way in, there would be no stopping them.

When the last freak in the area fell, he turned to where Hanson was slumped against the side of a building next to Carstairs and made his way over to them.

'You need to get to the airship. Being airborne is the best hope we have of taking down the freaks outside the walls without more casualties. Take Dale and Michaelson with you.'

Hanson shook his head as he straightened. 'I need to find Hannah. She's missing.'

Dread pooled in the pit of Jackson's stomach. Despite his worry for Hannah, he had to make sure the freaks were stopped. 'We'll find Hannah as soon as we get this situation under control. I promise. But we need that airship now.' He clasped Hanson on the shoulder. 'I need you to do this.'

Hanson's gaze was wild, but he nodded. 'Soon as that airship is in the air, I'm going to tear this town apart looking for her.'

Jackson managed a grim smile. 'And I'll help you.'

Then he gripped his firearm and strode off to where a group of the Brimfield guards stood alongside their captain. They were going to need a lot more ammunition to take down the freaks, and Flanders would have the key to the town armoury. It was time to bring out the big guns.

FORTY

Hanson glared at the new leader of the Legion as he stuffed the gun he had taken from one of her fallen soldiers into his holster. How could someone be so stupid as to create stronger freaks? He scanned the darkened alleys to either side. Hannah was out there somewhere. What if one of the freaks who had got past them found her first?

'We'll keep an eye out for Hannah, I promise,' said Leon.

He and the others had come aboveground when the fighting started, helping the Legion to take down these new freaks.

Hanson grunted. He should be the one looking for her. She was his friend. His best friend. If anything happened to her …

But no, he was on his way to the freaking council building to make Councillor Dillon hand over the airship. Jackson planned on using it to fire on the freaks amassed outside the town gate. They would never be able to get back to the compound with them there. A fierce grin bloomed on Hanson's face as he imagined what the cowardly councillor was going to say when Hanson showed up and took his airship again.

The grin soon faded. The last time he'd helped to steal the airship, Ben had died, killed by a freak. But there was only a handful of freaks loose in Brimfield now, so this trip should be less eventful.

He reached the council building and took the stairs to the front door two at a time. Carstairs, Michaelson, and Dale were close behind him.

'Mr Forsythe, wait,' a weak voice called from the edge of the building.

Hanson stopped, turning to see a man with his head swathed in bandages limping toward him. Pain was etched on his face as he approached, but there was a determined set to his features. Hanson recognised him as the councillor's assistant. The one who had given his blood so Hannah could make more of the vaccine.

Neil, she'd said his name was. She'd made no mention of his having been injured when she'd met him.

'Councillor Dillon has her. Miss Young.'

As the gasped words registered, Hanson bolted down the steps and landed in front of the assistant. 'What did you say?'

'The pharmacist told Councillor Dillon that I helped her. When I refused to help him capture you all, he set a trap. I'm sorry, I tried to stop them taking her, but I was too late.'

'Where is she?'

'According to one of the guards who thinks as I do, that we all owe Miss Young our lives, the councillor has her handcuffed to a shelf in a storage room down the hall from his office. Hendrix is waiting on the ground floor for you. Two guards are with Miss Young, but Hendrix will help you rescue her. Councillor Dillon is planning to use her to make you surrender to him. If you don't turn yourself in, he said he will kill her.'

'Freaking hell, he will,' Hanson said as he spun and launched back up the stairs to where Carstairs and the others waited.

'Get to the roof and get the airship running. I'll meet you there with Hannah.'

'Maybe one of us should come with you?'

Hanson shook his head. 'I've got this.' He was going to rip Councillor Dillon apart.

Carstairs nodded and set off with the others, while Hanson burst into the foyer, startling the lone guard standing beside the front reception desk.

The guard's eyes widened. 'Thank goodness you are here. You have to save her.'

Before Hanson could answer him, a snarl came from behind. He spun around to see a female freak in the open doorway. He had a moment to hope the injured Neil had got away before she'd appeared, and then the freak lunged toward him.

He aimed his gun at her head and pulled the trigger.

Click!

Shit. He was out of bullets.

The guard shot in front of Hanson, hand shaking as he fired at the freak.

'I'll take care of the freak. You help Miss Young. The councillor's office is on the top floor.'

As the guard fired at the freak again, his hand steadying and the shot taking her between the eyes, Hanson ran for the stairwell. As he swung the door open, he heard more snarls behind him. He glanced over his shoulder as two more freaks bounded inside, one of them tackling the guard and forcing him to the ground.

A shrill scream came and was abruptly cut off. Then the freak, blood bathing its face, looked up and spotted Hanson.

He bolted through the door and set off up the stairs as fast as he could go, aware the freaks would be on his heels soon enough. He reached the first landing as the door below opened. Despite the ache in his leg muscles and the gasping of his breath, he increased his speed. He had to get to the top floor. He had to get to Hannah.

With the freaks seconds behind him, he reached the exit door to the top floor and burst through it, running into the hallway and taking a precious moment to get his bearings. He spotted a sign on the door opposite the stairwell.

'Councillor Kelvin Dillon.'

Neil had said the storage room Hannah was being held in was just down the hall, but he had no time to get to it, not with freaks on his arse.

He dived across the hall and wrenched open the door to Dillon's office, throwing himself inside and slamming the door closed seconds before the first freak hit the landing. He thumbed the lock and began looking around for something to barricade the door. These freaks were strong, and a locked door wouldn't hold them for long.

He cursed when he spotted the man sitting behind a large, ornate timber desk.

Councillor Dillon's face was suffused with rage as he pointed a finger at Hanson. 'Murderer!' He got to his feet, gripping the desk with one hand as the other scrambled on top of it. He picked up a letter opener and swung around the side of the desk, almost stumbling in his haste.

'I'm going to kill you.'

A bang on the door behind Hanson pulled his attention away from the irate councillor. 'We'll both be dead soon if you don't shut up and help me barricade this door.' Another thud on the door had it rattling on its hinges and Hanson leaned all his weight against it.

The councillor didn't seem to hear or care about what he'd said. As soon as he was close enough, he lunged at Hanson, the letter opener aimed like a dagger. Hanson took one hand off the door to grip the councillor around the wrist, squeezing and twisting until he dropped the makeshift weapon.

Then he pulled the councillor closer. 'Listen to me, you freaking moron, there are super-charged freaks outside this door and they are going to burst in here and kill both of us if we don't do something about it. You want to kill me, fine, but wait until after we stop them coming in here and ripping us apart.' These new freaks were savage, seemingly more intent on carnage than on infecting their victims. Hanson had no intention of dying that way. Not that he was going to sit back and let the councillor kill him once they'd secured the room.

As another thud came on the door, some of the rage left Councillor Dillon's face. 'The freaks? They're here? Where are my guards?'

'No idea,' Hanson said, though from what he'd seen, most of them were in the streets hunting down the remaining freaks.

'What are we going to do?' Dillon pulled on his hand, a quiver in his voice as he eyed the door.

As it appeared the gravity of their situation had cooled his bloodlust, Hanson chanced letting him go. 'We need to move the desk in front of the door. That will buy us more time.' Time to do what, he wasn't sure. But he'd figure it out.

He had to.

Hannah was stuck in the same building. He had to find her and get her out of here. His heart ached at the thought of him not being able to save her before the freaks found the storeroom where she was locked up. He would not lose her, not when he was just figuring out how much she meant to him.

Dillon shook and then returned to his desk, ineffectually tugging at one corner. 'It's too heavy,' he said with a whine in his voice. 'We'll never move it.'

With a snarl, Hanson bounded across the room and vaulted over the desk. As ominous thuds came from the door, he pushed and shoved at the desk with all of his might while the stupid councillor stood there wringing his hands.

'Help me,' he snapped, muscles straining to push the heavy timber desk across the plush carpet. It moved, but not enough.

Finally, the councillor settled in beside Hanson and began to push. His efforts weren't much, but it was enough for them to build up some momentum. Once the big desk was moving, Hanson did not stop until it was wedged up against the door. Then he collapsed across it, breathing heavily, as his muscles quivered from the effort.

The thuds on the door increased in volume, but the desk remained in place, and as Hanson pulled himself upright, he was sure it would hold for now.

Stopping the freaks from coming in was only part of the problem. He still had to find Hannah. He strode across the room to a thick red velvet curtain and pulled it aside, grinning when he found a large window. He prised at the latch, paint and dust flaking away as he pushed the window open.

'What are you doing?'

He glanced back at Councillor Dillon. 'We can't stay here. Sooner or later they'll bash a hole in that door, and we have nowhere to hide when they do.'

The thuds had not let up.

'You expect me to go out the window? It's four storeys up.' The whine in Dillon's voice rose in pitch.

'It's either that or wait for our friends out there to come get you.' Hanson didn't bother waiting for the councillor's response. The moron could stay there for all he cared, but Hanson was leaving. All that mattered was getting to Hannah.

He pulled himself up so his legs were slung through the window, feet groping for purchase on the bricks.

A shadow passed over him and he instinctively ducked. A scraping sound came as the letter opener he had taken from Dillon earlier slammed into the wall near his head.

'What the hell?' Hanson glared at the councillor. 'Are you freaking insane?'

'You murdered Cole.'

'He was a freak. He tried to kill me.'

'I don't care. He was my son.' Dillon's face was contorted with rage as he lunged for Hanson again.

Hanson rolled free of the window, landing heavily on the floor.

Dillon tried to adjust his aim, but he tripped over Hanson's legs and stumbled sideways into the open window.

Horror blotted out the rage on the councillor's face as he flailed his arms and managed to grab hold of the sill with one hand. Hanson scrambled to his feet and lurched forward, but he was too late. Dillon's grip slipped and he fell backward.

'No.' The scream echoed in the office as the councillor disappeared from view, cutting off with a thud seconds later.

Hanson winced and shook his head as he leaned out the window and saw the councillor's broken body in the laneway below. He hadn't liked the man, but that was a hell of a way to die.

A resounding thud came from the door behind him and he heard the stout wood crack, reminding him of the urgency of his mission. Within seconds he was out the window and clinging to the brickwork, thankful that whoever had built the town hall had employed shoddy workmanship. He did not look down, using the uneven placement of bricks as foot and handholds as he worked his way along to the window of the room in which Neil had said Hannah was imprisoned.

FORTY-ONE

THE LOW GROWLING ON THE OTHER SIDE OF THE WALL SENT shivers racing down Justice's spine, but she didn't stop. Crouched over, the box clutched to her chest, she ran as silently as she could behind Isaac. Renfield was at her heels. Neither of the mercenaries made a noise Justice could hear, but freaks had far better hearing.

The low growl became a chorus of snarls, and she could hear the freaks attempting to climb over the wall.

'Quickly,' Isaac whispered at the driver's side door of the four-wheel-drive. He waved for Justice to climb into the passenger seat as Renfield ducked around her and made for the back.

'Buckle up and hold on tight,' Isaac said as he started the engine.

Justice hastily complied, sliding the chest under her seat and bracing herself as best she could as the vehicle began to move.

Isaac used the large open area to turn the four-wheel-drive, positioning the vehicle so it pointed at the closed gate. On either side of the gate, Justice could see freaks clambering to the top of the wall, some of them already on the ground and surging toward the stationery vehicle.

'Any time now, Renfield,' Isaac called out as the freaks got closer, blocking the way to the gate.

Justice swivelled around to see Renfield manoeuvring himself through the sunroof, rifle in hand.

Booming shots rang out one after the other and Justice covered her ears as the scent of gunpowder filled the cab. In front of them, two of the freaks fell to the ground and did not rise, but there were many more to take their place.

Renfield continued to fire and soon all the freaks who had climbed into the monastery yard were down.

Then Renfield clambered back inside the vehicle and latched the sunroof. 'All clear, sir.'

'Roger that.' Isaac gunned the engine and the four-wheel-drive surged forward, toward the closed gate. Justice uncovered her ears and grasped the dash and the side rail as they picked up speed.

The vehicle hit the gate with a resounding crash, metal screeching as the wrought iron gate connected with the bonnet of the vehicle. Isaac did not slow his pace, and Justice knew better than to let go to cover her ears again.

The gunfire would have attracted all freaks within hearing distance, which could mean the whole town with their enhanced hearing. They were sure to be drawn to investigate. The sound of the four-wheel-drive crashing through the gate would be even more of a lure.

Sure enough, as they made their way onto the narrow streets, freaks emerged from houses and alleyways. They threw themselves at the vehicle, desperate to get to the humans inside, some of them moving into the roadway to block their path.

Isaac did not stop. He ploughed through the freaks, grim determination wreathing his features as he mowed down any in his path. Eventually, he was able to work his way through the mass and break into open ground. He increased speed, barely slowing down to take the corners as they made for the outskirts of town and out onto the open road. Justice looked into the side mirror and could see freaks chasing them, but their figures dwindled in the distance, unable to compete with the speed of the vehicle.

Would they keep after them?

So much was unknown about this new breed of freaks. For them to be able to withstand the pain of daylight and with an apparent increased resistance to injury, who knew what else they were capable of. The thought they might keep chasing them no matter the distance, that they might catch up to them at some stage, maybe while they were sleeping, was chilling.

To ward off those kinds of thoughts, Justice reached down and pulled the chest out from under her seat, inspecting it closely. There was no sign of a lid or a lock to open it, but there was a set of scales embossed on one side.

'You sure you're ready to see what's inside there?' Isaac asked, glancing over at her, one eyebrow raised.

'I have no choice.' Brother Owen and Sutherland had died so she could retrieve the chest. It had to mean something. It had to provide her with a clue how to stop humankind from the downward spiral that was set to destroy them all.

She placed her birthmark against the embossed scales and heard a faint click.

A crack appeared around the top of the box and she prised at it, feeling it give. She lifted it up and stared at the contents of the box.

'Huh?'

Nestled among decaying velvet were a dagger and a medallion. Both appeared to have been made of the same dull bronze metal, as was the chain looped through a hole at the top of the medallion. Justice pulled the medallion out by the chain, and as it swung in the movement of the vehicle, she could see images embossed on either side. On one side was a rendition of the dagger, and on the other a set of scales.

She inspected the dagger and saw it also had a set of scales embossed in the metal just where the hilt met the blade.

'I don't think a necklace and a dagger are going to be much help taking one of these new freaks down. Any ideas what you're supposed to do with them?' Isaac asked.

Justice shook her head. 'Brother Owen said I need to go to the place where the virus was first created. Maybe when I find it there will be more clues to tell me what I am supposed to do with these.' She clasped the medallion in her right hand, feeling a tingle in her birthmark when it connected with the scales on the medallion. She released the medallion and put it back in the chest, giving her hand a shake.

Then she picked up the dagger, twisting it this way and that, but when she placed her birthmark against the scales on the hilt, there was no tingle. She placed it back in the box and closed the lid.

'So, what you're saying is that we need to find one of these Legion guys to tell us where the lab is,' said Isaac. 'If they even know. It was five hundred years ago. Who knows what could have happened to the lab or their records since that time?'

Justice snorted. 'If they do know, I'm probably the last person they would tell. I ruined their plan to create the Apocalypse and make them rulers of Earth.'

'No need to worry about that, little sister. You just find me one of the Legion to question, and I'll make them talk.' He gave her a fierce grin.

Justice's smile was subdued in comparison, the thought of torturing someone to get information out of them unsettling. Yet it was imperative they find out where the original lab was located, or more freaks like those they had encountered in the monastery would be created and humankind would be doomed.

For now, though, there was nothing she could do about any of that until she returned to the mine compound to see if Hannah had any ideas about where the lab was or what she was supposed to do with the dagger and medallion. She slid the chest back under her seat before staring out at the barren landscape ahead of them. It would take them two days to get back to the mine and they'd had no contact with Jackson or the others to find out what was going on.

Had they had problems with these new freaks? Had Jackson been able to make the colonels see sense at High Command, or discovered why they had lost contact with the teams they had sent to Brimfield to collect blood and the airship?

She could only hope her friends were okay, and that Hannah's cure would work on these new freaks. She had a horrible feeling this virus was nothing like the original one and that the situation was going to get far worse before long.

FORTY-TWO

Hanson's grip on the brickwork was precarious, sweat making it hard to hold tight as he edged along the windowsill, eyes on the drainpipe at the corner of the building. If he could just reach it, he would be able to swing around the corner and be out of sight before the freaks entered the councillor's office.

A loud crack came from the room he had just left behind and he groaned when it was followed by a thud. The door was down. He took a deep breath and leapt for the drainpipe, slippery fingers scrambling for purchase. He hit the frame holding the pipe to the building and grabbed on with his fingertips, his feet finding toeholds in the bricks on either side.

He didn't dare wait to get a better grip. Snarls and growls came from within the office and he knew it was only a matter of time before the freaks' keen sense of smell told them where their prey had gone. He swung around the drainpipe to the other side of the building and froze, desperate to still his rasping breaths in an effort to avoid detection.

The snarling and growling grew louder, but he couldn't afford to shift his position to see if the ruse had worked.

Eventually, the sounds receded and he heard banging and

crashing coming from inside the office for a moment before all went silent.

Hanson finally let himself gulp in a breath as he reflected on the idea that Councillor Dillon had saved him. The smell of his dead body must have confused the scents in the air and made it hard for the freaks to know if more of their prey was about. That was a kind of irony he was sure the councillor would not appreciate, even if it was the most helpful thing the man had ever done.

Now, though, Hanson had to focus on getting to Hannah. Neil had said she was handcuffed and defenceless. If the freaks sniffed out which room she was in before Hanson could rescue her, she would be easy prey.

He stretched out along the brickwork, taking the time to test each foot and handhold. He wouldn't help Hannah if he slipped and ended up splattered on the ground like Dillon.

But if anything happened to her …

No. He would get to her in time, and together they would find a way to escape a building swarming with freaks out to kill or infect them.

She was so smart; she'd come up with something for sure.

The image of her sparkling hazel eyes and her throaty voice had a lump rising in his throat. God, she meant so much to him, more than he had wanted to admit until now. Andy was right: he was crazy about Hannah.

She'd had so much pain in her life already, and yet she'd remained hopeful for the future, determined to save people with her cure. She didn't deserve to die at the hands of some rabid freaks someone had cooked up in a lab. She deserved better.

Better than him.

Breath catching, eyes going wide, the thought froze him in place.

Hannah deserved better than him. She deserved a man who could give her everything she ever wanted. A man who had his shit together and knew who and what he was. A man like Carstairs, not a half-breed who kept getting people he cared about killed.

Moving as fast as he safely could, he placed one foot on the edge of the windowsill of the storage room Hannah had been locked in and reached for the latch to open it.

The window opened as his fingertips grazed the latch and he gave a strangled yelp.

Hannah stuck her head through the opening, eyes wide when she spotted him. 'What are you doing?' Her voice was a whisper.

'Rescuing you,' he said just as quietly.

A wry twist to her lips, Hannah gestured for him to move back. 'I've blockaded the door but that won't hold them long.'

Hanson adjusted his grip on the drainpipe and held out his other hand to steady Hannah as she clambered out onto the windowsill.

'Neil said you were handcuffed to a shelf.'

'I picked the lock when the guards left to investigate the gunshots,' she said, holding up a hairpin.

Of course, she picked the lock. She'd got herself free and was well on the way to rescuing herself. She didn't need him to take care of her.

His foot slipped, and Hannah reached out to steady him.

He grinned at her. Instead of saving her, it looked as though she was going to be the one to save him. She was freaking amazing.

'Are you just going to hang there waiting for the freaks to come get us or are we getting out of here?' Hannah asked, a frown creasing her brow.

He wiped the goofy smile off his face. 'Up or down?'

Snarls from below had them both looking down and he swallowed a groan as he saw a number of freaks prowling in the alley. They had probably been drawn by the sounds of Dillon's screams as he fell. Now they milled around the alley, but it wouldn't take them long to realise there were more uninfected about.

One lifted her head and gazed upward, her snarls intensifying when her bloodied gaze latched on to him.

'Up,' Hannah said, gesturing for him to start climbing.

He started to scale the drainpipe, wishing Dillon's office had been on the side of the building with the external ladder. A clang sounded as Hannah reached out to grip the drainpipe and climbed up after him. He hoped it would hold both of their weight for the short climb to the roof.

An alarming number of groans and creaks came from the pipe and the bolts fixing it to the bricks on either side. He went as fast as he dared, not wanting to make it fall with Hannah below him.

He reached the overhang for the roof and shuffled sideways for Hannah to grab a more secure perch.

'What are you waiting for? Get to the roof.'

The pipe continued to groan and he looked down to see the freak who had spotted them was climbing up. With all sense of self-preservation burned away by the virus, she was travelling much more swiftly than they were. He gestured for Hannah to go ahead of him.

'I need to dislodge the pipe.'

She gave him a solemn nod, and then swung herself over the edge of the roof. Once she was safe, Hanson pulled and prised at the bolts, working as fast as he could to dislodge them. He got one loose and then started on the other.

The snarls from below were getting closer and louder. He risked a glance to see two more freaks had followed the first, their weight causing the pipe to creak alarmingly. If he could just get this last bolt undone and prise the pipe away from the wall, gravity should take care of the rest.

Sweat stinging his eyes, conscious he was running out of time, he wrenched out the last bolt. The muscles in the arm holding on to the bricks quivered, a cramp in his fingers telling him he didn't have long to go. He persevered. He would not let the freaks gain access to the roof where Hannah was crouched.

With one last effort, he pulled on the pipe and it swung away from the building, the snarls below cutting off as the freaks swung in mid-air. Then the rest of the pipe pulled free of the brackets holding it in place, thanks to the weight of the freak just below Hanson's feet. As the pipe dropped, the first freak launched herself at him. He tucked his feet up as high as he could, knowing it would not be enough.

She latched onto his ankle, the wrench as she began to fall to earth, pulling him from his precarious perch. He yelped as he fell away from the building, hands flailing to find purchase against the bricks.

A second wrench came as someone grabbed hold of his arm, nearly dislocating his shoulder from its socket, and he gritted his teeth against the pain even as the freak still pulled him downward. Hannah would not be able to hold the weight of both of them.

He looked up to tell her to let go.

Carstairs' face was red as he leaned over the edge of the roof, both his hands wrapped around Hanson's forearm.

He could see the shapes of more people up top and broke into a fierce grin. They'd made it.

Now he just had to get rid of the freak hanging on to his ankle.

Looking downward again, he lifted his free leg and smashed his foot onto the freak's hand, trusting in Carstairs and the others to keep hold of him.

He bruised his own shin in the process, but kept going, swinging his unencumbered leg to stop the freak from grabbing him with her other hand.

As she snarled and did her best to keep her grip, he smashed his heel down on her fingers again and again, until finally she let go. He surged into the air as she fell to the ground, and he winced at the sound of her body hitting the pavement. Then he put his all into helping Carstairs get him over the overhang and onto the roof.

Panting, on his knees, every muscle and joint in his body aching, he struggled to suck in air.

Arms came around him from behind and he twisted around to wrap his arms around Hannah, burying his face in her hair. A long moment passed before he could make himself let go. Then he remembered his resolve to step aside so she could be with the better man. The man who had saved him. Lieutenant bloody Carstairs.

Before he could say a word, Hannah's mouth was on his.

He forgot everything. His good intentions. His aches and pains. The only thing that mattered was the feel of the woman in his arms and the knowledge that they were both alive.

When he finally came up for air, he stared down at her.

Hannah's cheeks were flushed, her lips swollen from their kiss. Then her gaze dropped and she cleared her throat before detangling herself from his arms. 'Thanks, for … ah, coming to rescue me.'

'Ah … no problem,' he said, reaching up to scratch his head. Was that all this was? A thank you kiss? Not that she'd even needed him to save her.

Better if it was just a thank you; then he wouldn't have to walk away knowing she felt the same way about him.

He dragged himself to his feet and eyed Carstairs, aware of the speculative look in the warden's eyes as he glanced from him to Hannah. 'What are you waiting for? It's time to get this airship going.'

Hannah took off for the airship, while Hanson avoided Carstairs' gaze, hoping the other man wouldn't mention the kiss, even as he scrambled for something to say.

But neither of them got a chance to speak.

The door to the roof smashed open and Hanson jumped around as a stream of freaks poured through the doorway.

For a second, he froze, remembering being in this situation several weeks ago, when Councillor Dillon's son had become a freak and killed Ben. Hanson shook off his paralysis. He spun to pinpoint where Hannah was, relieved to find her in the interior of the airship, along with Dale and Michaelson. Carstairs threw him a fresh magazine and as he loaded his gun, he ran toward the doorway and started shooting. In moments, he and Carstairs had taken care of the freaks and they lowered their weapons.

Hanson grimaced as he realised the door would never shut again properly. He could hear the sounds of people in the stairwell coming up to the roof.

He called Carstairs over. 'Get Hannah and the others out of here. I'll hold them off and meet you at the front gate when I'm done.'

Without waiting for a response, he hurtled through the doorway and ran down the first two flights of stairs. The footsteps below were getting louder and he aimed his pistol, ready to take out the first freak.

A male appeared and Hanson began to squeeze the trigger.

Then he focused on the man's eyes, clear eyes with no blood pouring from them.

Hanson released the trigger and lowered the pistol to his side. 'Call out next time. I thought you were a freak and was about to shoot you,' he told the council guard.

More guards were in the stairwell below him, all of them armed, weapons at the ready. He recognised the guard he'd almost shot as one who had caught him earlier.

'Councillor Dillon is dead.' The guard's eyes narrowed. 'Did you have something to do with that?'

Hanson stiffened. 'The freaking bastard fell out the window when he tried to kill me.' He shook his head. 'I tried to save him, but all he cared about was getting his revenge.'

The guard stared at him for a long moment, then gave a

short nod. 'We've cleared the rest of the building and are heading to the roof to do the same.'

'No need. My team cleared the roof.' Hanson holstered his pistol and took the steps to the level just ahead of the guards. 'How many freaks are left out there?' He tossed his head to the side. Surely there couldn't be many more. Jackson and the others had been working their way through town.

'There's a bunch of them in the half-breed zone. We were heading there next after we made sure the councillors were okay.' His expression was grim, and Hanson didn't think it was just because Dillon was splattered on the ground in the back alley.

'The other councillors … they make it?'

'Councillors Nash and Petersen were downstairs in the main chamber when the freaks came in. They didn't stand a chance.'

Hanson grimaced. 'What about Neil? Is he okay?' After the help Dillon's assistant had given him and Hannah, it would be a shame if anything bad happened to him.

The guard gave a fleeting smile. 'He's fine. He barricaded himself in the files room with the Councillors Mandalay and Higgins. Last I saw of him, he was lecturing them on how to run Brimfield without the other three around.'

Hanson snorted, well able to imagine the little man taking charge and making sure the next council did things the right way.

'If he's got the situation under control here, then why don't we see what we can do about those freaks harassing the half-breed zone?' Though none of the people living in the zone he'd been raised in were from Brimfield, or half-breeds, they didn't deserve to be set upon by freaks. Dillon had kicked out the troublemakers and sent them back to Harlington, but the ones who had remained in Brimfield were innocent people just looking for a safe place to live.

That safe place had turned out to be far more dangerous

than the one they had left behind. But not for long, not if he could help it.

As he strode alongside the guards, men and women who would have gladly handed him over to Dillon to be hanged a short time ago, he marvelled at how much the world had changed in a short space of time. A common enemy had pulled them all together: humans, half-breeds, wardens, and even those from the Legion. He had better make the most of this tenuous peace while it lasted.

Hanson cast a sideways glance at the guard as they passed the end of the alley where Dillon had met his end. 'We good with this?' He indicated down the alley. He didn't want to fight alongside these guys and then have them turn around and charge him as an accessory to murder or some such rubbish. He had no one else to back up his claim that the councillor's death had been an accident.

The guard gave him a measured look. 'Neil told me everything, about how Councillor Dillon lied to make everyone believe you lot were responsible for the attack on him. How he did everything he could to besmirch the name of the wardens and flouted the law whenever it suited him just to paint your lot as the bad guys.'

He shook his head. 'I knew he was a hard man, but losing his son unhinged him. Some of the orders he was giving … they were enough to make your skin crawl. Councillor Kelvin Dillon was an arsehole who would kill his own mother if he thought it would give him an advantage, but unless he was voted out of the council, we were stuck with him, and he had Nash and Petersen firmly in his pocket. They were all the same: greedy and cruel. Now that the three of them are gone, the remaining councillors can make sure the three who get to join them are nothing like Dillon.'

Hanson hoped that was the case. For all that had gone down in Brimfield, the way he and the other half-breeds had been treated, it was still his home. Living in the mine command wasn't bad, but maybe one day, if the new council agreed, they'd be able to return and make the town one where everyone really was safe and welcome. No more freaks, no more prejudice. Just a place where they could all live together and prosper.

It was probably a fantasy, what with generations of animosity between them all, but if Justice could do what she said and cleanse the world with the power of Gaea's ritual, then maybe there was a chance his dream could come true.

FORTY-THREE

Justice sat up straight as they drew near Cadel. The town gates were wide open, with no sign of any guards.

'Renfield, wake up,' said Isaac.

Renfield had been lying down in the back but he now sprang up, showing no signs of lingering sleepiness. 'What's up, Commander?'

Isaac nodded ahead. 'The not so friendly people of Cadel have left their gates open.'

'Think they've got trouble?'

'That I do. The question is, what kind of trouble? We're low on fuel, seeing as we didn't get a chance to refuel back at the monastery. This is the best possible place for us to stop and gather more supplies, but it could be risky.'

'Do we have a choice?' Justice rubbed at her eyes. They were sore, gritty, like the rest of her.

Isaac shot her a strained smile. 'Nope. Either we stop here and get what we need or we'll wind up walking the rest of the way back to your man.'

She would walk, if that was what it took, but she knew getting more supplies now was their best bet for getting back to the mine compound in a reasonable time frame. With the threat of new freaks looming over their heads and no idea when the final axe would fall on Gaea's promise of doom, speed was of the essence.

Justice nodded. 'Let's do it.' She reached into the back and grabbed one of the stun guns Jackson had insisted she carry with her at all times.

Isaac grinned in response and then faced forward, tension visible in the rigid way he held himself as they drew closer to the Cadel gates. They reached the open gateway, and Justice peered ahead, trying to see what awaited them in the streets. There was no movement. The entire town could be deserted for all she knew.

Over the roar of the engine, she could hear no other sound.

Isaac and Renfield were vigilant as they drove farther in, making their way down what appeared to be the main street. Closed signs were hanging in the shop windows they passed, even though it was mid-afternoon, with no lights on inside the buildings that she could see.

Shadows filled the cross streets and laneways, all with no sign of life.

Was her first impression right? Had the town been deserted?

A loud bang sounded a split second before the four-wheel-drive lurched sideways. Justice cried out as she was flung against her door, pain flaring in her shoulder, causing her to lose her grip on her stun gun.

It clattered to the floor at her feet as the four-wheel-drive righted itself. Then another bang came, and the nose of their vehicle dipped into a crater that appeared in the road in front of them.

Isaac cursed as he fought to reverse out of the crater even as more bangs sounded, softer than the ones from before. Someone was shooting at them.

'I see them,' Renfield shouted, forcing his way through

the sunroof and taking aim with his rifle. The sound of his return fire echoed inside the four-wheel-drive, and Justice once more covered her ears, though it only dulled the noise. More gunfire erupted around them and Renfield grunted, slumping back inside the vehicle, blood streaming from one shoulder.

'I've been hit, but I took out three of their guys. There's still at least four of them left, from what I can tell.'

'Who are they?' Justice asked as she scrambled over into the backseat to grab their medical supplies to try to staunch the bleeding from Renfield's shoulder. He was pale, a pained grimace covering his face as she worked as best as she could in the cramped surrounds.

'Mercenaries. The same outfit that ambushed us the night of the storm, if I'm not mistaken,' Isaac said, his tone calm despite the continuing gunfire. 'Here,' he added, shoving Justice's stun gun over to her. 'Get ready. They'll swarm us now that they know they have us pinned.'

Hands slick with Renfield's blood, Justice took the stun gun, willing her hands to stop shaking. This was not like the time when she had shot General Butcher to stop him from killing Jackson. Then she had been filled with certainty, focused on protecting the man she loved. Now she was scared, trapped in a stationary vehicle with an unknown number of enemies outside.

Still, she would do what she had to. She had to get out of here, get back to the compound and Jackson so they could figure out where to go to fulfil the final part of Gaea's prophecy. With his good arm out of commission, Renfield gripped a pistol in his left hand and faced one door. Justice squared her shoulders and faced the other, leaving it to Isaac to guard both front doors.

When the door was wrenched open, Justice did not hesitate. She fired into the chest of the person on the other side. The mercenary fell back, but another took his place and

Justice fired again. She kept firing until her doorway was clear, sweat stinging into her eyes and blurring her vision.

When no other figure appeared in her doorway, she risked glancing around. Renfield was gone, his door gaping open, but Isaac was still in the front seat, a pistol in both hands. A small round canister landed in the spot where Renfield had been, and Isaac's eyes widened.

'Get out now,' he shouted, throwing himself out the driver's door.

Justice hurriedly followed suit, landing heavily on the ground, dust choking her throat as she scrambled away from the four-wheel-drive. A loud boom came from behind her, followed by a wave of heat and air that smashed into her. She felt her body being lifted up and her limbs flailed as she flew through the air before landing with enough force that she couldn't breathe, couldn't think. Her ears rang and tears streamed from her eyes, body aching all over as her lungs fought to get air.

As the pain in her chest eased and she could breathe again, she clenched her hands into fists, surprised to find she still held the stun gun. She rolled over, using her free hand to brush dirt from her eyes as she struggled to a sitting position. She could hear grunts, the sound of someone being hit, and a derisive laugh.

'Not so righteous now, are you? Not without all your men to hide behind.'

'Fogarty, you coward,' Isaac said, sounding winded. 'You're the only one here who likes to hide behind others. That's why so many of your men desert your little group and come to join my company. They know you'll only get them killed, while you run off with all the profits.'

A snarl sounded, followed by what had to be another blow, and Justice heard Isaac groan as she pushed herself to her feet. Every inch of her body still hurt as she stumbled around what remained of the four-wheel-drive. Isaac was curled up on his side as a skinny man in camouflage gear kicked him in the stomach. Two other men stood beside the leader—Fogarty, she presumed—their backs to Justice, attention focused on Isaac.

More bodies lay scattered on the ground. One of them Renfield, who was not moving. Justice sucked in a deep breath and aimed her gun at Fogarty.

He must have caught sight of her out of the corner of his eye, and he spun to face her, lifting his own weapon.

She fired first, hitting him directly in the chest and knocking him off his feet. Then she fired into the backs of the other two as they turned.

They dropped to the ground and Justice lowered her arm, the effort to hold it up beyond her. If there were any more of Fogarty's men in the area, they were done for. She stumbled over to Isaac, who gazed up at her with a fierce grin on his face despite the blood and contusions covering every inch of bare skin.

'Nice shots, little sister. We'll make a mercenary out of you yet.'

She slumped to the ground beside him, holding back a cry when pain flared through her body. 'No thanks. I don't think I'm cut out for this business.'

'Well,' Isaac said as he painfully dragged himself into a sitting position, one hand pressed against his torso, 'the offer still stands if you ever change your mind.'

Justice gave him a weary smile, closing her eyes.

She was too sore and too tired to open them when she heard running footsteps. If it was more mercenaries, let them come.

'Miss, I'm here to help you. Can you tell me where it hurts?'

A frown creasing her brow, Justice tried to prise her eyes open. She knew that voice, didn't she?

As gentle but firm hands poked and prodded at her body,

she realised where she had heard it before. It was the doctor who had given her medical supplies for Brother Owen when they had first approached Cadel and been turned away.

She opened her eyes a slit and stared at him. 'My friends, are they okay?' She tried to turn her head, to check on Isaac and Renfield, but her neck spasmed in pain and she cried out.

'It's okay, we'll take care of them. You need to remain still while I assess your injuries.'

Justice let her eyes close again, content to let him do his work, though she couldn't stop a hiss of pain each time he touched a sensitive spot.

'It's okay, you don't appear to have any broken bones, though you will be sore and bruised for some time.' The doctor placed an arm under her shoulders and helped her to sit up. The pain of the movement made her dizzy and she rested for a moment before accepting his help to stand. When she was upright, his arm around her back making sure she didn't topple over, she looked for the others.

The mercenaries she had stunned, hands bound, were surrounded by guards, while Isaac was on his feet, looking just as bruised and battered as she felt.

Renfield …

He was still on the ground, blood soaking the bandage she had hastily applied to his shoulder wound. That blood mingled with a chest wound.

Tears pricked her eyes at the sight of his lifeless body. First Brother Owen, then Sutherland, and now Renfield. How many more were going to die? Was all this death going to be worth it in the end?

She bowed her head and allowed the doctor to lead her away, not caring where he was taking her, tears obscuring her vision as they went. It wasn't until she was seated in his surgery, Isaac standing beside her, that she lifted her head.

'You have some explaining to do, Doctor,' Isaac said, his voice hard. 'Your council refused to let us enter Cadel when we had an injured man and yet it appears you had no qualms in opening the gates to Ian Fogarty and his men.'

The doctor flushed. 'They tricked us, said they had been sent by the wardens to protect us from the new freaks. It wasn't until we opened the gates that we realised they had lied. By then, it was too late. They'd taken over the council chambers and threatened to burn our town to the ground if we didn't help them to capture you. They said you were a very dangerous man and were wanted for crimes against humans, and that Fogarty was only here to collect the bounty and would leave town once he had captured you.'

Isaac leaned against the wall behind them, eyes closed. 'I may be dangerous, but Fogarty would have burned your town anyway. He has a vicious streak. If I were you, I'd make sure he never wakes up.'

The doctor paled at hearing this.

Then Isaac opened his eyes again. 'What now? Your council better not have any ideas of keeping me here and collecting that bounty themselves.'

The doctor shook his head. 'I'm sure they won't do that. I'll make sure they let you go.'

As it turned out, they had nothing to fear from the council. All their ire was directed at Fogarty and his men, who had been locked away in the town detention centre to await trial.

After spending an uncomfortable night in the doctor's surgery, Isaac helped himself to one of Fogarty's vehicles. They left town after retrieving the chest and what other supplies they could salvage from the mangled wreck of their four-wheel-drive.

As they drove away from Cadel, Isaac looked over at Justice. 'Any chance you can convince Kyle not to kill me when he sees what state you're in?'

Justice managed a wry smile. 'Don't worry, Isaac, I promise to protect you.'

FORTY-FOUR

Jackson was grim as Michaelson directed the airship toward the mine compound. Below, hundreds of dead freaks littered fields that had once been filled with crops. It would be a lean season for Brimfield, but he was sure that under Neil Barrowman's leadership, they would survive.

A small smile formed as he remembered the newly elected lead councillor's promise that Jackson and his wardens were welcome back in Brimfield. More than welcome. He wanted them to take an active part in securing the town's future. That would have to wait until after they had taken care of these new freaks.

The destruction of the horde that had been outside the town gates had been brutal and bloody, but thanks to the airship, there had been no further casualties. They'd been able to fire down on the freaks in safety, though the task had left a bitter taste in Jackson's mouth, and he was sure many of the others felt the same—even the ones from the Legion.

He looked over to where Rona Maguire stood with a small group of her people. The rest, along with some of his wardens, were driving to the mine. He'd insisted she come with him so he could keep an eye on her. And he wasn't the only one. Hanson had stayed close to the Legion leader the entire time they had been aboard, clearly not trusting her apparent turnabout.

For his part, Jackson was inclined to believe Rona really did want to make amends for creating the new freak virus. She fought alongside him in Brimfield, showing no hesitation in shooting down those of the Legion who had become infected. Guilt over her actions in the name of vengeance was evident in her harrowed gaze. Still, it would be a long time before he could bring himself to trust her fully.

'Has there been any word from Justice?' Hannah asked him.

He turned to face her and shook his head. 'No, and we haven't been able to get through to Lieutenant Jensen either.'

Jackson gazed at the ground below them, wishing the airship could go faster, eager to get to the compound and find out what was going on. Maybe Justice would be there, waiting for him, with everything she needed to stave off humankind's destruction. When they finally drew near, he realised Brimfield hadn't been the only place to get a visit from a freak horde.

A sea of freaks massed in front of the compound gates, clambering over each other as they sought to get the people on the other side. There were not as many here as had attacked Brimfield, but there were still too many to count easily.

A line of wardens lined the top of the wall, firing down at the freaks, while others were picking off those climbing the rocky ridges to either side of the gate. Jackson unholstered his gun and called out for the others to do the same. He picked his first target, aiming for the head, and looking for his next target immediately after his shot. Systematically, he worked his way through the horde, striving not to think about all the lives lost to this new virus.

When the last freak fell, he ordered Michaelson to land the

airship. Then, with Hanson, Hannah, and Carstairs at his back, he strode toward the opening gates.

Jensen came out, a weary smile creasing his face as he approached Jackson. 'Good timing,' he said as he scanned over them. His smile widened when he stepped forward and clasped Hanson on the shoulder. 'Glad to see you made it. We were getting worried about you.'

Hanson waved at the dead freaks scattering the ground around them. 'Looks as if you had just as much trouble as we did.'

Jensen's smile faded as he faced Jackson. 'I take it the new freaks made it to Brimfield as well.'

Jackson nodded. 'I'll fill you in on everything that happened, but first, is Justice here?'

His heart sank when Jensen shook his head. 'No, sir, but we have had visitors who say they are from the Legion.' His expression darkened. 'They said more of their people were on their way to Brimfield. I tried to warn you, but the storm knocked out our communications and then this happened.' He looked down at one of the dead freaks.

Pushing down his worry for Justice, Jackson indicated for Rona to join them. 'This is Rona Maguire. She's the new leader of the Legion. She'll be helping us take care of these new freaks.' He didn't add that she was responsible for them. That would come later, during the debriefing. For now, they had to see to the dead.

By the time the rest of their people and the members of the Legion arrived, all the dead freaks had been carted away from the compound and their bodies burned to minimise the risk of infection. Black smoke from the funeral pyre spiralled into the air.

Jackson stood on the wall looking out at the road leading to the compound, willing Justice to appear. There was no sign of her or any other vehicle. As he returned to the ground and strode toward the main building for the debrief, he hoped she had not encountered any of the new freaks. The mercenary commander and his men might be accomplished fighters, but there were only three of them, and if they chanced upon one of these hordes, that would not be enough.

FORTY-FIVE

Hannah sidled around the lead Legion scientist, Bryant Montgomery, not happy to have him and the others taking over the lab. Sure, it had been their lab originally, but they had abandoned it, same as the rest of the compound, after they'd been defeated by the wardens. This was her lab now and she did not like these strangers coming in and messing up how she had everything arranged.

Despite that, she was intrigued to know how they had come up with the gas to control the freaks in the first place.

'I don't understand what changed. The bloodwork is still consistent with our initial testing. The gas should still work,' said Bryant.

'Maybe we made a mistake and allowed some foreign body to contaminate this particular batch,' suggested one of the others, a woman called Tara Baldwin. The other scientist had yet to say a word, or bother to give his name.

'Perhaps,' Bryant said, 'but I can't find any trace of a contaminant and nothing else has changed.'

'If it isn't the gas, then maybe it's the virus,' said Hannah.

All three scientists jumped. They'd been ignoring her since

they entered and took over the lab, so maybe they had forgotten she was even there.

Being ignored was bad enough. To be forgotten … Well, maybe it was time to remind them who this lab belonged to now.

'Do you have any samples of the virus you created?' It felt wrong even saying it.

After all the misery and death that had resulted after the first virus was created five hundred years ago, it was still hard to blame these people for making the same mistakes as their ancestors. But how many people were going to die because the Legion believed it was their right to rule the world?

She shook off her anger with effort and moved forward to commandeer the microscope. 'I took samples from the freaks that attacked Brimfield, so we can compare the two to see what has changed that may have made your gas ineffective.'

'Ah, yes, we have samples of the initial virus in storage.' Bryant waved at a pile of refrigerator boxes stacked in the corner.

Hannah gave him a cool smile. 'While you get those samples unpacked and prepared for examination, I'm going to see what effect my vaccine has on the Brimfield samples.' There, let them squirm with the knowledge they were in the wrong and that she had been the one to come up with a cure. She grabbed her samples from the fridge under the desk and prepped the slide to see what effect, if any, her vaccine would have.

'Ah, I don't think your vaccine is going to work on this new strain,' said Bryant. 'We made sure it was resistant, for when our freaks came up against the wardens you had inoculated. Our initial testing proved we had been successful.'

Hannah straightened and glared at him. 'You people never learn, do you? If we can't get your gas working, or come up with a new cure, the whole country could be overrun with freaks within months. Weeks even. If I were you, I'd be doing everything I could to get this mess sorted out.'

Then she turned back to her slides, dismayed to see he had been right. Her vaccine had no effect on the new virus strain. After all the effort to get blood, the sacrifices Neil had made to help her escape Councillor Dillon's clutches, it had all been for nothing. If she couldn't fix this, all the deaths from the incursion to Brimfield would be a waste.

To do that, much as she hated it, she would have to work with the Legion scientists. From what she had heard, the scientists who had created the original virus had been among the first victims. These ones were alive and well. If they had made the thing, there was a chance that locked in their brains was a way to unmake it. She just had to find it.

She turned to Tara, the only one who had shown any hint of interest in Hannah since walking into the lab. She was watching on as the other two found the samples they needed and began to compare them to the new samples Hannah had collected.

There was a collective groan from the three of them that told Hannah without words that the two samples were no longer the same.

'Your virus has mutated, just as the original virus did after it was first created,' she said in a flat tone.

'But we took steps to ensure that didn't happen,' said Bryant. 'I designed the strain to make it impervious to mutation.'

'Clearly whatever it was you thought you did didn't work,' Hannah said, her tone getting even flatter. These people, with their arrogance and their belief in their evil cause, were so stupid.

Tara frowned and crossed her arms. 'I told you we needed to test that strain longer before we told Rona it was ready.'

Bryant glared at his compatriot. 'There was no time for further testing. Rona wanted the virus ready to go as soon as possible. It was not possible to test for every eventuality in the time we were given. She should have given us more time.'

Tara snorted, and Hannah didn't blame her. Throwing the blame for this catastrophe into another's face wouldn't help them. She gestured for the woman to join her on the other side of the lab.

'I need you to tell me every single step you took to create this strain,' she said. 'Don't leave anything out.'

'What does it matter? If the virus has mutated beyond our original creation, then there's no point.'

'My mentor Daniel once told me that the only way to truly defeat an enemy is to understand them. So, if I'm to come up with a cure, I need to know this virus better than I know myself.' Who knew, maybe she would get a chance to use the precious blood she had taken from Neil after all. Either way, she would do her best to cure this virus if it was the last thing she did.

FORTY-SIX

ANDY RACED DOWN THE HALLWAY AT HANSON'S HEELS AND burst through the large double doors and out onto the wide stone stairs that led to the main parade ground for the compound, relieved to be back following orders instead of giving them. 'I hear you and Hannah are a couple now.'

Hanson shot a startled expression at him over his shoulder, missing a step and stumbling down the next couple of stairs before he caught his balance. He shook his head. 'Who said we're a couple? Did Hannah tell you that?'

'Come on, everyone can see it. Something obviously happened to get the two of you to finally admit you have feelings for each other.'

'Feelings? Who said anything about feelings?'

Andy grinned at the squeak in Hanson's voice. 'You mean you didn't get all cosy with her when the two of you were hiding from the guards? From what Leon said, he was interrupting some serious moment when he and Carstairs found you. I hear there was also a kiss, on the roof, when you were getting the airship.' The airship was now tethered to a line hooked to the building they had just left.

Hanson's expression darkened. 'Leon wouldn't know what

he was interrupting. And the kiss was nothing. Hannah was just thanking me for saving her life. That's all.'

'We've all saved Hannah's life at one time or another. So how come you're the only one who got kissed?'

'It's not what you think. Hannah and I are friends. Good friends. That's all.'

'Good friends. Right. That's why you look like you want to punch Carstairs in the nose anytime he talks to her.'

'He's just got a nose built to be punched. Come on, don't tell me you haven't thought about it at least once. I saw him talking to Felice just before and the two of them were definitely having a cosy moment. From the way I see you watching her, that has got to make you want to punch him. You want the girl? You better make a move before it's too late.'

It was Andy's turn to miss a step. He shook his head, forcing away the thought that the smooth lieutenant from Harlington might have Felice in his sights now that Hannah was clearly unavailable. No matter how much Hanson might protest, it was clear to anyone with eyes that he and Hannah were the perfect couple.

But Felice—she deserved more than being a rebound or whatever it was Carstairs was looking for. Bloody Michaelson had also been showing an interest in the feisty young woman who had taken over control of the mine compound as if she was born to be in charge. She would have made an amazing warden if they'd not been so hung up on excluding half-breeds.

Andy felt ashamed that it had taken him so long to realise they were all the same, that half-breeds were not less than warden or human. If they had been welcomed into the Wards, allowed to fight alongside them, they may have eradicated the freaks generations ago.

It had taken Justice and Hannah to show him the error of five hundred years of prejudice. Meeting Felice had cemented it. Unfortunately, the rest of the country still held the same prejudice as their ancestors. It would take years before they were truly accepted as equal.

Not that it appeared Carstairs—and Michaelson—had any qualms about starting up a relationship with half-breeds. Or trying to. Andy hadn't seen Felice respond to any of his fellow wardens' overtures, and he frowned at the thought of Carstairs trying the same.

He pushed that aside. 'I'm not talking about me and Felice. This is about you and Hannah.'

'You admit there is a "me and Felice" thing to talk about,' Hanson said, waving his hands as emphasis.

'No, I'm not admitting anything. Stop talking about this. There is nothing going on with me and Felice.' Much to his disappointment.

She challenged him at every turn, made him feel like a bumbling teenager on occasion, and had been his back up more times than he could count since that first battle to rid Brimfield Ward of freaks. She was one hell of a woman, and a man would be lucky to have caught her eye. But even with all the time they'd spent together, running the compound, she'd given no sign she would appreciate his interest. He'd have acted on it if she had. Not that Hanson needed to know that.

'Hey, you're the one who brought it up.'

'Did not.'

'Did too.'

'Boys, did you both get hit on the head and regress twenty years?'

Andy spun around at the sound of Felice's voice, heat swamping him. How long had she been standing behind them? How much had she heard?

There was a twinkle in her eye as she gazed at Andy. 'I'd expect such juvenile conversation from Hanson, but I thought you were more mature than that.'

'Ah … I … ah …' Andy spread his hands, struggling to find something to say that wouldn't make him sound like even more of an idiot. 'It was just Hanson being Hanson. It didn't mean anything. I swear.'

'Way to dig yourself deeper, man,' Hanson said, clapping him on the shoulder and giving a low chuckle. 'You'll never win the girl this way.' Then he gave Felice a cheeky grin and a wave. 'I've got real work to do. He's all yours.'

As he strode off, Felice never took her eyes off Andy. 'Win the girl? What, is this a competition? Some macho bonding thing?'

'What? No, of course not. It's nothing like that.'

She crossed her arms in front of her chest and glared at him. 'What is it like then?'

He shook his head, mouth opening but no words coming out.

Felice gave an exasperated laugh, then leaned forward and patted him on the cheek. 'When you figure it out, you come find me. I'm not interested in Lieutenant Carstairs or any other warden.' Then she turned around and sauntered off, leaving Andy not sure if he should be relieved or terrified.

She'd heard the whole stupid conversation with Hanson and made it clear Carstairs and Michaelson had no chance with her. But Andy did.

A smile crept over his face at the thought. Worried he was wrong, he wiped it off.

She did mean he had a chance, right?

As he hurried off in the direction Hanson had taken, his brain offered up all the smart things he could have said in response to Felice's question instead of just standing there like an idiot. But there would be time later to fix it. He would find her after they'd taken care of all the new freaks. Then he would make it clear once and for all what it was that he was interested in.

FORTY-SEVEN

HANNAH WAS ALONE IN THE LAB, BLISSFULLY ALONE. THE Legion scientists had retired to the rooms they had been assigned, Bryant grumbling because the room he had occupied previously was now taken by Andy. With so many people added to the mix, many of the Legion had been bunked down in the mine complex. They were being watched. Just because they said they were there to help fix the mess they had made didn't mean they were trusted.

Hannah had agreed to let Tara bunk in her room. She couldn't justify keeping the room to herself, seeing as it had two single beds, though that meant there was little chance for privacy anywhere in the compound.

She hoped by the time she finished this last experiment, her new roommate would be fast asleep and Hannah could slip quickly in, get cleaned up, and go to bed.

A head poked in the door. 'You know, the lab will still be here in the morning.'

Hannah smiled at Barrett. 'I know. I just need to finish this up and then I'm done.' She waved him off. 'You should get to bed too. Lots of new people to feed tomorrow.'

He grimaced and said, 'Don't remind me. Trev has me running in circles getting everything prepped.' He yawned.

Hannah yawned in sympathy, eyes watering. 'I hope the Legion people won't be here for long, and life can get back to normal.' If they could figure out the gas or a cure.

'Something to look forward to,' Barrett said before he wished her goodnight.

Alone once more, Hannah began packing up the supplies she had used for the test. The machine beeped and she leaned over to check the display, sighing when it gave her the same result as the last three times. She dutifully recorded the results in her lab logbook and then packed the last few items away. But her mind was not on the task, or the most recent failed test.

She had hardly seen Hanson since they had left Brimfield. When they had crossed paths, he'd barely spoken two words to her before bolting off. It was the kiss, she was sure of it.

He was embarrassed and was now avoiding her because she'd done something stupid.

She hadn't meant to kiss him. She'd just been so relieved he was safe, that he hadn't fallen to his death or been infected by a freak. She'd gone to hug him and without thinking about what she was doing, her lips were on his.

He'd kissed her back, sure, but that was probably an automatic reflex, a spur of the moment thing he was clearly regretting. Now he was putting as much distance as possible between them, probably thinking she was going to throw herself at him at any moment. Not that she would.

The kiss had been a crazy impulse, a way of celebrating that they were both alive. It hadn't meant anything. It couldn't.

One lapse of judgement had already put their friendship in jeopardy.

With luck, after he realised she was never going to repeat

it, Hanson would stop avoiding her and they could go back to normal. She missed him, more than she thought she would. Sure, he was cheesy, often arrogant and too sure of himself, but he was a good guy, and had risked his life countless times to save her and others. He'd even been acting less like a jerk and more like a leader thanks to Jackson's influence.

The thought that he might never want to be her friend again made her chest ache. She had Justice. If she ever came back from gallivanting around with monks and mercenaries. Justice was her best friend. But Hanson was …

She ran her hand over her mouth, remembering the way his lips had coursed over hers. For a brief moment on the roof of the council building, she had forgotten about everything else. Nothing had mattered except for Hanson and the way her body moulded to his, the taste of him, the warmth spreading over her body. That warmth enveloped her now as she remembered the kiss, but she had to push all thought of that moment aside and focus on repairing the damage she had caused.

It was probably because it had been her first kiss. Crazy to think she had reached twenty-six without ever knowing what it felt like to be held like that, to lose herself in someone's arms. That's what came from being raised in a Ward headquarters, where most of the wardens hated her and none of those who tolerated her would ever have considered kissing her.

Hanson was a half-breed, like her.

She needed him in her life. As a friend. Not someone she should be thinking about kissing, no matter how good it had felt. He challenged her—in a good way. She would be devastated if the kiss cost her his friendship for good.

Tears pricked her eyes at the thought and she shook her head. It wasn't tears. No, it was because she was tired, that's all.

So tired she wasn't thinking straight. She had to put the

kiss out of her mind and focus on fixing the gas to control the freaks or coming up with a cure that didn't require intervention from Gaea.

Justice should be back soon. They hadn't been able to contact her since she'd left, the storm damaging most of the radio network. Maybe she would come back with a way to fix everything. She might even know what Hannah could do to fix her relationship with Hanson.

Focused on her thoughts, Hannah switched off the light to the lab and slipped out the door, locking it behind her. She pocketed the key, not wanting Bryant or the others to be in there without her. That meant she would have to be up early to allow them access in the morning. After breakfast, though.

Her stomach grumbled, reminding her it had been some time since dinner, and she had been too preoccupied to do more than pick at it. Maybe she should find herself a snack to tide her over until morning. She would sleep better with something in her stomach, she was sure. In the morning, when Hanson returned from a scouting missing Jackson had sent him on, she would explain to him that the kiss hadn't meant anything and he would stop avoiding her.

Most of the lanterns had been extinguished to conserve oil, but a couple were lit to aid the wardens on duty to navigate the compound in the near darkness. She was able to find her way outside and to the dining complex without banging into anything, but she stopped before opening the back door into the kitchen area.

A rustle came from the lean-to off the side that housed the generator. Shadows flickered in the low light.

'Hello?' Hannah kept her voice low, not wanting to startle whoever it was. Probably one of the night patrol.

The shadows stilled for a moment, then they moved forward, the light from the lantern hanging on the pole behind Hannah allowing her to distinguish three figures. As they came closer, she realised they were all members of the Legion, and none of them looked happy to see her. Sounds came from inside the lean-to and she realised there were more people about.

She backed up, taking in the scowls on their faces as she opened her mouth to ask them what they were doing. These people should not be here. She banged into something and an arm wrapped around her middle as a hand came up to cover her mouth. Hannah rammed an elbow back into the stomach of the person holding her and they let go. She didn't stop there. She kicked out, knocking her attacker to the ground, and bolted for the dormitory where the bulk of the wardens were sleeping, shouting for help as she ran.

The noise of footsteps came from behind her and she was tackled, slamming onto the ground with a heavy body on top of her.

Her shouts had done their job. Wardens streamed out of the dormitory in their night attire, and the weight on her back shifted.

'Stand down.'

Hannah got to her feet and looked over to the door of the main building to see Rona standing there, still dressed in red body armour. Jackson was at her side, though he now wore jeans and a shirt. He and Rona strode toward them as the wardens rounded up the Legion people who had been hanging around the lean-to.

'What's going on?' Rona ignored the wardens and Hannah, stopping in front of one of her people. His face was twisted into a snarl.

'It's not right, Master Maguire. This is our stronghold. These wardens don't belong here.'

'What were you planning to do?' Jackson asked, arms crossed in front of his chest.

The man sneered at him and shook his head.

'They were in the lean-to,' Hannah said, pointing to it.

Jackson's eyes narrowed. 'You were tampering with the generator?'

The man stiffened. 'I don't answer to you.'

'You answer to me,' Rona said, lunging forward and grabbing the man by his throat with one hand. The other held her pistol and she rammed it into his stomach. 'What were you going to do?'

'You'd side with them, over your own people?' He gave no sign he was bothered by either the weapon shoved into his stomach or the hand at his throat. 'Your sister would be disgusted with you. And so would your father. You've betrayed the Legion by allying with this lot.'

Bang.

Hannah jumped as the man fell backward, blood soaking the side of his shirt. Rona stepped back and let him fall to the ground without a second glance.

'Rona, that was not necessary.' Jackson eyed Rona as he called for a medic to attend to the man now groaning in agony.

'It's a flesh wound. He'll live,' she said. Then she eyed the other men and women from the Legion. 'I am only going to say this once. We will work with the wardens to destroy the freaks we created. Anyone who doesn't agree is welcome to leave. Now!' She pointed her pistol toward the gates.

The Legion members shuffled their feet, eyes downcast.

When it was clear none of them was going to take Rona up on her offer, she holstered her pistol. 'So, which one of you are going to tell me what this idiot was planning to do?'

After a number of varied glances, a woman was shoved forward. 'He planned to use the fuel from the generator to set the dormitory on fire. Make it look like an accident. Reduce their numbers so we could take back control of the compound.'

Hannah sucked in a breath. The sleeping wardens would have been burned alive.

Any sympathy for the wounded man fled and she could see on the faces of the wardens surrounding him that he would be hard pressed to find anyone to care if he was injured. As for the people who had been with him, Hannah glared at them all. It may have been the injured man's idea, but they had been willing to go along with it.

Jackson stepped forward, calling Lieutenant Jensen over. 'Lock these people up in the mine. We'll deal with them in the morning. Without bloodshed,' he said as he eyed Rona.

She shrugged. 'He was a traitor. I was within my rights to shoot him.'

'You agreed to abide by my rules. We don't shoot people, whether they are traitors or not. Once we investigate, and he's well enough, he and his co-conspirators will be exiled.' Now he turned to survey those co-conspirators. 'But make no mistake. If any one of you attempts to harm one of my wardens, you will face swift justice. As I'm sure you are aware, this mine has many chambers. You will be locked away, never to see daylight again, if one of my people comes to harm because of your actions.'

Heads downcast, avoiding eye contact with those of their own people who had come out thanks to the commotion, the traitors were led away by Jensen and his wardens.

Jackson then turned to Hannah. 'Are you all right?'

A shiver swept over her at knowing what might have happened if she had just gone up to her room and not in search of a late-night snack. Her appetite was gone now, but she managed a nod for Jackson. He clasped her arm and accompanied her back to the main building.

'Get some sleep,' he said as they reached the landing on the top floor. 'You look as though you need it.'

'You too,' she said, noting the lines around his eyes. With everything that had happened at High Command, and then in Brimfield, he had to be near his limit. She was sure he would not rest well until Justice was back.

For her part, despite what had happened, her eyes closed as soon as her head met the pillow. The last thought she had was that she hoped Hanson had not run into any trouble on his mission to Harlington. The memory of his kiss followed her into sleep.

FORTY-EIGHT

THERE WERE SO MANY NEW FACES WATCHING ON AS ISAAC drove into the mine compound, none of them appearing too friendly, that for a moment Justice began to worry they'd been overtaken by a hostile force. That would explain the lack of radio contact on the journey from Cadel. Then she spotted Felice in the midst of one group and her fears subsided. Whoever these newcomers were, her friend had them in hand and appeared to be directing them in tasks to clear up what looked like storm damage.

'Looks as if the storm that hit us the night we left also caused problems here,' said Isaac. 'Probably the reason for the radio silence.'

Her nerves settled at his suggestion. The storm had to be the reason she hadn't heard from Jackson for days. Nothing sinister at all. As soon as the vehicle stopped, she climbed out and made her way over to Felice.

'Welcome back,' her friend said as she leaned in to hug Justice. 'Though you may have wanted to delay your return until we had the place cleaned up more. It's not exactly comfortable living around here at the moment.'

Justice accepted the hug and laughed. 'After the conditions I've been living in lately, anything would be an improvement.'

Felice frowned. 'Rough trip, huh?' She looked over at the vehicle where Isaac was just getting out. 'Brother Owen stay at the monastery?'

Throat choking up, Justice shook her head. 'He didn't make it,' she managed to say. 'We lost Renfield and Sutherland too.'

Felice's arms surrounded her once more, and Justice allowed herself a moment to grieve. As Isaac joined them, she pulled away and met her friend's eyes. 'Where's Jackson? Is he back from High Command?'

The skin around Felice's eyes tightened. 'He's back, all right. He's inside, with Rona Maguire.'

Isaac stiffened. 'Rona Maguire?'

Movement in her periphery caught Justice's eye and she looked up to see Jackson exiting the main building, a statuesque redhead in tight-fitting red body armour at his side. His head was inclined toward the stranger, all his attention on whatever it was she was saying. Her features were animated as she pointed at different areas of the compound. Then her gaze landed on Justice's small group, and her expression hardened.

'Justice.' The delight in Jackson's voice had Justice smiling, and she ran toward him, forgetting about everyone else as she threw herself into his arms.

It was a long moment later before she became aware of a low-voiced argument going on behind her. She turned around, still cradled within Jackson's arms, to find the redheaded woman glaring at Isaac.

Then she turned that glare on Jackson. 'You didn't tell me you were allied with mercenaries.'

'Better to be a mercenary than a terrorist,' Isaac said sardonically.

'I take it you two know each other,' Jackson said, wary amusement in his tone.

'Know *of* would be a better description,' said Isaac. 'Miss Maguire here has a nasty reputation for doing whatever it takes to get her point across.'

'I was protecting my people. Your mercenaries were attacking them.'

'My mercenaries were doing the job they were hired to do by the town your terrorists were attempting to take control of. You blew up the council building, with the council and numerous innocent people inside, when it was clear you were on the losing side.' Isaac shook his head. 'You value your cause more than you value people's lives.'

'You know nothing about me.'

'I know enough to know I don't like you or what you stand for.'

'If that's true, then why were we able to hire some of your mercenaries? Where are your vaunted morals when it comes to a paying job?'

'We don't take jobs that hurt women and children, unlike you. You don't care who gets hurt, as long as you get what you want.'

The woman—Rona—gave a low growl and reached for the gun holstered on her hip. Jackson let go of Justice and moved forward as Isaac pulled his own weapon and went into a fighting stance.

'Okay, that's enough,' Jackson said, getting between them. 'You guys clearly have history, but it ends now. We have a common goal—at least I hope we do.' He eyed Rona. 'Fighting among ourselves is not going to solve the problem of your freaks. We're allies, not enemies.'

Your freaks.

Justice sucked in a breath. 'You made them.'

The words hung in the air as Justice watched emotions play over Rona's face. Anger was chased out by shame. 'I didn't know what would happen. I thought we could control them with the gas, the way Marcus did, but I was wrong.'

'You're from the Legion.' Justice reeled, pulling away when Jackson went to grab her hand. 'What is she doing here? She's part of the Legion. Brother Owen and Sutherland and Renfield are dead because of her freaks. They nearly killed us.' She was aware her voice was rising, a hint of hysteria creeping in, but was unable to stop it. This woman Jackson had called an ally was one of the people who had tried to kill her over and over again, just so they could bring about the Apocalypse.

She glared at Rona. 'Is this your new plan to be gods? Get your pet freaks to kill as many of us as they can so you can rule over the survivors?'

'Wouldn't surprise me,' Isaac said in a disgusted tone.

'Not helping, Smith,' said Jackson.

He moved until he stood in front of Justice, blocking her view of Rona. He cupped her face in his hands. 'I know it's a tough ask, but I need you to trust me. Rona and her people are here to help. Her scientists are in the lab with Hannah right now, trying to figure out a way to stop these freaks.'

Justice shook her head, but he didn't let go, his deep blue gaze pinning her in place. 'I would never bring her here if I thought she was a danger to you or that we didn't need her.'

Justice wanted to believe him, to let it go, but seeing this woman, knowing she was part of the group that had destroyed everything that was good in her life, she couldn't just shake hands and pretend it was all okay. The Legion had killed her mother and all the monks. The men who had become her reluctant bodyguards had delighted in telling her how she would one day die at their hands.

It hit then, all those new faces watching her and Isaac as they'd driven in. They were all from the Legion. Any one of them would have gladly killed her to stop her from fulfilling her purpose. What was to stop one of them from trying again?

If they found out her purpose had only been partially completed …

Justice pulled away from Jackson and held up a hand to ward him off when he moved to touch her. 'Please, don't.'

She felt an arm wrap around her shoulders and looked up to find Isaac glaring at both Rona and Jackson. He gave her a squeeze. 'Don't worry, little sister. I've got your back.'

Jackson gave him a grave nod, while Rona's eyebrows rose. Then the new leader of the Legion cast a dark glance at Jackson.

'Come and find me when your half-breed has some news,' she said before striding off.

Justice's hands curled into fists as she watched her go.

'Smith, do you mind giving us a moment?' Jackson said.

Isaac turned Justice to face him. 'Is that what you want?'

Justice managed a sharp nod, and his arm fell away from her shoulders.

'Very well,' said Isaac. 'But I won't go far. I meant what I said. As long as the Legion witch is here, I'll be keeping a close eye on you.'

He cast a dark glance at Jackson and then strode off to grab their gear out of the back of the purloined vehicle. Justice almost called for him to grab the chest out from under her seat, but then thought better of it. There was no need to let Rona and the people from the Legion know anything about what she had been given at the monastery. The less they knew about the mission with Brother Owen, the better.

'I'm sorry about Brother Owen,' said Jackson. 'And for not being there.'

Justice gave him a teary smile. 'Thank you.' He reached out to her, and she let his arms envelop her, revelling in the solid feel of him. He was her rock. Together, they would get through this.

She pulled back a little. 'How did things go in High Command?'

Jackson grimaced. 'They voted me in as acting-general.'

'What?' Justice stared at him. 'You're the new general?'

'Acting. Until we get the mess with the new freaks sorted out and they can do a proper election to determine who will be the next leader for the Wards.' He grimaced again. 'If there are any Wards left.' He told her of the reports coming in from towns all over the country, of how they were being overrun.

'I arranged for several large contingents of wardens to go from town to town to clear out freaks, but it is too late for some. So many have already been lost because the previous acting-general was more concerned about preserving the wardens than he was about upholding the charter. If we don't get a handle on these new freaks, if Hannah can't come up with a way to control or cure them, soon there may be no one left for the Wards to protect.'

Justice shook her head, understanding his concern. 'They overran the town of Shelton. That's when we lost Sutherland and Brother Owen.' She filled him in on what had happened at the monastery, casting a look around to make sure no one was in earshot before mentioning the chest she had found in the secret room.

Jackson's focus sharpened. 'Do you know what you are supposed to do with them, the dagger and medallion?'

It was her turn to grimace. 'Brother Owen died before he could tell me. All I know is that I have to get to the place where the virus was first created and cleanse it with blood. I'm assuming that means my blood, and I cut myself with the dagger, but I'm only guessing.'

'It's okay, we'll figure it out,' Jackson said, leaning close and embracing her again. 'We have to.'

She never wanted to leave Jackson's arms, but too soon his duty called him away and, after collecting the chest, Justice made her way to the lab to see Hannah. Maybe her friend would have some more ideas about what to do with the items it contained. At the very least, there was a safe in the lab where she could put the chest so Rona and any of the Legion people could not get their hands on it.

Maybe there was something in the books she had missed, a vital clue, anything that would tell her where the Legion had created the virus in the first place.

Of course, she could just ask one of the Legion scientists who were supposedly working with Hannah to come up with a new cure, but while Jackson might trust them enough to allow them access to the compound and the lab, Justice wasn't sold on the idea. These people had been hunting her all her life, determined to kill her. Their ancestors had created the freak virus in the first place, and after failing to kill her, the new lot had then gone and set loose another virus.

She'd thought Marcus Callaghan had been the worst kind of evil she would ever encounter. If Rona thought unleashing a wave of freaks not even the wardens could fight had been a good idea, she had to be even more deranged than Marcus and his old masters.

In the lab, Justice hovered in the doorway. Two men and a woman, all of them wearing lab coats that had seen better days, were huddled on one side of a desk as Hannah peered into a microscope.

Heaving a sigh, Hannah lifted her head and gave a glum look to her companions. 'It didn't work—again. We need to go back to the start.'

Justice made to leave. Hannah was busy, with important work to do. Justice would find another time to catch up with her friend and someplace else to hide the chest. But Hannah turned around and spotted her, a wide smile brightening her tired features as she pushed away from the desk and hurried over to the doorway.

'I'm so glad you're back.' She wrapped her arms around Justice and hugged her tight, squeezing the chest between them.

'Ouch,' Hannah said as she released Justice and stepped back, rubbing at her torso. 'What's that?'

With a glance at the scientists, who had stopped talking and were staring their way, Justice simply said, 'I'll tell you later. You're busy. I shouldn't be disturbing you.'

Hannah shook her head and latched on to Justice's arm. 'No, it's fine. I need a break anyway. We're going around in circles, coming up against the same problem. My head is spinning and nothing is making sense. I need to come at it from a different angle. First, you need to tell me what happened at the monastery. Did Brother Owen tell you how you are supposed to fulfil Gaea's purpose?'

Not liking the intent way the Legion scientists were watching them, Justice pulled on Hannah's arm and led her out of the lab. 'Let's talk about it somewhere private.' Not only did she not want the scientists listening in as she detailed what the contents of the chest were, she didn't want to tell Hannah how Brother Owen had died with strangers watching on.

They headed to the common room and a wave of home-coming swept over Justice as Barrett bustled away to get her and Hannah something to eat. As he fussed over them both, she settled into her seat in a corner of the empty dining room, took a deep breath, and recounted what had happened. After she was finished, it was her turn to bombard Hannah with questions.

'What happened in Brimfield? Last I heard, Andy had lost contact with both teams and was sending someone to rescue you and Hanson and the others. Where is Hanson? Is he okay?'

To her surprise, Hannah blushed.

'I kissed him,' she said. 'Hanson.'

'What?' Justice stared at her friend, amazed as the blush in her cheeks deepened.

'He rescued me. Well, he was going to, but I'd already

escaped. Then he was hanging off the roof, a freak attached to his leg, and I was sure he was going to fall and die like Councillor Dillon. Then he managed to kick the freak off his leg and Carstairs got him onto the roof. And I was just so relieved I latched on and … kissed him.'

Justice's head reeled. Councillor Dillon was dead? Hannah had kissed Hanson? 'What did he do?'

'He kissed me back. And then he shoved me at Carstairs and went off to fight more freaks. We haven't really spoken since.' Hannah frowned. 'I think he's been avoiding me.' Then she gave a rueful shrug. 'Not that I've been out of the lab much since we got back here, and he's been busy doing missions for Jackson. But I get the definite feeling he is avoiding me.'

Her blush faded, and sadness filled her eyes. 'He is one of my best friends and I screwed it up by kissing him. He must be so embarrassed; he doesn't want anything to do with me anymore.'

Justice shook her head. 'I don't believe that.' From what she'd seen, Hanson cared deeply for her friend. For all his bravado and cheeky nature, she was sure he was not the kind of guy to kiss a girl and then walk away. Something else had to be going on.

Before she could say something, Hannah gave herself a shake. 'Anyway, enough about Hanson. I am so glad you are back. Things have been really hectic since Rona and her people showed up. My head is still spinning from the fact she deliberately made a new virus and was planning on using it against us, all because she blamed us for her sister's death. Now that she knows it was Marcus that drove her sister to do what she did, she's been trying to do everything she can to help, but the virus is out there. So many people have died, and she can never make up for what she allowed to happen. But if I could just figure out why the virus mutated, we might be able to come up with a way to control these new freaks.'

At the mention of Rona, Justice stiffened. 'Her sister?' Then she listened in horror as Hannah told her why Rona had targeted the wardens.

'She went to Brimfield planning to kill everyone who she felt played a part in Karline's death. She was about to kill Hanson, with Councillor Dillon egging her on, when Jackson arrived and talked her out of it and told her what really happened to Karline. Then a horde of the new freaks showed up, and she fought at Jackson's side. He saved her life, and that's when she realised she was wrong.'

Too little, too late, Justice thought as she remembered Brother Owen's death and the way Shelton had been devastated by freaks. Hannah was right. Nothing would make up for what Rona had done, but perhaps they did need her help to stop the new freaks. If Hannah couldn't find a cure or reconfigure the gas to be able to control them, more people were going to die.

Justice put the chest on top of the table and placed her hand on the scales. Hannah gaped as the previously seamless chest opened up.

Justice reached in and grabbed out the dagger and the medallion. As before, she felt a tingle in the birthmark when she clasped the medallion, but when she switched hands, she still felt nothing from the dagger.

She placed the dagger and medallion back in the chest, closed it, and faced Hannah. 'I need to know where the Legion first created the virus, five hundred years ago. That's where I should have been to dispense Gaea's justice. The site needs to be cleansed with my blood. Do you think the Legion scientists would know where their ancestors made the virus?'

'I do.'

The words hadn't come from Hannah. Justice twisted in her seat and found Rona standing behind her, Jackson at her side.

Swallowing down her instinctive dislike of this woman, Justice stood up. 'Tell me.'

'The original Legion labs are located beneath the place that later became the centre for fighting the freaks.'

Jackson's eyes widened. 'High Command.'

Rona nodded.

Justice gave a hard smile. 'Well, it's a good thing I know the acting-general.'

FORTY-NINE

From the safety of the airship, Jackson looked out over High Command.

The sea of freaks roaming in the streets of what had once been the safest town in the country made it impossible for them to set foot in the place. The parade ground directly in front of the citadel teemed with freaks, blocking access to the medical centre Rona said they needed to reach to access the Legion's underground lab. Bleakness wormed its way into Jackson as he noted the number of wardens among the infected. He'd only been gone four days. How could the freaks have taken over and infected the wardens living there so quickly?

He'd sent a large number of wardens under his command to fight the freaks in the towns, but there should have been plenty of wardens remaining to stop the freaks from taking over.

Where was Captain Murphy? Was he one of the freaks now prowling the parade ground, with blood streaming from their eyes as they stared into the sky, trying to work out how to get to the uninfected people flying above their heads?

A splash of white in the periphery caught his eye, and he

turned his head, a grin forming at the sight of a familiar face on top of the citadel roof.

Captain Callum Murphy.

A large number of wardens crowded behind him, all heavily armed. Many of them looked weary, but remained vigilant as they patrolled the edges of the building.

Jackson called out for Michaelson to direct them closer to the citadel roof so he could talk to Murphy.

'You're a welcome sight, Acting-General Kyle,' Murphy said, head tilted and a hand shading his eyes as he gazed up at Jackson. 'I hope that thing is fuelled up. It's going to take dozens of trips to get all our people out of here.' He waved toward the wardens arrayed around him and then pointed at the nearby roofs. More clusters of wardens stood guard, and it gladdened Jackson's heart to know that most of those he had left here were still alive.

Then he delivered the bad news to Murphy. 'This isn't a rescue. We need to get under the citadel, to stop all this.'

Though he was aware Justice had doubts about what she was supposed to do here, he was sure she would figure it out in time. She had to.

If not, it would be better to go down fighting than not try at all.

Murphy's expression tightened as Jackson filled him in, then he turned to survey the wardens on the citadel roof with him for a moment. 'We do this, make it to the lab, then we finally get that second chance you were telling me about, right? A chance to decide our own destiny, choose our future.'

'That's right.'

'Well, that's something worth fighting for.'

With a grim nod, Murphy moved away to talk to the leaders among his gathered wardens. Then he returned to Jackson. 'They're in. It's what we were created for, after all, to fight freaks. Time to fulfil our charter and get rid of every last one of them.'

Pride swelled in Jackson as he surveyed the men and women under his command. Using hand-held radios, they filled in those stranded on the other rooftops on the plan. All these wardens were ready to sacrifice their lives so that he, Justice, and their crew had a chance to get to the underground labs.

Onboard the airship, Jackson turned to face the people he would be going into battle with for the last time, meeting the eyes of his wardens and those who had joined them along the way.

Justice met his gaze with a determined nod. At her side, Hannah and Hanson stood ready, while Jensen and the remaining wardens from Brimfield handed out weapons. Rona stood to the left of Justice, while the mercenary commander was loitering between both women. Despite his dubious occupation, Isaac Smith was a good man, and Jackson knew he would do whatever it took to protect the woman he called his little sister. No matter what, all of the people on this airship were committed to getting her to the lab. Nothing else mattered.

FIFTY

As the airship hovered over the citadel roof and wardens began to descend rope ladders to join Captain Murphy's forces, a tingle started in Justice's hands and she gasped. This was just like when she had been chained up in the dining room back at the mine compound on her twenty-fifth birthday. The tingle had signalled the approach of sunrise when she was to dispense Gaea's justice and it had spread to her entire body as dawn got closer.

It was the same tingle she felt when she clasped the medallion in her hands. Surely this meant they were in the right place. Rona had been telling the truth when she said the hidden lab had been underneath the army barracks that became High Command after the virus was unleashed.

The gall of the first Legion masters must have been incredible, to choose this place to make their virus.

Back then, the barracks had been situated close to the main medical centre where the scientists had been working on a cure for the common cold. Perhaps some of those soldiers had been members of the Legion, as well as some of the scientists?

The tingle in her hands deepened, spreading to her arms,

and Justice wondered if she needed to land at all. Maybe this was close enough and Jackson wouldn't have to fight through hundreds of freaks to get her to the underground lab.

She knelt, pulled off her backpack, and grabbed out the chest, placing her birthmark on the embossed scales. As she opened the chest, a shadow blocked out the sun.

Justice looked up and frowned when she spotted Rona standing over her.

'What are you doing?' The leader of the Legion's voice was harsh, expression suspicious as she glared at Justice.

Justice snapped the chest lid down. 'None of your business.' She clutched the chest close and scrambled to her feet.

'If it has anything to do with why we need to get into the old lab, then it is my business.' Rona rubbed at her arms and then curled her hands into fists.

Justice didn't want to expose the contents of the chest to her, but maybe Rona was right. This was to do with the Legion, after all. Besides, she still wasn't sure what she was supposed to do with the medallion and dagger, and maybe there was something in the history of the Legion that would give her a clue. With a sigh, she reopened the chest and showed the contents to Rona.

'I retrieved these from Gaea's monastery. Her instructions are for me to wash clean the sins of the fathers with blood. I'm guessing that means my blood is needed for some kind of ritual, but your freaks killed Brother Owen before he could tell me exactly what I was supposed to do.' Her tone was accusatory.

Rona winced, then stretched out a hand to run her fingers over the medallion. Justice watched her closely to see if she had a reaction. Rona gave no indication of it as her hand moved to the dagger. She snatched her hand back, shaking her fingers.

Justice's eyes widened. 'You felt it. The tingle.'

Rona stiffened. 'I don't know what you're talking about.'

'Then why did you pull away so fast?'

'The dagger is sharp. I didn't want to cut myself on it and taint this ritual of yours with my blood.'

The explanation made sense, but Justice wasn't buying it. Whether she wanted to admit it or not, Rona had felt something when she touched the dagger, though not the medallion.

Justice prised the medallion from the velvet interior and slung the chain around her neck, tucking it into the front of her body armour. The tingle in her body intensified when it came in contact with her skin. Then she picked up the dagger and held it out to Rona.

The other woman backed away, hands in front of her, palms facing out. 'I told you, I don't want to taint your ritual.'

'Fine,' Justice said, sticking the dagger in the sheath on her belt. There would be time to sort out what role, if any, Rona was meant to play once they reached the lab.

For now, she knew in her heart that being above the lab was not going to cut it. Instinct told her she needed to get to the source of the virus. She only hoped that when she did, Rona would be willing to admit she had felt the tingle in her fingers when she'd touched the dagger.

She closed the empty chest and shoved it back into her backpack before going in search of Jackson. He was busy arranging his troops, both those on the airship and the ones ringing High Command in an assortment of vehicles. They needed to wait until all their combined forces, warden and Legion, were in place before attempting to get to the lab.

Isaac had also put out a call for his mercenaries to head to High Command, but with the sketchy radio service since the run of severe storms, it was hard to know how many had heard him or if they were in a position to come.

The wardens had done all they could to protect the town, but without walls there had been no way to keep the freaks out. So, the wardens and the rescued townspeople were now holed up in buildings with barricades on all the doors and windows. They were fast running out of supplies and the situation was getting dire.

Justice had to get to the underground lab for any of them to have a hope of surviving.

That is, if she survived the trip to the lab.

FIFTY-ONE

The whistle blew, signalling the last of his people were in place. On the roof of the citadel with Justice and his team, Jackson gave the order to move out. Many of those fighting alongside him today would die, and their deaths would be on his head. Despite the weight of guilt that pressed down on him, Jackson knew it had to be done. The only way to secure a future for the survivors was to get Justice to the lab.

Rona, too, if what Justice suspected was true.

As he moved along the line of wardens waiting to use rope ladders taken from the airship to descend the side wall of the citadel, he looked over to where the leader of the Legion waited for her turn with a small group of her people. Despite her being from the Legion, he had to admire her guts for admitting her mistakes and committing to fix them. In that, she reminded him of Miranda Wilson. He only hoped the quest for revenge for her sister's death wouldn't lead Rona to her death as well.

The first group of the wardens reached the ground and took up positions at the parade ground end of a driveway that led to the transport depot behind the citadel. Thanks to a large metal gate blocking access from the parade ground, the freaks had been unable to get around to this side of the citadel, but that safety net would not last long. With dozens of freaks roaming the parade ground, they would soon be spotted once they moved out.

In the distance, shouts and the sound of gunfire rose as wardens stationed on the roofs within the city itself started their diversion.

With luck, most of the freaks amassed in front of the citadel would leave to investigate the sounds of violence, leaving fewer for Jackson and his team to wade through. He wasn't counting on it. He had his best men going first to clear the parade ground before he allowed Justice to set foot on it.

When it was her turn to descend one of the rope ladders, he was at her side. They reached the ground, and waited for Rona to join them before setting off along the driveway toward the gate that was the only thing separating them from a horde of freaks. His men were ahead of them, ready to take point, and he gave the signal.

The gates opened, and his wardens streamed through, shooting at the freaks waiting for them.

Snarls and gunfire filled the air, and soon a voice called back that the way was clear. Jackson ushered Justice to the gate and peered through. The bodies of over a dozen freaks were sprawled on the parade ground, and there was no sign any of his wardens had been injured.

More freaks were swarming out of the buildings on the other side of the parade ground, rage contorting their faces as they headed toward them.

The wardens raced forward to meet them, firing as they went, while Jackson and his smaller team ran diagonally across the parade ground, making for the medical centre. From there, they would be able to reach the tunnel that not only led to the old medical centre where Wallace had died, but also, according to Rona, hid the access tunnel to the underground lab.

She ran alongside Justice, pistol in her hand, features drawn. She still wore the red body armour, refusing his offer of Ward armour. He hoped hers was as sturdy as theirs as she was going to need good protection.

The sounds of fighting behind them were dwindling, the gunshots coming further apart. The sheer number of freaks was overwhelming his wardens. He urged Justice and the others to hurry, desperate to get to the medical centre as fresh sounds of fighting came at his rear. He didn't need to look over his shoulder to know that some freaks had got past the first team and were harrying them from behind.

He reached the door to the medical centre and wrenched it open, ushering Justice and Rona inside, the rest of the team behind them.

He called out to Isaac. 'Get Justice to the lab. I'll hold the door.'

Justice shot him a horrified look, but Isaac grabbed her arm, dragging her away as Jackson turned to face his team.

Jensen glared at him. 'You should be with Justice.'

'I need to stay here to stop any freaks from getting in.'

Jensen shook his head. 'We'll hold the door.' He gestured to the others arrayed around him, Hannah and Hanson among them. 'If there are any freaks in the tunnels, Justice will need you to protect her.'

Though torn, Jackson nodded and saluted. 'Good luck, Lieutenant.'

'You too, sir.'

Then Jackson turned to follow Justice, determined to get this done so he could return to his wardens. He caught up at the tunnel entrance, finding Justice arguing with Rona.

'I am not going without Jackson.'

'Don't be stupid. If you are the only one who can complete this ritual, you have to go. You're more important than any one man.'

'That's a bit harsh, don't you think?' Jackson called out as he came around the corner.

'Jackson!' Justice wrenched her arm free of Isaac's grip and ran toward him.

'She's not wrong, you know,' Jackson said as he hugged Justice. 'Getting you to the lab is more important than anything.'

'Not to me,' she said. 'What's the point of securing a better future if you're not in it?'

'Let's get this done then.' He urged her toward the door blocking the tunnel access. Time to end this.

FIFTY-TWO

Hannah wiped sweaty palms on her armoured pants and gripped her pistol tight as she waited for the first freak to get through the door to the medical centre, trying to ignore the nausea roiling in her belly.

She could do this. They had to buy Justice time.

'You shouldn't be here. You should have gone with Justice.' Hanson's voice was grim. 'It's not too late.'

She shook her head. 'I'm not leaving. You guys need me.' The number of freaks they were facing was staggering. It would take all of them to stop the freaks from gaining access to the tunnel.

Hanson gave a low growl. 'Fine, but stay behind me. I won't let anything happen to you.'

She stared at him, getting caught in his intense gaze, the depth of feeling in his voice. Maybe she was wrong, maybe he did have feelings for her after all, and she hadn't ruined everything with her kiss.

She wanted to ask him, to tell him how much she cared about him, but a scream rang out nearby and Hanson turned to face the door again. Hannah forced herself to focus. After the battle, after Justice had completed her ritual, she would confront Hanson then.

The first freak appeared, and Jensen shot it in the head. Then more appeared. Soon there was no time to think about anything other than staying alive. She lost count of the number of freaks she shot, even as they were pushed back further into the medical centre.

Screams, shouts, and gunfire drowned out all sounds.

Then she heard Hanson call her name.

She spun around and found a freak had come at her from the side, so close she couldn't raise her pistol in time. The freak reeled backward, a bullet hole appearing in its forehead. She looked up to see Hanson lowering his gun, and she gave him a quick smile even as more freaks swirled between them. Someone grabbed her arm, and she spun to see Carstairs beside her. He pulled her back down the corridor, and she struggled against his grip.

'I have to help Hanson,' she yelled.

Carstairs didn't let go. 'There's too many freaks between us and them. You'll never make it.'

The truth of his words stung, but Hannah still wasn't ready to give up. She peered over her shoulder, looking for Hanson.

He spotted her and gave her a look filled with so much anguish it caused tears to sting her eyes. 'Carstairs, get her out of here,' he called out. Then he disappeared from view.

Gulping back sobs, Hannah stopped resisting as Carstairs pushed her ahead of him and through a doorway. She stumbled into the room when he released his grip on her arm.

'I'll come back and let you out when it's safe,' he said.

She spun around in time to see him slam the door shut, with him on the other side. She ran to the door, grabbing the handle and trying to wrench it open, but he must have jammed the lock. She banged on the door, but there was no response. She was trapped in there, while everyone she cared about was fighting for their lives.

'Damn you, Carstairs,' she yelled, scanning the room for another way out, but there were no windows. She sank to the floor, her back to the door, tears filling her eyes as she thought about Hanson.

What if he was dead? What if she never got the chance to tell him she loved him?

FIFTY-THREE

The confined quarters of the tunnel got on Rona's nerves as she followed Justice. Jackson was behind them, along with the infuriating mercenary commander, Isaac Smith. Rona curled up her mouth at the thought of him. Typical of his type, not caring who he fought for as long as he was getting paid. Though she had to wonder why he had taken on a job as bodyguard to Justice. That seemed a step down for a commander. Surely he could have passed the job off to one of his men. But then, maybe the wardens were paying him a substantial amount to cover having the best of his team protect Justice.

At first, when Justice and Isaac had arrived at the compound after what appeared to be a trip of numerous days, Rona had thought they were romantically involved. That would have explained why he had agreed to act as her bodyguard. He was certainly attentive enough. One look at Jackson and Justice together had wiped that notion out of her head.

The two were clearly devoted to each other, and his actions earlier, offering to sacrifice himself to get Justice where she needed to go, and her unwillingness to go on without him, showed each would do anything for the other.

And she'd detected no animosity or jealousy on Isaac's part. He treated Justice more familiarly than anyone else, but without showing any sign of romantic interest. So, it had to be money keeping him at Justice's side. As soon as he got her to the lab and was compensated, he would no doubt disappear to take on the next high-paying job that came along.

The lab.

Her nerves twinged.

Was she doing the right thing, showing Justice where her ancestors had created the first freak virus?

The virus had been meant to level the playing field, to make humanity take notice of the damage they were doing to the Earth and show them they needed to work together to ensure a better future for all. After it all went wrong, and the wardens had been created, the Legion had come up with a new purpose, to take control in the chaos to force the survivors to play fair. That purpose had been distorted even further over the years, until the masters had been determined to rule the Earth at any cost.

The death of Justice had been instrumental to their plan, a plan that had gone the way of all the others.

Now Rona had a chance to fulfil the promise she had made to her father. Not to stand at her sister's side while she ruled the Legion. With Karline's death, that dream was lost forever, but she could still help to create a better world.

She'd thought that by getting rid of the wardens, the humans would be able to achieve the Legion's original dream, for everyone to be equal. With their enhanced genetics and superior strength, wardens would never consider themselves the same as the humans. At least, that's what she'd thought.

Then she'd met Jackson, a man determined to create a future where there was no need for segregation, or for wardens to protect humans. Without freaks, their role as protectors would be obsolete. The current wardens would have to assimilate into society, find jobs, mix with humans and half-breeds. It wouldn't be easy for them, after generations of prejudice between the different groups, but she had to admit it was almost the same as the vision her father had worked toward.

An intersecting tunnel appeared ahead and Justice stopped, waiting for Rona to tell her which way to go.

This was it. One way led to the labs, while the other led to the quarters used by the scientists sequestered here. She could take them to the quarters and lose them in the rabbit warren of rooms and tunnels on that side. Or she could do what she had promised and lead Justice to the lab so she could perform her ritual with the dagger and medallion.

Rona's fingertips tingled with the memory of the jolt she'd received when she touched the dagger.

Ever since, she had felt as if a current was running through her body, not unpleasant but slowly building in strength the closer she got to the lab. Justice knew she'd felt something, and from the way she rubbed at her arms, Rona guessed the other woman also felt the current. She would know if they were to go in the wrong direction.

With a sigh, wishing she didn't feel so conflicted, Rona pointed to the tunnel that would take them to the labs.

'Sure this is the way?' Isaac brushed past her and shone his torch down both tunnels. Then he eyed her, with eyebrows raised and a sardonic twist to his lips. 'You wouldn't be trying to get us lost, would you?'

Rona glared at him, hating that his observations were too close to the mark. 'Unlike you, I keep my word.'

His eyes widened. 'What's that supposed to mean?'

She snorted. 'As if you don't know.' He was the commander of the Righteous. All jobs were under his control. He was also the only one who could have given his men the order to withdraw from the battle her father had paid them to assist with. If they hadn't withdrawn, the Legion forces would have won. Instead, they had been overrun and her father had died in the hasty retreat.

'Listen up, I don't know what you've heard or why you think I would dishonour my word, but I'm telling you straight that I have never reneged on a contract.'

'Unless someone offers you more money, of course. Tell me, Commander, how much would it take for someone to contract you to kill Justice? Double what the wardens are paying you to protect her? Triple?'

His eyes glittered, mouth flattening into a line. 'They're not paying me anything.' He turned and walked down the tunnel toward the lab.

Justice frowned as she glanced at Rona. 'Isaac is a good man. Whatever it is you think he did, I'm betting you're wrong.' She followed Isaac into the tunnel.

Conscious of Jackson and the others watching on, she hurried after Justice, thinking over what had just happened.

Isaac Smith was not the kind of man to risk his life for nothing.

Maybe she was wrong about him not having feelings for Justice. To think otherwise, that he might be doing this because it was the right thing to do, did not sit well with her perception of him.

And if she was wrong about this, what else was she wrong about?

Rona strode past Justice and caught up to Isaac. He cast her a sideways glance but otherwise ignored her as they traversed the tunnel, the light of their torches casting shadows ahead of them. Then the shadows lessened, the light became more apparent, and an uneasy feeling settled in the pit of Rona's stomach. She switched off her torch and gestured for Isaac to do the same.

After giving her a measured look, he complied.

Instead of being plunged into darkness, light still caused shadows to appear in the tunnel ahead of them. Indicating to

Isaac and Justice to remain silent, Rona crept forward, dirt and rocks under her feet. There were more rocks than in the tunnels they had already travelled through. She reached the next turn and peered around the corner, stifling a groan at the splash of sunlight illuminating a pile of rocks and dirt in the centre of the tunnel.

Part of the roof had caved in. She listened intently, but could hear nothing save for her own breathing. She turned and made her way back to where she had left the others, the light behind her making it hard to see anything.

She banged into something unyielding and swallowed a gasp. Her hands ran over the obstacle and found body armour encasing a muscular torso. A light bloomed and she looked up to see Isaac smirking down at her.

She pushed away. 'What is it with you people and black clothing?' she muttered quietly.

His smirk deepened. 'It's easier to hide the bloodstains, and to sneak up on people in the dark.'

She scowled. He would have had no trouble seeing her. Yet he had made no effort to stop her banging into him. She switched her own torch back on, taking satisfaction in shining it in his face and making him wince.

She looked over to where Justice was standing beside Jackson. 'The lab is just around the corner but part of the roof has collapsed in the tunnel heading to it. It's open to the outside. We'll need to be quiet as we work our way past the blockade.'

She didn't need to tell them why.

With the tunnel exposed, any freaks aboveground could access the tunnel system. It may have just been pure luck none had found their way down here already. The thought of fighting these new freaks in the confines of the tunnels sent a shiver down her spine. She stiffened her shoulders and turned back the way she had come, quickly rounding the corner and making her way to the pile of debris blocking the centre of the tunnel.

Isaac brushed past her and aimed his weapon into the open expanse above the tunnel, then gestured for Justice and the others to make their way to him. Without taking his eyes off the hole, Isaac put out a hand to help Justice clamber over the dirt pile. He made no such gesture when it was Rona's turn. Not that she needed or wanted his help.

Rona breathed a sigh of relief once they had all passed the hole without incidence. There was only a short distance to go to get to the lab, and they would be able to lock themselves in so Justice could perform her ritual in safety.

A scramble came from the tunnel to the left of Rona and a freak sprang for her.

A loud crack sounded, and a hole blossomed in the middle of the freak's forehead. Rona spun around to see Isaac lowering his weapon.

'Hurry,' he said in a tense tone. 'That will draw more of them for sure.'

Ahead, Jackson and Justice started to run, and Rona hurried to catch up with them. The sound of snarling came from deep within the tunnel and she knew Isaac was right. More freaks were on their way. They had to get inside the lab before any caught up to them.

If the lab was still intact.

With freaks closing in, Rona dreaded arriving at their destination and finding more holes in the roof or walls. She ran the last hundred metres and threw herself around the corner, running into Justice's back.

Jackson stopped in front of a solid metal door, prising at the electronic lock while Justice held the torch to give him light.

'Move aside,' Rona said, roughly brushing Justice out of the way in her haste.

Shots came from behind her; Isaac firing at the freaks on their heels.

Forcing the realisation that they were trapped from her

mind, Rona focused on the keypad. After five hundred years, there was no guarantee the code would still work, but it was all she had. She was just thankful the lab ran on self-perpetuating energy and there would be power to disarm the lock.

Sweat stinging her eyes, she punched in the code and almost sagged in relief when the red light changed to green. She pushed the door open and ushered the others in. Isaac entered last, and she looked behind him to see three dead freaks, all neatly shot between the eyes, on the floor of the tunnel. She could also hear more of them on their way. Many more.

If Justice's ritual didn't work, there would be no way for them to leave the lab.

She slammed the door shut and reengaged the lock before switching on the lights and turning to scan the space they were now in.

The lab was small, much smaller than she had anticipated. It seemed inconceivable that the virus could have originated in this tiny lab. As more and more lights turned on, she realised her initial impression was mistaken.

The first room was small, but a long corridor led away on the other side and it seemed to go on for ages. On either side of the corridor, she could see heavy-duty doors with reinforced glass windows.

That must have been where they housed the humans they had been testing the virus on before things got out of hand.

Indeed, the closer she looked, the more she could see the damage caused when the freaks created by the mutated cure had got out. Tables in the lab were scattered or broken, and so were many of the glass windows in the holding cells. It appeared the reinforced glass had been no match for the rage-enhanced strength of the test subjects. Rona was just glad the labs had been cleared out before the citadel above became the hub for the special forces soldiers who volunteered to become the first wardens. They would not have to navigate around skeletal remains as Justice performed her ritual.

She looked over to find Justice and the others standing together in the middle of the lab.

Justice had the medallion around her neck and held the dagger in both hands.

At the sight of the dagger, the current in Rona's body surged, and she held back a gasp, determined not to make a sound.

Even so, Isaac's head swung around and he fixed a hard gaze on her.

She lifted her chin and glared back at him. He may have saved her life back in the tunnel, but that didn't mean she was willing to forgive him for reneging on the contract, an action that had ultimately led to her father's death.

He gave her a smirk and turned back to Justice. 'Well then, little sister. We got you to the lab. Now what?'

FIFTY-FOUR

The tingle in her body bordered on painful as Justice stepped further into the dusty and dank old lab. She spun in a slow circle. To help focus, she closed her eyes and listened to what her body was telling her.

There.

The tingle was stronger in that direction.

Justice opened her eyes and walked forward, starting down the long hallway. Most of the doors to what had once been containment cells were closed, though a few gaped open and Justice shivered as she passed them. In the middle of the long hallway, she stopped in front of a partially open door, the shiver enveloping her entire body. She stretched out a hand to push the door fully open, expecting to see another bleak containment room, but instead it opened into a narrow corridor that led to a closed door with a hazard sign at eye level.

Justice moved down the corridor, conscious of the barred windows on either side that would have allowed the scientists to see into the closest containment cells. Dark stains covered the room on her left, turning the walls into a patchwork of rusted brown and faded white. She pulled her gaze away and focused on the door in front of her. Like the one that had led into the main lab area, this one was locked with a keypad, the red light flashing steadily.

'Rona,' Justice called out, stepping to the side so the other woman could approach the door. 'Does the same code work for this door?'

Rona gave her a tense look. 'No.'

'We can get in through there,' Jackson said, pointing to the stained containment room beside them. 'The window into the room behind that door has been smashed.'

Justice grimaced at the thought of entering the cell.

'You're sure that's where you need to go?' Isaac asked.

'Yes.'

Justice gazed at Rona. They'd answered at the same time, confirming her suspicions that the woman from the Legion was feeling the same thing she was. They had to get into the room behind the locked door, the sense of urgency compelling her to step past Isaac and follow Jackson.

There was no doubt the dark stains on the floor, walls, and ceiling were blood. Something terrible had taken place in this room, but Justice did not allow herself to contemplate what that might have been. The glass shards sticking to the windowsill had long since fallen away, and she allowed Jackson to lift her over and into the room beyond.

Isaac offered to help Rona, but she sneered at him before climbing over the edge.

Soon Jackson and Isaac joined them and they surveyed the new room.

As with the main area, the lights had come on with their entry, illuminating a compact laboratory that reminded Justice of the setup at the mine compound. Hannah would have loved it, if it had still been in working condition.

A wall of what appeared to be refrigerator units had been smashed almost beyond recognition, while every item of furniture and equipment had been destroyed in what had clearly been a bloody and brutal event.

A shiver swept over Justice and she rubbed her arms, sure no one would have escaped this lab alive or uninfected. There was no telling how many scientists had been in here when their test subjects had turned on them. Still, it was not the signs of the past carnage that Justice fixed on.

Her gaze was drawn to a metal bed frame that had been turned on its side, the mattress long since rotted away. Chains were still attached to the side of the bed frame, for all the good they had done.

It was here, Justice knew, that she had to perform the ritual. She gestured for Rona to join her as she stepped closer to the bed. Rona shook her head, staying back against the wall near the broken window.

'I need you, Rona. You are part of this as well.'

'This has got nothing to do with me,' said Rona. 'This is your ritual, so get on with it.'

Justice frowned at her but let it go for now, sure Rona would not be able to deny the truth much longer. Going by the sensations surging through her own body, Rona would have to give in soon. For now, she simply pulled the medallion from the neckline of her body armour and slipped it over her head. She awkwardly clasped the medallion as she took the dagger from its sheath and cut a diagonal slash into her right palm, through the centre of the birthmark of Gaea's scales.

She couldn't explain why she did so, the actions feeling right as she wiped the dagger on her leg and sheathed it. Then she placed her bloodied palm onto the scales embossed on one side of the medallion and held it over the bed frame, watching as drops of her blood fell and dripped onto the chains that had bound the original freak in place for the Legion's scientists to experiment on.

Nothing happened.

Justice looked up, meaning to call Rona over so they could

complete the ritual together, but a loud crash and yelling distracted her. It was coming from the main room. Justice heard Hanson's voice, but it was quickly drowned out in a sea of screams.

Jackson jerked, weapon coming up as Lieutenant Jensen appeared in the doorway of the cell behind Rona, features contorted with rage as he sprang forward. More yells and the sound of shots firing came from behind him in the main lab area, but Justice couldn't think about that. All she could see was Jensen, blood pouring from his eyes.

Jensen jumped over the windowsill and landed in a low crouch as Rona lifted her weapon as she hurried backward.

Jackson fired, and Jensen's body jolted.

Jackson had used his stun gun, firing again and again to hold Jensen back.

'Hurry up and compete your ritual,' he called to Justice, distraught. 'Before we lose him for good.'

FIFTY-FIVE

'RONA!'

Pulling her eyes away from the infected warden, Rona looked over to where Justice held out a hand for her.

'I need you.'

The tingling in her body intensified, and Rona held back a gasp as she felt herself being tugged forward. It was as if her body no longer belonged to her. She wanted to turn around, to aim her pistol at the warden and shoot him between the eyes. Kyle's sentiment toward his man would get them all killed. However, her body was locked on course, pulling her to Justice until she stood facing the young woman her people had been trying to kill for twenty-five years.

A bitter twist to her mouth at the fate that had seen them working together, Rona fought to stop raising her hand. It was impossible. Whatever had her in its grip was far stronger, and as waves of tingles swept over her body, she could no longer hold back a gasp.

Justice's eyes widened, and she plucked the dagger from her sheath and placed it in Rona's outstretched hand.

As soon as the dagger touched her palm, the force holding Rona prisoner let go, the release so sudden she stumbled sideways and would have fallen onto the bed frame if Justice hadn't reached out to steady her.

'Do it. Now, before it is too late.'

Impelled by the horror in Justice's voice, feeling as though she was watching all this unfold from above, Rona holstered her pistol and used the dagger to slice into her palm as she had seen Justice do. Justice held the bloodied hand that still clutched the medallion out and Rona grasped it with her cut palm. Blood dripped from the cut to fall onto the mangled bed frame, mingling with Justice's blood.

Sensation bombarded her body, and she cried out as light flared all around her and Justice. She closed her eyes, unable to bear the light as a gigantic wave of energy swept through her body and burst out of her.

Then the light faded, and she opened her eyes to silence.

The only sound was that of her breathing and Justice's.

She looked behind her to see that Kyle and the others had frozen, the warden who had been infected suspended in mid-air as he sprang for Isaac, a snarl on his face and blood splatters hanging in the air in front of him.

What the hell was going on?

She turned back to Justice and saw that instead of looking at the frozen battle behind them, her eyes were fixed on a spot to the left. Rona looked that way and gasped, brain scrambling to process what she was seeing.

FIFTY-SIX

Justice gaped at the floating apparition that hovered a foot above the floor of the lab, a nimbus of light surrounding it.

Gaea.

She looked exactly as she had when she had appeared to Justice in the void. Impossibly beautiful, so bright and wondrous, that she hardly seemed real.

As Rona's startled oath rang out, Justice remembered to breathe, to blink as Gaea floated toward where they still stood with their hands clasped around the medallion, their mingled blood dripping on the mangled bed frame.

'Well done, my daughters. You have completed the tasks set down for you before you were born.'

Justice heard a strangled gasp from Rona before she said, 'I'm not supposed to be here. This was not my destiny. It was hers.' Rona pulled her hand free from the medallion and pointed at Justice.

Gaea shook her head, ethereal tendrils of glowing hair floating around her face. 'No, my child. This was always your destiny. It was why you were born to the Legion, to make amends for the wrongs that have been perpetrated against humanity. I needed children born from each side to come together to ensure true justice would prevail.'

'I don't understand,' said Justice. 'There was never any mention in the myths or the Book of Justice of someone else being involved.'

'That was to protect Rona and Karline. If the Legion had discovered one of their own was to take part in the ritual to cleanse humankind of the taint they had created, they would have done whatever it took to destroy their line.'

'Karline was supposed to do this, wasn't she? Not me.' Rona's voice was thick, tears brimming in her eyes when Justice glanced her way.

'No, Rona. Your sister had a different destiny. She was supposed to take control of the Legion and to stand at your side as you and Justice completed the ritual. She would then have led the Legion on a new path, one dedicated to healing the Earth. Instead, she chose to take her life to stop Marcus Callaghan from subverting the Legion and creating an even darker future.'

'Bring her back.' Immense grief throbbed in Rona's voice. 'You brought Justice back from the dead, and the monk. You can bring my sister back too.'

Gaea shook her head. 'Were I to undo your sister's sacrifice, to return to life those who have fallen to see destiny prevail, it would take all the power your ritual has generated. There would be nothing left to cure those afflicted by the disease you yourself unleashed. Is that what you want? To bring your sister back and let those afflicted with the new freak virus to remain as they are?'

She then turned to Justice. 'If I do this, those who have fallen while protecting you would also be restored. Your mother, and the monks who raised and cared for you. Humankind would then have to make their own way without my intervention. They would live or die according to the vagaries of fate, starting with those assembled here with you today.'

Gaea's gaze shifted from Justice to Rona. 'Think hard, my daughters, because your choice cannot be undone.'

Justice looked to Rona, seeing hope warring with uncertainty in her eyes.

'Please,' said Rona. 'My sister did not deserve to die.'

The pain in Rona's voice, the hope in her eyes that Justice would agree to let Gaea bring their loved ones back, tugged at her heart. But at what cost?

She looked to where Jensen was suspended in mid-air, poised to kill or infect Isaac. More frozen freaks could be seen in the cell, ready to enter the lab and rip everyone inside apart. Many of them wore Ward armour, while in the lab and aboveground, brave wardens and their allies were fighting to give Justice a chance to fulfil her destiny.

If she chose to turn her back on that, her loved ones might be returned to life, but they would come back to a world that was tearing itself apart. To resurrect their loved ones, returning them to a world where the freaks were out of control, would only sentence them to death a second time.

Justice shook her head. 'I'm sorry, Rona. We can't.' She heaved a deep sigh. 'My mother would not want me to save her life at the expense of millions of others, and I don't think your sister would want that either.'

Rona's shoulders slumped, but she nodded and held out her hand.

Justice placed the medallion in her hand and they clasped their free hands as Gaea smiled down on them. The Goddess placed her hands on their heads. Justice screamed as raw power ripped through her body, dimly aware of Rona also screaming.

The light that had dimmed now bloomed so brightly her eyes stung before she could screw them shut. The light continued to bombard her as she felt an immense wave of power building up within, twin to the power she could sense filling Rona.

It was as if the two of them were connected, no one person capable of holding this much power. Justice was sure every atom of her body was about to explode.

The power burst from their bodies, channelling into the floor.

The mangled bed frame was obliterated in the blast as the power spread to encompass the ceiling and walls.

Though they were still there in the old lab, eyes closed, hands clasped, Justice felt as if she was riding the wave of power alongside Rona as it travelled through the ground and up into High Command, ramming its way through the frozen bodies of the wardens, humans, half-breeds, and freaks as it went.

It didn't stop there, travelling to every inch of the country and beyond, with Justice and Rona caught in its grip. Only when the power had scoured the Earth clean did it relent and release them.

Justice fell to the ground, dimly aware her connection with Rona had been cut.

The last thought she had before darkness fell was that this was how she had died last time.

FIFTY-SEVEN

Jackson groaned as consciousness returned. His head ached, throbbing so hard it was all he could focus on for a moment. Then memory hit.

'Justice.' He forced his eyes open and found he was lying face down on the ground of the old lab. He turned his head and saw Lieutenant Jensen sprawled out beside him, blood covering his face. He was still, silent.

Was he dead?

Where was Justice?

With another groan, Jackson got his arms beneath him and pushed up onto his knees, dizziness swamping him with the movement, while nausea swirled in his gut. He forced his discomfort aside as he scanned the room.

Justice was lying on her side beside Rona, both of them still clutching the medallion between them. As he got to his feet and stumbled over to Justice, his heart stuttered at the pallor of her face.

Then she gave a low moan, eyelids fluttering.

She was alive.

Relief toppled him and he fell to his knees beside her,

gently leaning in to brush her hair back from her face. Slowly, she opened her eyes and gazed up at him.

'Did it work?' Her voice was croaky, and he wished he had water to soothe her parched throat. His was dry and scratchy and he was sure the forced unconsciousness was to blame.

'You did it.' He helped her to sit up, wrapping an arm around her as she leaned against him. 'At least, you knocked us all out with that wave of power and light.' He shrugged, eyes going to where Jensen was still lying motionless, though now that his head had stopped throbbing so madly, he could hear the lieutenant's even breathing, as he could for Smith, Hanson, and the others. 'If it cured the freaks, I guess we'll find out when Jensen wakes up.'

Justice looked over at the lieutenant, and Jackson felt her body stiffen when he began to move. He held her tightly with one arm, while with the other he gripped his pistol and aimed it at Jensen's head.

Jensen sat up, hands going to his head as he rocked backward and forward. Jensen lowered his hands and stared over to where Jackson waited with the trigger cocked.

'What the hell happened?' His voice was slurred and just as croaky as Jackson's and Justice's were.

Jackson lowered his weapon and smiled at his lieutenant. 'Justice cured you. The ritual worked.'

At that, Jensen's eyes widened, then a dark expression filled his face as he looked at the blood coating his hands. That expression was one Jackson was intimately familiar with. He'd seen the same expression every time he looked in the mirror after Justice had cured him. It would take his lieutenant a long time to come to grips with what he had done while he'd been infected. If he ever did.

Jackson was still aware of the darkness lurking within, the memory of his time as a freak ensuring he would never take for granted what he was capable of ever again.

For now, he simply gave Jensen a firm look. 'On your feet,

warden. We need to get the injured aboveground and make sure they are taken care of.'

Recalled to his duty, some of the darkness left Jensen's expression, but he would be haunted by memories for a long time to come. He nodded and did as he was ordered.

The others were starting to come around, Hanson being the first to revive fully. 'It worked?' he asked as he stood on wobbly legs and surveyed the others, who were slowly coming to.

'It did.'

Then Hanson stiffened. 'Hannah, I left her in the medical centre.'

'Go.'

The young half-breed spun on his heels and was gone. Jackson returned his attention to those still remaining. Some of them would not be waking up and he buried his sadness as he worked on those that would.

The able-bodied helped the injured back through the tunnel system, and Jackson thought about what he was going to do next. Evidence of the cured freaks met him at each turn, and he knew the time of the wardens was at an end. With no freaks left to fight, they were no longer needed.

When he reached the citadel and saw the damage that had been done, he knew no amount of repair would make this place operational again. Sure, manpower and materials could repair the buildings, but what it stood for was gone.

Beside him, Justice sighed. 'It's really over, isn't it?'

He handed the warden he had carried out of the lab over to the medics amassed on the parade ground, before smiling at Justice.

'We made history today. Not only did you destroy the freak virus and give humankind a second chance, but you also brought about the end of the Ward.'

She gripped his hand. 'Are you sad, to have it all be gone?'

He shook his head. 'I was proud to be a warden, to do my

bit to protect humankind. Now I can be proud to have been part of the last Ward. From here on we get to make our new destiny.'

'And what will that destiny entail?'

'Whatever we want.'

Truth told, he already had some ideas about where to go from here, and with Justice at his side, he knew the future was going to be great. But first he had to do right by everyone who had fought at his side: warden, half-breed, or human. Even people he would once have considered the enemy, like the Legion.

He hadn't missed seeing that it had taken Justice and Rona together to complete the ritual. The last thing he remembered seeing before light had overwhelmed him had been the two of them holding hands.

If Rona could put aside a lifetime of enmity toward the person her people had been trying to destroy for twenty-five years, and work with her to complete Gaea's ritual, he was sure that all of humankind could learn to work together. If not, well, maybe he could take steps to make for a smoother transition.

FIFTY-EIGHT

Hanson scrambled up through the hole in the ceiling of the tunnel, leaving Jackson and the others to take care of the mess in the lab after the battle to stop the freaks from overwhelming them before Justice could complete her ritual. Once he was aboveground, he sprinted in the direction of the citadel. The last time he had seen Hannah was when he'd told Carstairs to get her out of the old medical centre.

With all the fighting going on, none of the different groups had been able to maintain radio contact, and now that it was over, Carstairs was the only one who hadn't responded to Kyle's calls to check in.

Maybe he hadn't heard the call.

He wouldn't contemplate any other reason for the radio silence from Carstairs.

Hannah had to be okay.

He tore around the side of the medical centre and rammed through the door, head swivelling as he listened for signs of life.

Nothing.

It was all silent.

No sign anyone was in the building.

'Hannah!' He raced through the narrow corridors, making for the section that led to the newer medical centre in the citadel.

'Hannah, where are you?'

No one responded to his call, and as he emerged into the new medical centre and spied bodies sprawled on the floor of the hallway, his throat choked up. Most of the bodies wore body armour, blood seeping out of rents in the tough fabric. He feverishly dived into the pile of bodies, turning them over to search their faces, wrenching the helmets off those still wearing them.

Hannah was not among the dead. At least, not this group, though his gut churned at finding familiar faces.

He forced the nausea down and continued on, finding more bodies scattered throughout the centre. He would not stop until he found Hannah.

A groan up ahead had his heart racing, and he turned a corner to find a number of freaks, or what used to be freaks, sitting on the floor of the main foyer holding their heads. They were splattered in blood, many suffering visible wounds and no doubt struggling to wake up from the hell the virus had subjected them to. He didn't stop to reassure them.

He couldn't help anyone until he had found Hannah.

He stepped around the former freaks and sped up. He was nearing the door that led into the citadel and could see sunlight ahead.

He raced through the doorway, taken aback as he surveyed the carnage littered over the parade ground. Smoke wreathed through the air as wardens ran about putting out flames, while others were tending to hundreds of injured dotted all over the place. Hanson had eyes for only one person.

Hannah.

She kneeled beside one of the injured, and as he ran toward her, he vaguely realised it was Carstairs. Hannah was wrapping a bandage around the top part of his head.

Hanson reached her side and grabbed her arm, pulling her to her feet. 'I thought you were dead.' He enfolded her in his arms, hugging her tight, tears dampening his cheeks at finding her uninjured.

'You are uninjured, right?' He loosened his grip, sliding his hands down her arms and moving back to survey her. Blood was splattered over her armour, but there were no tears. It was someone else's blood.

He grabbed her again and buried his face in her hair. Though she smelled of blood, smoke, and other stuff he didn't want to think about, none of that mattered. She was alive. He hadn't lost her.

She hugged him back just as tightly and the hard knot that had settled in his stomach eased.

Too soon, she let go of him and twisted out of his arms. 'I'm glad you're okay, too, but I have to finish binding Carstairs' wound.' She bent down and expertly finished applying the bandage. Then she straightened and scanned the parade ground before picking up her medical bag and walking off.

'Where are you going?' He grabbed her arm and pulled her to a stop.

'There are more injured to treat. The medics need all the help they can get. And we need to organise someone to take care of those who have been cured.'

She set off again and Hanson kept pace with her. 'I'll help you,' he said. There was no way he was letting her out of his sight. Not now. Maybe not ever.

For the next couple of hours, he carried the injured they found to the hospital tent the wardens set up, following Hannah's directions. He was exhausted, but there was no way he was going to stop. Not until Hannah did.

Dark circles were under her eyes and she stumbled as she got to her feet after taking care of her latest patient.

'Okay, that's it. You've done enough.' Hanson took hold of her elbow and helped her stay upright.

'But there are still so many people to treat.'

'Let the medics handle it. You're no good to anyone if you can't keep your eyes open.'

She opened her mouth to protest, but a yawn cut her off.

'See?' Hanson tugged her along, wrapping an arm around her back to provide more support as he scanned the parade ground for a place she could rest. There were no real options, so he headed for the driveway that led around the side of the citadel in the hope that somewhere on the other side of it he would find a place he and Hannah could crash for a while.

They had just rounded the corner when Hannah stumbled. He stopped walking and turned to wrap his other arm around her, gently cradling her against him. Her hands were on his chest and she looked up at him with a tremulous smile.

'Guess I'm more tired than I thought I was,' she said, a wry grin curving her full lips.

Hanson went to answer, but then her tongue peeked out to wet her top lip, and every coherent thought fled. All at once he was aware of the feel of her soft curves pressed against him, her beautiful hazel eyes gazing into his.

Time stood still as he stood there staring at her, unable to tear his eyes away.

Her pupils dilated and she sucked in a deep breath, the movement pressing her breasts more firmly against him.

He groaned, low and deep, and his arms tightened around her as heat surged throughout his body. All he had to do was bend his head and he'd be able to taste her, to see if her mouth tasted as sweet as last time.

But this was Hannah.

His best friend.

He released her and stepped back, body trembling as he held back his desire.

Hurt filled her eyes, and she looked away.

Damn it. He hadn't meant to hurt her.

'Hannah,' he said, resisting the urge to step forward and sweep her into his arms again. 'You're my best friend. I don't want to ruin what we have.'

Hannah took a deep breath, her gaze meeting his. 'Hanson Forsythe, I am only going to ask you this one time and if you lie to me, I swear I will make your life miserable. Do you love me?'

Breath stilled, he stared at her, amazed by the determination that had replaced the hurt in her gaze.

He couldn't lie. Not to Hannah. Not to himself.

'Yes, but—'

A smile lit up her face as she held up a hand to cut him off and stepped toward him. 'I love you, too, so shut up and kiss me.'

If he'd thought her beautiful before, she was glorious now and he didn't hesitate to follow her order.

As his mouth covered hers, he realised that being in love with your best friend was the best kind of feeling in the world.

FIFTY-NINE

Andy ran a hand through his hair, avoiding the eyes of the wardens he passed on the parade ground. Surely they would hate him. He'd been infected, he'd attacked them, tried to infect and kill them. He'd tried to resist the virus, as Captain Kyle had when he'd first been infected, but it had overridden his humanity, turning him into a monster.

The ritual Justice and the woman from the Legion had completed may have cured him and all the others who had been infected, but it could never remove the stain from his soul. Part of him wished she hadn't cured him, wished that he'd been killed.

He'd begged Hanson to do it, but he'd refused. Then, with his last conscious thought, he had lunged for Captain Kyle, sure he would put him out of his misery. Instead, he'd stunned him, which had only momentarily stopped him from trying to kill the others. The reprieve had not been enough. He'd woken with blood on his hands.

Whose blood, he did not know, but as a team of wardens carried the bodies of those who had fallen in the battle to a makeshift morgue, he had to wonder how many of them had died at his hands. He'd washed his hands repeatedly but still felt the weight of blood and death on them, and knew no amount of scouring would absolve him of what he had done.

He rounded a corner of the citadel, seeking privacy to wallow in his shame. Instead, he almost barrelled into Hannah and Hanson, not that he thought they would notice him.

The two were wrapped in one another's arms, kissing passionately.

As much as he was pleased to see that his young friend had finally done something about the feelings he'd been trying to hide for so long, part of him despaired. Would he ever feel the touch of a woman again? How could he let himself accept the affections of another now he knew a monster lurked inside him?

He turned away from the oblivious, happy couple and went in search of another place to hide out. Striding across the parade ground, he headed for the medical centre. It had been cleared of bodies, so no one would disturb him there.

'Where do you think you're going?'

He went rigid, steps slowing despite himself at the sound of Felice's voice. He didn't stop. Nor did he turn around. He only had a short distance to go to reach the medical centre.

'I need to get something,' he said, striving to keep his voice normal. It came out harsh, strained, and he increased his pace. A moment later, he reached the centre's door and stepped inside.

'Hey, stop and talk to me for a second.' The sound of fast footsteps came from behind him and then a hand gripped his arm.

He was tempted to pull away, to just keep going, but he did as she asked. Turning to face her, he kept his gaze focused on a spot on the wall to her left, not wanting to see censure or disgust in her eyes.

Her hand shifted from his arm to his cheek. 'Andy, look at me.'

Unable to deny the entreaty in her voice, he lifted his gaze and stared into her eyes. They were a beautiful colour, a light hazel shot through with green that seemed to shift colour with her moods. Right now, they were shining with unshed tears.

'Don't,' he said, voice hoarse. 'Don't cry for me. Please.'

'Who said I'm crying for you?' She let go of his cheeks and wiped her eyes. 'Maybe these are happy tears because Hanson finally stopped being an idiot and realised Hannah is the best thing to ever happen to him.'

He snorted. 'Took him long enough.'

Felice's mouth twisted into a wry smile. 'Well, some men can be completely clueless about what is standing right in front of them. Until the woman gets sick of waiting and takes matters into her own hands.' She shifted her hands to her hips and sent a challenging gaze his way.

Andy took a step back, hands coming up in front of him. 'Felice, I think you are an amazing woman, and any man would be lucky to have you take him in hand.'

Her chin lifted, a militant glint in her eyes. 'But?'

'You deserve a man who is worthy of you, who doesn't come with blood on his hands. You deserve better than that.'

Her eyes narrowed. 'Andrew Jensen, what happened was not your fault. You were infected. The virus took control of you and made you attack others. No one is blaming you for that, especially not me.'

'I'm blaming me. I should have fought harder, to stay uninfected, to stop the virus from taking over.'

'What makes you so special?'

'Huh?'

'The new virus was so virulent that no one could resist. And from what I hear, you did hold off for longer than most. You did everything you could to fight that virus. You can go on blaming yourself for actions that were beyond your control all you want, but there is no way I'm letting you off that easy. Even if I was willing to walk away, you owe it to your friends, the other wardens, yourself, to do everything you can to make sure the world gets to enjoy the second chance they've been given. And I'll be beside you every step of the way, whether you're ready for that or not.'

She stepped closer, hands coming up to wrap around the back of his neck as she gazed up at him. 'If ever there was a man who needed a woman to take him in hand, then it is you, Andrew Jensen. And I am just the woman for the job.'

Then she pulled his head down and claimed his mouth with her own.

Andy resisted at first, arms at his sides, but as the warmth of her body pressed against his, the hard core of pain inside him began to ease. He wrapped his arms around her and pulled her even closer as he tasted her mouth, warmth spreading through his body.

A long time later, he lifted his head and gazed down at her. She wore a satisfied smirk as she met his eyes and he was unable to stop an answering smile curving his lips.

He still didn't think he deserved this, deserved her, but maybe he wasn't as unredeemable as he thought. After all, if a woman like Felice was willing to accept him as he was, he figured he'd be an idiot to walk away. She stepped back and took his hand, and he allowed her to lead him back to the parade ground to where his fellow wardens were striving to make the best of the situation.

He still felt as if the monster lurked inside him. Maybe in time that feeling would pass. And until it did, he would do everything he could to help the wardens regroup and have relevancy in the new future that beckoned.

SIXTY

CALLUM LOOKED AT THE RUIN OF THE CITADEL. GRENADES HAD proved effective in taking down large groups of the freaks, but it had made a mess of the place where wardens had come together to decide the best way to protect humankind.

At least, that had been the goal for hundreds of years, until those in command had become so puffed up with their own importance, and the supposed superiority of the wardens as a whole, that they schemed to make sure they would never be rendered obsolete. To think, for the last decade, he had been following the orders of generals who were willing to sacrifice their own people to make sure the freak virus was never eradicated.

That was in the past. Not only had Justice been successful in completing the ritual that had cleansed the world of the freak virus for good, but Jackson Kyle was now Acting-General of High Command. Or what was left of High Command. The town itself had not fared much better than the citadel, with fires still burning in some areas. The wardens were exhausted, resources stretched, and they could only focus on those fires closest to the citadel where the wounded were being treated.

So many wounded, and even more dead. The ritual cleansing had not occurred soon enough to prevent the deaths of thousands of people, many of them wardens. But if not for Justice, there would have been no one left uninfected. Shaking his head, he turned away from the carnage and looked to where Acting-General Kyle stood with a small group of people, among them the leader of the Legion, the mercenary commander, and his former lieutenant Max Carstairs.

Callum strode over to them, sure that Kyle was rallying his troops for the mammoth effort it would take to get High Command operational once more.

'If you give us a couple of days, we can have the mine compound ready for you and your people to move back in. Now that we're welcome back in Brimfield, it's time for us to return home,' Kyle said as he stood with an arm around Justice's shoulders, both of them facing Rona Maguire.

'You're leaving? What about High Command?' Callum shook his head. 'Or are you planning on leading from Brimfield from here on?'

Though High Command had been a fixture in the lives of all wardens for five hundred years, it would take a long time to get it back to optimal service. Maybe Kyle intended for Brimfield to become a temporary base of operations while the work was completed. It would be far more comfortable, and Callum didn't mind the thought that Kyle and his wardens would be close to him in Harlington over what were sure to be the next few turbulent years.

Kyle shook his head. 'High Command is finished. We're obsolete. No one needs our protection anymore, thanks to Justice and Rona. It's time for every warden to make their own path.'

Callum stiffened. 'You can't just abandon them. The Ward is all they know.'

Kyle inclined his head. 'I'm not abandoning anyone. Any warden who wishes to come with me to Brimfield is welcome to do so. I expect you and all the other captains to offer any who wish to remain in your Wards the same courtesy.' He waved a hand at the citadel behind them.

'This place is finished. We need to move forward. We'll take everything we need and return to our Wards, and give our people time to get their feet under them as they decide what they wish to do with their lives now the Ward charter has been fulfilled.' Kyle's expression was grave. 'In time, there will be no wardens, no half-breeds, no separation between us and them. We'll all just be people.'

Callum fought back a sigh, knowing it would not be an easy transition for many of the wardens to make, or for the humans and half-breeds. But Kyle was right; the Ward was obsolete. Time for them to plan for a new future. Still, any warden who needed it would have a place in his Ward for as long as it took them to discover their path. As for him, he would remain in his Ward. After a lifetime as a warden, he couldn't imagine being anything else.

Before he moved off to find the other captains to see what could be salvaged for transport to the various Wards, Callum turned to Carstairs. 'Harlington Ward would be happy to have you back, Lieutenant. Unless you feel your place is in Brimfield with Kyle.'

Carstairs wore a chagrined expression. 'To tell the truth, sir, I'm not sure what I want to do.' He cast a glance behind him and Callum followed his gaze to find the two young half-breeds who had played a major part in Kyle's Ward were embracing. Hannah Young and Hanson Forsyth.

When Carstairs looked back, a hint of pain filled his eyes before he cleared his expression. 'Maybe it would be best if I did return to Harlington with you.'

'Or you could come with me.' The mercenary commander, Isaac Smith, shrugged. 'I'm always looking for good people to join my company, and I've seen you fight. You're welcome to join the Righteous.'

Rona Maguire snorted. 'And you wouldn't even have to change the colour of your uniform.'

Isaac laughed.

With a wry smile, Carstairs said, 'Actually, joining the Righteous sounds like just the thing. It's time for me to forget about being a warden and see how the other half operate.'

Though saddened by his lieutenant's decision, Callum guessed he would have to get used to his wardens leaving. Not all of them would want to return to the Wards after everything that had taken place. Many of them were rightfully disillusioned by the mismanagement at the highest level.

He hoped more of them would not decide to throw their lot in with mercenaries. Even though, with their skill set, it was a viable career choice, he shuddered to think what less scrupulous commanders than Smith might do with augmented forces at their disposal. Maybe he could forge a place for his wardens after all, keeping those mercenaries in check and making sure no one group gained too much power.

Filled with a new purpose for the future, he bade farewell to the others and set off to gather provisions to aid his wardens in finding their place in the new world.

SIXTY-ONE

Justice scanned the room she had shared with Jackson at the mine compound, reflecting on the memories they had made in the short time they'd been here. And the even shorter time that they had been here together. It was strange to think that a place to which she had once been brought by an enemy had become a home. Not that she was sad to hand it back to Rona and the survivors of the Legion.

Her true home was wherever Jackson was, and it seemed fitting that they were returning to Brimfield to start the next chapter in their lives. It was where he had first become her bodyguard, where she had given her heart to a freak and was sure they would never have a happy ending. Her sacrifice had changed all that, and now there were no more freaks and they would be helping Brimfield to rebuild after the chaos Councillor Dillon had unleashed there.

As she picked up the bag of her belongings, she shook her head. Strange that both Dillon and Rona had been enemies with similar goals. But the councillor's quest for vengeance had ended in his death, while Rona's had led them to becoming allies. Justice wouldn't say she and Rona were friends, but she respected the leader of the Legion for being able to see the error of her ways and to do whatever was needed to make amends.

With Rona as their leader, the Legion would be able to move on from the troublesome path their ancestors had set them on and forge a new destiny. Though what that path would entail was yet to be determined. Justice hadn't missed the discomfort Rona displayed anytime one of her people called her 'master'.

That was Rona's problem to figure out. It was time for Justice to join Jackson and the others for one more farewell.

Down in the large space in front of the main building, Justice smiled to see Barrett and Trev lecturing the Legion people on how to keep the kitchen and garden working properly. On the other side of the space, Felice was busy organising the wardens and half-breeds for the exodus. This process seemed much more intensive than when they had originally been chased out of Brimfield, even though they had more time and weren't worried about a mob at the gates. Lieutenant Jensen was beside Felice, face solemn, arms crossed in front of his chest. He was having a hard time dealing with being turned into a freak near the end of the battle, but she hoped with Felice's help and understanding he would find his way out of the darkness.

The thought that he, like so many others, was dealing with the aftermath of actions undertaken while he had been infected dimmed her smile. Jackson still had nightmares where he lost his humanity and couldn't claw himself back, just as she had nightmares that she failed in her purpose and everyone she cared about died.

Then her eyes fell on where Jackson stood alongside her friends, Hannah, Hanson, Isaac, and Carstairs. Rona was there too, a strained look on her face as she listened to Isaac and Carstairs banter with each other.

Justice carried her bag over to Felice, who handed it off to one of the wardens packing all their gear in the trucks, and then moved to stand beside Jackson.

'So,' he said as he wrapped his arms around her waist and pulled her against him, 'you ready to go home?'

'Absolutely.' Not that it was Ward headquarters they would be returning to, seeing as Dillon had set it on fire along with all the garrisons after they'd escaped his mob. The small cottage she and Jackson had taken refuge in when he'd first become her bodyguard was still empty, and she was looking forward to filling it with new memories.

Newly elected head councillor Neil had assured them there would be places for all who chose to make their home in Brimfield. Jackson had been elected to the council, along with Hanson. It would be the first town to ever have a warden and a half-breed among its council members. It was going to be an interesting time as all the different factions learned to live together, starting with demolishing the half-breed zone so new housing could be built there and on the grounds where headquarters and the Ward garrisons had once stood.

'I'm going to miss the lab here,' Hannah said, a wistful tone to her throaty voice. 'But Neil said I can use the empty doctor's surgery. It has a house attached at the back, so that's where we will be staying.'

'That's only until my crew can get a new lab built for you,' Hanson said, sliding his arm around her. 'I've already started work on the design and it will put this old lab to shame.' He waved a hand toward the main building.

'There is no way you are designing *my* lab without me,' Hannah said, nudging him in the stomach with her elbow. 'You may know how to design buildings but you know nothing about setting up a proper lab.'

'Good thing I have you around to set me straight then, isn't it?' he said, tweaking her nose.

Hannah giggled, a radiant smile on her face as she gazed up at him.

Of all the things to have come out of this, seeing her two friends finally admit they had feelings for each other was one of the best. It was great to see them happy, and to know that she would not have to say goodbye to them.

Unlike Isaac and Carstairs.

Justice moved out of Jackson's arms and walked over to Isaac. 'You make sure you come and visit,' she said as she leaned in to hug him. 'And make sure you bring Carstairs with you, too. I'm really going to miss you guys.'

He hugged her back. 'Of course, we'll come visit, little sister. You didn't think you were going to get rid of me that easily, did you?'

Beside him, Rona snorted, and Isaac turned to look at her. 'Do you want me to come visit you too, while I'm in the area? I know you're going to miss me.'

She snorted again. 'What I won't miss is all this black you lot have going on.' She waved a hand at his black uniform and the Ward armour Carstairs was wearing. 'It may hide blood-stains, but it's so boring, especially when you are all dressed the same.'

She waved a hand at the yellow armour she was currently wearing. Like her red set, it accentuated her curves and high-lighted her tall frame. 'It doesn't have to be ugly to be functional.'

Isaac barked out a laugh. 'If you were one of my merce-naries, we'd be able to use you as bait. No one could miss you coming in that armour.'

His eyes narrowed. 'In fact, that's not a bad idea. Fancy giving up your role as Master of the Legion and becoming one of the Righteous? As I said to Carstairs, we're always looking for good fighters.'

Rona's eyes widened, and Justice was sure she was about to tell Isaac just what he could do with his offer. She made no secret of her disdain for him or mercenaries in general.

SIXTY-TWO

Rona's breath caught in her throat at Isaac's offer. Become a mercenary. Walk away from the Legion and a destiny her father had groomed her for since she could walk.

No. Her destiny had been to stand at her sister's side. To watch Karline's back as she led the Legion.

Karline was gone and Rona had become the leader by default, even though everything the Legion had been working toward was no longer a concern. She cringed every time someone called her 'master', and the thought of staying here at the compound and forced to lead made her shake.

Jackson had offered her a place in Brimfield, but she'd declined. How could she live among people who had been so adversely affected by her actions?

Her plan had been to travel alone, avoiding the townships and people she had wronged as much as possible. Maybe travelling with a mercenary company would be a better option. Lone travellers were easy pickings for those seeking to take advantage of others, and it would give her safety of numbers and something to occupy her thoughts while she figured out how to make proper amends for all the damage she had wrought.

She met Isaac's challenging stare. 'I'm not taking orders from you, and don't expect me to wear black, but I am open to playing bait.'

Who knew, maybe whoever they baited would take her out of the equation so she would no longer have to face the knowledge of what she had done.

Isaac's eyes widened, and then he grinned. 'That sounds reasonable. Though if any of my people decide they need to be colourful, I'm holding you responsible.'

Great, one more thing to feel responsible for. But a uniform choice was far better to be blamed for than the countless deaths on her head. 'When do we leave?'

'You have twenty minutes.' Isaac gave her a nod and then strode off to stow his gear in the back of his four-wheel-drive alongside Carstairs.

Rona turned to Jackson. 'Thank you, for everything.'

'Are you sure about this?' Jackson asked, waving a hand toward Isaac.

'No, but it's better than what I had originally planned.'

Justice's eyes narrowed. 'You were never going to stay here.'

Rona shook her head. 'I'm not leadership material. This lot will be better off without me. Though I hope you will keep an eye on them over the next few months. They're used to being led, so having the freedom to make their own choices may prove interesting.'

Jackson gave a tight grin. 'You can bet I'll be watching them.'

Sure that her people, *former people*, would be in good hands, Rona said a hasty goodbye and then strode off to her room.

A short time later, her gear was packed, and she was sitting in the passenger seat as Isaac started the engine and navigated through the gate. A small portion of the weight sitting on her shoulders lifted as she left the compound and the Legion behind. It was time to make her own fate.

'So, other than not wanting to wear black and refusing to obey my orders, is there anything else I need to know about you?' Isaac shot her a glance as he navigated the Jeep along the pitted dirt road.

Rona gave him a cool stare. 'Don't you think you should have asked that before you agreed to take me with you?'

He chuckled. 'What can I say? I like to leave room for the occasional surprise. Makes life more interesting, wouldn't you agree, Carstairs?'

In the backseat, Carstairs snorted. 'I'm a warden, or at least I was, so there were few surprises in my life until all this showed up.'

'Sounds boring. Bet you're glad to get out of that life and tackle some new challenges. Challenges that we get to decide the rules for. My second tells me the Righteous has been offered a job in this area, one that will require subtle handling. I'm thinking the three of us can sort it out before we meet up with the rest of my group.'

'Subtle?' Rona stared at Isaac, thinking there was nothing about either of them that was subtle.

'Yeah, it seems there's a bandit preying on the good people of Larkstone. One that has a fondness for accosting innocent young ladies as they go about their business.' He grinned at Rona. 'I'm thinking this is the perfect opportunity for you to play bait. You can pretend to be sweet and innocent, right? Though we may need to find you something frilly and flowing to wear.'

It was Rona's turn to snort. She couldn't remember ever being sweet and innocent, and this was not what she had imagined her first job working for a mercenary company would be. But taking on a bandit who was harassing women was something she could definitely do.

She gave Isaac as sweet a smile as she could manage. 'I'll wear a pretty dress, as long as you do as well.'

Isaac's eyes went wide as Carstairs chuckled loudly.

Rona faced forward and settled into her seat. Travelling with these guys was already shaping up to be an interesting pastime.

SIXTY-THREE

Jackson watched Justice as she flitted about the cottage, a gentle smile on her face as she caressed the home-made furnishings and ornaments left behind by the previous owners. They'd put what few belongings they had away and given the place a clean. After so long unoccupied, the dust had settled, but after a few hours all the surfaces gleamed and Jackson got to sit and watch Justice as she rearranged the knick-knacks in some kind of order that clearly made sense to her.

He'd suggested getting rid of a lot of it, but she wouldn't hear of it.

'The people who built this house filled every corner with the labours of their hands and attention. They're gone and we've taken their place, but that doesn't mean we can just throw out everything they made to make room for new stuff. Besides, I think all this makes it more of a home than a house.' Her expression was wistful, and he realised a home had been something she'd lacked all her life. She'd been raised in a monastery until she was ten and then had to go on the run for the next fifteen years.

The knick-knacks did give the place a homey feel, and

while he wasn't enthused about living in a house with the belongings of deceased people, he was content for Justice to have what she wanted. Besides, he was sure they would be filling their home with memories and knick-knacks of their own before too long. There would be no more running around, fighting for their lives. Instead, they would spend their days working to ensure the people of Brimfield remained safe as the world grew accustomed to the absence of freaks and the disbanding of the Wards.

He got up and walked over to where Justice was spinning a model aeroplane that hung from a fixture in the lounge room ceiling. He put his arms around her. 'I don't suppose there's time for you and me to take advantage of that nice big shower cubicle again?'

A knock on the door came before Justice could answer him. She grinned and patted his cheek. 'Later. You have work to do, Councillor Kyle.'

He chuckled. 'So do you.'

Neil had taken Justice on as his assistant, promising he would be a far more lenient boss than the former head councillor had been. With Hanson as a co-councillor, and knowing Neil had the best interests of all the people of Brimfield at heart, the town was in good if inexperienced hands.

The knock came again, and he released Justice, though he did grab her hand as they walked to the front door.

Hanson, dressed in a grey suit that had him pulling at his neck, stood beside Hannah. She wore a dress similar to Justice's, and Jackson gaped for a moment, having never seen her in anything but jeans or Ward armour. Hanson kept shooting Hannah admiring looks, and Jackson was pleased to see how smitten he was. They both deserved happiness.

Hanson nodded to the dark blue suit Jackson wore. 'Tell me councillors don't have to wear this stuff every day. I swear it's tried to choke me three times on the walk here.'

The doctor's surgery Hanson and Hannah were staying in

was only two blocks away, so they hadn't had far to walk. Jackson grinned at his disgruntled expression.

'Relax, it is only for formal occasions. You can be back in your construction gear after the ceremony.' He knew his young friend was eager to start building the lab he had promised Hannah.

They stepped outside, talking quietly as they walked through the streets toward where Ward headquarters once stood. People were coming out of their houses and soon there was a procession as they filled the streets. As they neared the site, the conversations stopped and Jackson sucked in a breath as he rounded the last corner and faced his former home.

The fire had gutted the buildings, and Councillor Dillon had everything left standing razed to the ground. The only part that remained untouched was the graveyard where wardens who had fallen in the battle to wrest Brimfield back from Legion control were buried.

Justice's hand tightened in his, though her steps did not falter as they drew closer to where a small dais had been set up in the middle of what had once been a parade ground. Waiting on the dais were Neil and the other two councillors, Mandalay and Higgins. Arrayed behind them were the wardens and half-breeds who had fought alongside Jackson. Many sported injuries, some were in wheelchairs or used crutches, but they were all in the best outfits they could find on their return to Brimfield the day before.

Jackson stopped and met the eyes of every one of them before he ascended the dais with Justice, Hannah, and Hanson.

The people who had followed them through the streets took up positions on either side of the dais and assembled wardens, a quiet shuffle taking place as they waited for the proceedings to begin.

After a nod from Jackson, Neil began.

'Today we stand on the point of our lowest moment.

Through our folly we, the citizens of Brimfield, turned against those who had risked their lives to save us. I would like to blame bad leadership for this betrayal, but know it would be a lie. We allowed the former leaders of this town to perpetrate this terrible act. We allowed flawed truth and veiled lies to sway our thinking. We allowed the good men and women standing before you today to be reviled and run out of town.'

He waved toward the graveyard. 'Wardens and half-breeds died to protect us and we vilified them for it.' He waited for a moment for that to sink in and then continued.

'For that alone, the Brimfield Ward would have been in their rights to wash their hands of us, to allow us to wallow in the ruins of our mistake. Yet when we were besieged by those wanting to take over our town, it was Jackson Kyle and his wardens who freed us from oppression. When a new kind of freak menaced our town, these wardens and half-breeds once again went into battle to save us all. Without their assistance, this town would have fallen to the freaks and we would all be dead or infected.'

He shook his head. 'Even though all they had ever done was try to help us, Councillor Dillon took it upon himself to discredit and destroy the wardens, an act that would have led to our downfall. It ultimately cost him his life and that of Councillor Nash and Councillor Petersen. While I am saddened, as we all are, by the loss of life, this gives us the opportunity to make amends, to start afresh and to ensure that from this day forward, Brimfield will be a town of safety for all. The Wards are no more, but with the inclusion of these fine men and women into our town, their spirit will live on and make us stronger. We are going to make Brimfield the best town ever.'

A round of applause met his statement. He smiled and then waved Jackson and Hanson forward.

'I present to you, citizens of Brimfield, your new council members, Councillor Kyle and Councillor Forsythe.'

This time the applause was thunderous and Jackson swallowed a lump in his throat as he looked out over a sea of faces. All of them beaming with happiness. He had been proud of his role as Captain of the Brimfield Ward, dubious about his promotion to acting-general, but this title, Councillor Jackson Kyle, was one he felt he had been working toward all his life.

All he had ever wanted to do was protect the people in his care. Before, the main threat had been freaks, but now the future was unknown. There was no telling what would happen in the coming years. But if this town could overcome generations of prejudice to accept a warden and a half-breed on their council, he was sure they could achieve anything. And he would do whatever it took to keep his people safe, all of his people.

He moved back to stand beside Justice as Neil called forth Hannah and some of the wardens and Brimfield security guards to be awarded medals. The wardens had been dubious about accepting such accolades, especially Lieutenant Jensen, but Jackson knew this was the town's way of thanking them.

As the lieutenant made his way up the dais stairs to accept his medal, Jackson supposed he would have to start thinking of him simply as Andy. Although, with Jensen and many of the others choosing to bolster the reduced numbers of the town guards, maybe he would have a new rank soon.

After the medals had all been given out, Felice supervised the setting up of tables for a feast that had been arranged by Barrett and Trev on the council's behalf. With her flair for organisation and the half-breeds' newfound love of catering, they would have no trouble getting customers for their fledging business.

As the food arrived and the official side of the proceedings evolved into a party, Jackson stole a moment to walk among the graves, to remember those who had fallen to achieve the peace they now had.

Soft footsteps sounded behind him, and he turned to find

Justice, Hannah, Hanson, and Jensen making their way toward him.

He put an arm around Justice's slender shoulders as they stood between the graves of Miranda Wilson and Daniel Zarb. Hannah and Hanson positioned themselves between Zarb's grave and that of Hanson's friend Ben Campbell, while Jensen was near the freshly dug grave of Geoff Anderson, having collected his body from Harlington before he had come to Brimfield. So many others had fallen and were buried elsewhere, but it was fitting that these people were buried here.

After a long silent moment, Jackson said, 'To the members of the last Ward, you will never be forgotten.' Then he saluted, unheeding of the tears streaming down his cheeks.

Jensen followed suit, while the others bowed their heads in remembrance.

Justice looked up at Jackson, tears glinting in her eyes. 'What now?'

He gave her a smile. 'Now we do whatever we can to make sure their sacrifice was worth it.'

With that he led them back to the celebration, and toward their hard-won second chance.

ACKNOWLEDGMENTS

Writing the end of a series is a bittersweet moment. I may have finished telling the story of characters who have lived in my head for years, but now I have to say goodbye to them. Justice, Jackson, Hannah, and Hanson have been my companions for so long, I am going to be lost without them. My mind is busy thinking up ways I can return to the world of *The Last Ward* and create more adventures with new and old characters. But for now it is time to let them go.

My characters are not the only ones to have helped me through this series writing journey. My family and friends have also been there every step of the way. I have bounced ideas off them, made them read sections and give feedback, and then hidden away in my writing cave for hours on end. As always, my mum has been my biggest supporter, closely followed by Donna, who is the best friend an author could have. My husband and children are long suffering and have grown accustomed to me being lost in daydreams of other worlds.

I would like to give special thanks to Sally Odgers for her expertise in whipping the first draft into shape, and to Michelle Lovi of Odyssey Books for giving *The Last Ward* a chance and for making sure *Dark Allegiance* is the best book it can be. Finally, thank you to everyone who has taken a chance and come along on the journey with Jackson, Justice, and their friends. I hope you enjoy this last chapter in their story.

ABOUT THE AUTHOR

Shelley Russell Nolan is an avid reader who began writing her own stories at sixteen. Her first completed manuscript featured brain eating aliens and a butt kicking teenage heroine. Since then she has spent her time creating fantasy worlds where death is only the beginning and even freaks can fall in love.

The first two books in her debut adult urban fantasy series, Lost Reaper and Winged Reaper, were published by Atlas Productions in 2016, with Silver Reaper published in 2017 to complete the series. 2018 saw the release of her Arcane Awakenings Novella Series, while Odyssey Books published the first book in a new post-apocalyptic series in 2019.

Born in New Zealand, moving to Australia with her family when she was seven, Shelley currently lives in Central Queensland, Australia, with her husband and two young children. They share their home with two wrecking ball kitties, and two crazy dogs on a mission to chew.

Shelley loves to hear from her readers so feel free to contact her on Facebook or leave a review wherever you purchased this book or on Goodreads.

https://shelleyrussellnolan.com

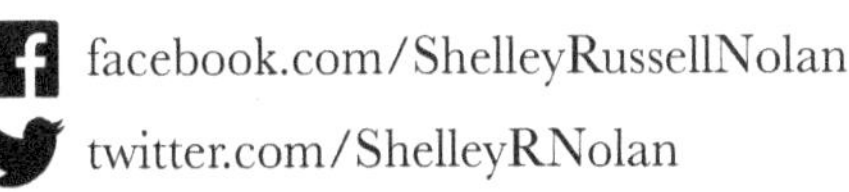

facebook.com/ShelleyRussellNolan

twitter.com/ShelleyRNolan